DARK SURVIVOR
AWAKENED

THE CHILDREN OF THE GODS BOOK 20

I. T. LUCAS

FOLLOW I. T. LUCAS ON AMAZON

CONTENTS

Prelude		1
1. Wonder		6
2. Wonder		10
3. Wonder		16
4. Wonder		20
5. Wonder		24
6. Anandur		30
7. Losham		37
8. Kian		41
9. Wonder		46
10. Anandur		51
11. Nick		56
12. Ruth		60
13. Grud		66
14. Anandur		70
15. Wonder		75
16. Anandur		80
17. Wonder		84
18. Ruth		88
19. Nick		93
20. Anandur		97
21. Ruth		104
22. Wonder		109
23. Ruth		115
24. Nick		120
25. Kian		125
26. Wonder		128
27. Anandur		134
28. Brundar		139
29. Wonder		142
30. Ruth		151
31. Brundar		156

32. Wonder   160
33. Anandur   165
34. Grud   170
35. Wonder   173
36. Anandur   180
37. Wonder   185
38. Brundar   190
39. Anandur   195
40. Wonder   200
41. Anandur   203
42. Wonder   209
43. Grud   215
44. Wonder   219
45. Nick   225
46. Ruth   230
47. Nick   235
48. Ruth   239
49. Nick   244
50. Wonder   250
51. Anandur   254
52. Brundar   257
53. Wonder   263
54. Brundar   268
55. Anandur   270
56. Grud   275
57. Brundar   279
58. Grud   281
59. Wonder   284
60. Anandur   288
61. Brundar   293
62. Wonder   297
63. Anandur   301

   The Children of the Gods Series   309
   The Perfect Match Series   325
   FOR EXCLUSIVE PEEKS   327
   Also by I. T. Lucas   329

PRELUDE

Nine months ago

There was water everywhere.

Awakened from a deep slumber, she took an involuntary first breath, but instead of air, her lungs filled with liquid.

She was submerged and drowning.

Panicked, she flailed uselessly in a weak attempt to swim up.

At first, the feeling of hot air on her fingertips did not register. When it did, she forced her enfeebled body into a sitting position, and as her upper torso cleared the water, a painful coughing fit expelled that which did not belong in her lungs.

With much difficulty, she opened her eyes.

The murky death trap she had imagined was only about a cubit deep. Thank the gods she was in shallow waters. The sting in her eyes was not too bad either, which she took to mean that it was not a pool of sea water she had been awakened in, but fresh water.

Was she in an underground cavern with a shallow river running through it? Or was it a very dark night? Had she suffered a bad fall into a small pond or a puddle?

She must have had a fainting spell.

But what was she doing there in the first place?

Was it a dream?

Panic rising, she realized that not only were the location and her reason for being there unknown to her, but also who she was and where she had come from.

No name emerged in her thoughts, not even an image. It was as if she had been born fully grown in that shallow pool like some goddess out of primordial waters.

Lifting an emaciated arm, she peered at the bony appendage with horror. She was a corpse. The skin was dry and shriveled, even though she had been submerged in water, and there was barely any flesh on it. Further inspection revealed that the rest of her body was in no better shape. Scraps of rotted fabric were all that remained of her original clothing, and it was not enough to cover her nakedness.

For a few moments, she sat in the water, breathing in the musky air and listening to her own heartbeat to reassure herself that she was indeed alive. Slowly, the steady rhythm calmed her enough to notice her terrible thirst. Ducking her head back into the pool, she took a few gulps of the muddy water only to spit everything up and cough.

There was too much dirt mixed within the life-giving liquid.

A bubbling sound, not too far off from where she was sitting, hinted that fresher water might be near, but not fresh as in a natural spring. It had a metallic scent to it, copper or something similar.

She was no expert in metallurgy. Copper and gold, that was the extent of her knowledge. Well, at least there was that. She did not know her own name, or where she came from, or why she looked like a corpse, but she could recognize those two smells.

Too weak to push up and stand, she crawled toward the bubbling until she reached a wall. It seemed that the sound and smell were coming from the adjacent cavern. But if the water was spilling over into hers, there must be a hole somewhere in the rock separating the two.

In the darkness, she patted the rock wall searching for the opening.

Her heart sank when she found it.

Even in her skeletal state, it was not big enough for her to squeeze through.

Except, as she gripped the opening, the soft sandstone crumbled under her fingers. Not all hope was lost. If she could enlarge the hole to half a cubit or so, it should be enough. She could squeeze through it then.

In her weakened condition, she could manage only a little at a time before having to take a break and rest. It took her a long time to enlarge the opening from one hand span to two, and then she had to take an even longer rest to let her hands heal before she could continue.

Sitting with her back propped against the rock wall, wheezing, her nails chipped and broken, her fingertips and the palms of her hands bleeding from numerous cuts, she felt like crying.

But what was the point?

It would be a waste of precious energy. She needed every scrap of it to keep on working.

Cradling her hands close to her chest, she waited for her body to repair the damage. Long moments passed until the bleeding stopped and the broken skin mended itself.

Somehow she knew that it had taken her much longer

to heal than it should have, probably because of her body's emaciated state.

Her nails were even slower to regenerate.

No matter. As long as the pain was gone, she could continue.

Hours must have passed as she worked and rested and then worked some more. When her task was done, and she squeezed through the opening, new cuts and scrapes joined the old ones, but she ignored the pain and kept pushing harder.

It was of no consequence.

Her mission was accomplished. She was on the other side of that rock wall. Now all that was left was to crawl toward the sound and smell of bubbling water.

At the source, she discovered a metal conduit that was obviously not natural. Smooth and round, it hung loosely from where it was attached to the wall with clamps, one of which had broken off, severing the two parts of the conduit or breaking one into two.

It was spouting what seemed like a never-ending supply of surprisingly clean water. The conduit seemed to be part of some sort of an underground water delivery system, which was odd since the cavern she had awoken in was natural and not part of a constructed dwelling.

Pushing her curiosity aside, she put her mouth to the water and drank her fill, then found an elevated dry spot and sat with her back propped against the wall.

After all that hard work, she needed a long rest. But the respite was way too short.

Her stomach rumbled, twisting painfully and reminding her that she needed food. Evidently, with her thirst quenched, her body's other needs had been awakened.

Still exhausted from her previous quest, she wished

they had not, or at least that they had stayed dormant for a little longer. To get to where she could find food, she needed to discover a way out of the caverns.

The water delivery system suggested that there were people living above ground. She was not far from civilization. And where there were people, there was food.

She also needed clothing to cover her nakedness. Not that there was much to see. The way she looked now, humans would run away screaming in horror, thinking her a walking dead—an animated corpse.

Humans. Somehow she knew that she was not one of them. She was different.

But how?

She was a female, she knew that, and if there were any flesh on her bones she would have looked like a human female, but she was not.

No matter, in time it would come to her.

Survival came first.

WONDER

*T*his was a strange new world she had awakened to.

Her memory loss must have been catastrophic because almost nothing was familiar. The language was foreign to her, with only a few words bearing some similarity to the language she thought in. Still, a full moon cycle had passed since her awakening, and little by little she was gaining a basic understanding of it—only a few words and phrases, but she was learning more each day.

There were tall buildings, wheeled vessels that moved fast on roads that must have been smooth at one time but were now in disrepair, and noisy, busy streets, teaming with humans.

She felt like an infant learning everything anew.

Stealing and manipulating the minds of humans were necessary for survival, but she hated having been reduced to thieving. The clothes she wore had been stolen from a clothesline, the sandals on her feet had come from a merchant whose mind she had manipulated to think they had been paid for, and the same went for food.

The merchants in the open market were probably shaking their heads when tallying their proceeds at the end of the day. Regenerating her tall body took large quantities of food, which their stands had provided free of charge, but not voluntarily.

She was getting stronger by the day, but a woman alone, even a tall one like her, was not safe at night. Not out in the streets. With nowhere else to go, she slept at the same construction site she had awakened in, making a bed for herself out of several empty sacks from the debris pile. She'd hidden it in one of the underground caverns that the tall buildings were built upon. The broken pipe had been fixed, and the arid climate ensured that the caverns had dried out in no time.

Most of her days were spent wandering the streets and markets while trying to learn everything she could about this land, its language, and its people.

The merchants flaunting their wares at the market were shouting that this or that was the best in Alexandria, and the street vendor with the large pages with writing on them was also yelling something to that effect.

The name was meaningless to her.

What she knew was that it was a port city and that the vessels moored in it were the size of villages. They were enormous monsters, the names on their sides written in a foreign language that bore no resemblance to the one on the shop signs and the large sheets of paper the street vendor was selling.

There was so much to learn.

The good news was that she no longer looked like a walking corpse, so hiding her frightening skeletal visage under the black outer garment she had stolen was not necessary.

What a relief.

Wearing it had been stiflingly hot, and yet many of the women she saw on the streets were wearing one just like that. The garment covered them from head to toe, leaving only a small opening for the eyes. Others wore long-sleeved shirts and scarves around their heads, covering their hair. Still, some of the women and girls wore form-fitting pants and plain short-sleeved shirts and no scarves.

Although everyone spoke the same language, many different people must have lived in the big city, bringing with them different customs from their homelands. The thing was, the varying levels of concealment were limited to the women. The men were all dressed more or less the same. Only a few covered their heads, and most did not concern themselves with modesty as much as the women did. They wore short pants that left their legs exposed and short-sleeved shirts that showed their arms—attire that made much more sense in the oppressive heat of the city.

There was much poverty everywhere, and she felt terrible for what she had been forced to steal to survive. Those few garments and foodstuffs were no doubt just as necessary to these poor people as they were to her.

But she had no choice.

Even the name she had adopted didn't belong to her.

Wonder.

A week or so ago, a little girl on the street had tugged her mother's sleeve and pointed at her. "Look, Mama, Wonder Woman!"

The mother had smiled apologetically, saying something in the language these people spoke, then scurried away with the child looking behind her shoulder and grinning.

When it had happened again with another child on the same day, it was settled.

Wonder Woman must have been the name of someone

important in this strange world she had awoken to, and since both times it had been said with a smile, it must have been a good one.

Wonder had a nice ring to it.

She just wished she knew what it meant.

WONDER

"*L*ook what we have here," the young man behind her taunted.

Wonder walked faster.

At first, she'd paid no attention to the four human males following her through the market. A lot of people crowded the narrow pathways between the stalls, and her only concern had been not to get caught stealing food.

Should she run?

But if she did, she would attract attention to herself, which was the opposite of beneficial to a thief. Especially one that had garnered plenty of curious looks as it was.

Not that she understood why people were looking at her.

Her dark coloring was no different than that of the locals, and the green color of her eyes, which was somewhat uncommon among the mostly browns she had seen, was not so out of the ordinary as to justify the stares. She was a tall woman, but she wasn't the only one. Wonder had seen several girls just as tall as her and a couple who were even taller.

Maybe it was her resemblance to that Wonder Woman person, who unfortunately she still had not figured out the importance of.

"Slow down, girly. We just want to talk," one of the men called out.

Wonder walked even faster. Once she cleared the market, she could run. The question was whether she could outrun them. If she couldn't, it would be better for her to stay where there were a lot of people around.

What did these young thugs want with her anyway?

She had no money they could steal. Was there anything else they might want?

Maybe they had seen her pilfering food?

If that was the case, she should run before they called a policeman, which was what people called the uniformed guards patrolling the market. She had seen them chase down a thief before and take him away.

Who knew what they did with criminals in these parts.

For some reason, her mind came up with whipping and enslavement, even though she hadn't seen anyone who looked like he or she was a slave. No one was in chains, and she hadn't seen anyone getting a whipping either.

Except, that didn't mean a thing. Slaves could have been kept somewhere else, and whipping might have been done away from the public eye.

It was better to run than discover what these people did to thieves.

As soon as the last stall was behind her, Wonder started running, slowly at first, then faster when she realized the four were still behind her.

Wonder was fast, her long legs eating the pavement with surprising speed. Ducking into an alley, she was sure she had lost them, but they must've cut through some other passageway, and two of them appeared in front of her. When she turned around to run the other way, the other two appeared at the mouth of the alley, blocking her way.

She crouched, instinctively getting into a fighting stance, her muscles tightly coiled and ready to launch an attack as if her body knew what to do even though her brain didn't. When a growl started deep in her throat, startling her, she didn't know where that came from either.

What was happening to her? Was she turning into a feral creature? Where were those responses coming from? Were they part of her nature, or a muscle memory from a life she couldn't remember?

"Come on, girly, no need to get all hissy. We just want to play," one of the guys said as he sauntered closer, his friend following closely behind him.

Wonder didn't answer.

Her knowledge of their language had gotten good enough to understand basic communication and to speak a few necessary words, but not good enough to form sentences. The vocabulary needed to answer the thug was beyond her capabilities.

Instead, she bared her teeth and growled louder. On an entirely instinctive level, she was aware that the men should run from her and not the other way around. But it seemed they were too stupid to realize that they were not dealing with an ordinary human girl.

Their mistake.

Her body knew what to do as soon as the first one reached to grab her. Without having to think it through, she closed her hand around his wrist and pulled, throwing him over her shoulder with such brute force that he hit the side of a building with a thud, then slid down and never got up.

Was he dead?

She didn't look back to check, her hearing good enough to confirm that he was out of commission.

For now.

Enraged by their friend's fate, the other three lunged at her all at once.

As Wonder's arms and legs punched and kicked, her fast moves soon turned into a blur. Her goal was always the same—get leverage and hurtle the assailant across the alley. In seconds, the sounds of battle were over, and four bodies were strewn about the alley's dirty pavement.

In the silence that followed, Wonder's own heartbeat thundered in her ears for a long moment. When it quieted enough for her to hear the others, she could discern only three aside from her own.

She had killed one of them. It was the first one she had flung against the wall. No heartbeat was coming from his direction.

Bile rising in her throat, Wonder bent over and emptied the contents of her stomach.

She was a killer, a murderer, a taker of life.

The policemen would come for her and put her in chains. When the other three awoke, they would never admit that they attacked her first, and she had no words to defend herself with.

With one last glance at her terrible handiwork, Wonder turned and ran. With no money to pay for transport, she could think of only one way to get out of the city as fast as she could—sneak onto one of those huge boats leaving the harbor.

It shouldn't be too difficult.

As she ran through the busy streets, desperate to distance herself from what she had done, Wonder didn't give much thought to how she was going to accomplish that.

Her haggard state was her biggest concern. A bruised woman, wearing dirty, torn clothing, could not avoid notice. But shrouding herself in her current state was above her skill level. Ignoring the looks, she kept on running until she reached the harbor.

The security was much tighter than she had expected.

Standing on the dock, she observed as the crew and passengers showed the guard some sort of a booklet before being allowed onboard.

She was in deep trouble.

In order to get in, she had to summon her most powerful shroud to conceal her bruises and the state of her clothing, not an easy feat on a good day, and nearly impossible to maintain for more than a few minutes when shaken down to her core by the events that had brought her there.

On top of that, she would have to thrall the guard to believe she had the same booklet as the other passengers.

Taking several deep breaths, Wonder imagined herself wearing nice new clothing and holding the required documentation in her hand, then got in line behind a hefty older woman dragging a large wheeled case behind her.

Poor thing needed help, but Wonder couldn't offer it. First, because she didn't have command of the language, and secondly because she needed to focus on holding the shroud.

"Here you go, young man." The woman handed the official her booklet together with another piece of paper. "I'm so glad your vessel is taking on passengers. I didn't know cargo ships did that, and for such a low price too. Now I can finally visit my daughter and my grandchildren without having to go on one of those flying machines." She shook her head. "People are not meant to fly through the sky like birds."

The guard examined the documents and handed them back. "You are free to pass, Mrs. Rashid."

"Thank you." The woman folded the piece of paper, put it inside the booklet, and stuffed both in her large bag. "Good day to you."

"Have a pleasant trip, Mrs. Rashid."

Holding her breath, Wonder pushed her thrall at the guard and followed behind the older woman without stopping. A few tense moments went by as she expected him to order her to halt, but the call never came.

Wonder exhaled a relieved breath and kept on walking.

WONDER

"I brought you dinner, sweetie," Mrs. Rashid said as she entered the cabin. "They think I'm an old fat woman who eats too much." She chuckled as she put the plate down on the table.

"Thank you. I don't know what I would've done without you." Wonder sat down and lifted the utensils.

Hasina, as Mrs. Rashid insisted Wonder call her, waved a dismissive hand. "You make this voyage tolerable. I would've been bored out of my mind if I were all alone in this cabin with nothing to do."

A retired English teacher, the kind lady who had taken pity on her and invited a stowaway girl to share her cabin, had also taken it upon herself to prepare Wonder for her new life in the United States of America, which was where the ship was heading.

Day by day, Wonder's vocabulary was growing, and her use of the language was becoming more and more natural. Mrs. Rashid was very impressed with her progress. She was even teaching Wonder to read and write in the English language as well.

"I'm forever in your debt, Mrs. Rashid."

"Pfft, it is my pleasure. And please call me Hasina, as I have asked you over and over again. You're such a stubborn girl," she said with a smile, letting Wonder know she wasn't really angry at her.

"But that's good." She patted Wonder's head. "Your stubbornness probably saved your life, you poor thing. I don't know who's the son of a donkey who beat you up, because you refuse to tell me or really can't remember anything. I can only assume he is an abusive husband and that you had no choice but to run for your life. If you were found, God only knows what he would have done to you."

Hasina shook her head. "Terrible things happen to women, and there is no one to help them. I was lucky to have been married to a good man, but not every woman is so fortunate. If you're telling me the truth and you really can't remember anything, then he must've beaten you up quite severely. You might've died."

Wonder said nothing, letting Hasina believe what she would. It was better than telling the kind lady more lies or partial truths.

Once she had enough command of the language to communicate, Wonder had told Hasina that she had woken up covered in bruises and no memory of what had happened to her, or who she was.

It wasn't a lie, but it wasn't the complete truth either. If the woman knew the real reason behind Wonder's plight, she might not have been as eager to help her. No one wanted to aid a murderer, even one who had killed in self-defense.

Wonder finished the meal and wiped the empty plate clean with a paper towel. "Thank you for the food, Hasina."

"You're welcome, dear. Are you full? Or would you like me to bring you more?"

Wonder was still hungry, but it was nothing new. Hunger had been her constant companion throughout the voyage. Mrs. Rashid could bring her only so much food, and it wasn't enough, but she wasn't going to upset the old lady by admitting it.

"I'm quite full, thank you."

Mrs. Rashid eyed her suspiciously. "You don't look full to me. I'll get you some dessert. They think I'm fat anyway." She patted her big protruding belly. "In the meantime, get some more studying done. I want you to copy chapter twelve while I'm gone."

"Yes, Mrs. Rashid."

The teacher utilized what tools were available to her. Television was one of them, and books from the ship's library were another. Apparently, there was another thing named a laptop that could've been very useful, but Mrs. Rashid hadn't brought hers on the voyage and couldn't find anyone to borrow one from.

"I'll be right back."

After the chapter had been copied, and the delicious chocolate cake eaten, Mrs. Rashid went out to mingle with the other passengers, and Wonder settled in for another evening in front of the television.

Watching stories enacted in such a realistic way was fascinating. She'd learned a lot about the new land the ship was sailing toward. Unfortunately though, Wonder had learned nothing new about herself.

It was as if she had been born the day she had awakened in that cavern. Well, that wasn't entirely true, just mostly.

She knew now that Alexandria was the name of a city in a country called Egypt, and that the language people spoke there was called Arabic. Some of the words in that language sounded familiar to her, which was not the case with English.

Hasina had told her that she'd never heard anyone speak Wonder's language or anything similar to it. Wonder had a feeling that the teacher suspected her of making the language up.

Sometimes, Wonder suspected it too.

Maybe when they arrived in the United States, they could find someone who'd heard it before and could tell them in which country it was spoken.

Wonder had spent many nights fantasizing about that land.

WONDER

"Wonder Woman, go check the ladies' room," Tony said in Wonder's earpiece. "I hear yelling all the way to my office."

Tony liked to make fun of her adopted name, but she didn't care. Now that she knew who Wonder Woman really was, she liked it even better.

Her new legal last name wasn't Woman, though, it was Rush. Wonder Rush courted even more snickers than Wonder Woman, but she didn't care about that either. She'd chosen it because it sounded a little like Mrs. Rashid's last name. The woman was the closest to family Wonder had. She owed her so much.

"I'm on it, boss," she said as she pushed her way through the crowded dance floor towards the back of the club.

It had been two months since she had arrived at the shores of San Francisco and six weeks since she had started working in Tony's nightclub.

Serena, Mrs. Rashid's daughter, had arranged everything, from Wonder's refugee status and all the necessary documents, to the job at the club.

Initially, she'd been hired as a cleaner.

There wasn't much else an uneducated woman like her could do. If not for her unusual strength, Wonder would have still been mopping the club's floors and scrubbing its toilets instead of acting as its only female bouncer.

It had taken one major brawl between a bunch of drunken college girls for the owner to realize Wonder's unique capabilities. As the male bouncers had stood watching, helpless to do anything since they couldn't touch the women, Wonder had untangled the mess in seconds.

Tony, being the wise businessman that he was, had realized that a woman who was as strong as a man was a perfect solution for when ladies got rowdy. Well, Wonder was probably stronger than the human male bouncers, but she wasn't about to correct the misconception.

Frankly, she would have preferred to keep on cleaning.

Even though it got disgusting at times, especially when she had to wipe up vomit off the floors and clean the mess people left in the bathrooms, it was peaceful work that she was good at. Transforming a space from dirty to sparkling clean provided a sense of satisfaction and immediate gratification that breaking up fights and throwing out drunkards did not.

Not for her, anyway.

Acting aggressive and pretending to look threatening went against Wonder's gentle nature. Even though it seemed like she was a natural born fighter, Wonder hated violence in any shape or form.

The upside was better pay.

"You lying bitch! You told Rachel I hooked up with her boyfriend and now she is telling everyone that I'm a colossal slut!"

As Wonder took a deep breath and pushed the ladies'

bathroom door open, the one who was shouting lifted her hand and slapped the other girl's face.

Shocked, the girl cupped her injured cheek. "You're crazy! I've never said anything like that!" She lunged at the offender, grabbing her hair.

It was Wonder's cue to step in.

"Break it up, girls!" she said, catching the hair-grabber's wrist and holding it firmly. "Let go!"

"She started it!" the grabber whined. "She slapped me!"

"Let go, or I'm throwing both of you out. You have two seconds to disengage."

Hissing, the grabber released the other's hair and took a step back. "Throw her out. I did nothing wrong. The bitch is crazy."

Wonder pushed herself in between the combatants, forcing them apart. "Calm down. I'm giving you one minute to fix yourselves up and then you can either behave and go back to the club or leave and resume your fight outside. But if I hear one more shout from either of you, I'm going to remove you from the premises and get you banned from ever coming back."

The last threat finally did the job.

"Fine," the slapper said and walked out.

"How am I going to go out there like this?" The grabber pointed at her red cheek.

"Would you like me to bring you some ice?" Wonder offered.

"Oh, so suddenly you're nice to me?"

"I'm just doing my job. Do you want the ice or not?"

The grabber sighed. "Yeah, I guess. Sorry for yelling at you. It's not your fault that bitch is insane."

"Apology accepted. I'll be back in a minute."

"Thank you." The grabber turned to the mirror and

reached inside her purse to pull out a tube of cosmetic concealer.

Human girls used a lot of products on their faces, but the only one Wonder had tried to date was a black pencil to outline her green eyes. She still wasn't sure whether it made her look better or worse. Not that it mattered. The only reason she used it at all was to make herself look a little older.

A bouncer who looked younger than twenty didn't project the necessary authority or inspire compliance.

Wonder wished she knew how old she really was, but that information was lost with the rest of her memories, and it didn't seem as if any of them were coming back.

In fact, she was starting to doubt what little she thought she knew about herself. Was she really immortal?

It was hard to argue with her body's rapid regeneration from injuries, or with her ability to influence the minds of others, but maybe she was just a human freak?

After all, not only had she not encountered any other immortals, but it seemed no one knew of their existence. From what she had learned, gods and immortals were considered mythical creatures and not real living breathing people.

Perhaps she had dreamt it up while unconscious?

A disturbing possibility since being an immortal was the only sense of self she possessed.

5

WONDER

"*H*ey, Wonder, mind walking me to my car?" Natasha asked. "Since those murders started, I'm afraid to walk from the front door to the parking lot. I'm freaking out all the way until I'm locked inside my car."

"No problem. Let me just tell Tony I'm stepping out for a few moments."

"He was the one who suggested I ask you. He said none of us should go out by ourselves at the end of our shifts, but Tina, who is supposed to be my partner, is not ready to go yet and I have to get home pronto. My two-year-old is complaining of an earache."

Funny that Tony hadn't suggested Wonder partner up with anyone at the end of her shift. Apparently, bouncers were excluded.

"Let's go." She patted her holster.

The recent wave of murders had prompted Tony to give all of the club's bouncers Taser guns and send them to a class on how to use them. According to the newspapers, the murders all occurred in the vicinity of clubs and bars, which was basically every other building on both sides of the street that Club Nirvana was on. Thankfully, none of the murders had happened nearby, but that didn't mean they wouldn't. In an area that was packed with clubs, pubs, restaurants, and bars it was highly probable.

The Taser gun was a good weapon, mainly because it wasn't lethal when handled properly, and also because of its range. There was no need to get close to the attacker. The main disadvantage was that it was good for only one shot.

The nonlethal part was what Wonder liked about it the most, though. She wasn't sure she could've fired a real gun.

One killing was enough for a lifetime, although she had done that one with her bare hands. Evidently, her strength was also a lethal weapon when not used properly. She hadn't known how strong she was prior to throwing her attacker against the wall. If she had, she would've been more careful.

"Did you end up getting that other job you had applied for?" Natasha asked as they stepped outside through the back door.

"Yes. I get to clean six warehouses to start with, and if they are happy with my work, they might give me more."

As someone who didn't need more than five hours of sleep, working the one shift at the club left Wonder with too much time on her hands. Other than her coworkers, she didn't have any friends to hang out with, and since Mrs. Rashid had returned to Egypt, there was no one to assign her homework and insist that she keep on learning either.

Not that she'd discontinued her studies entirely, but she wasn't putting as much effort into expanding her knowledge. Most of it consisted of watching television and the occasional reading of a few pages of a book. The thing was, Wonder preferred to fill her days with work. She needed to save up enough money to move out of the shelter and into her own place.

"I don't understand why you went after cleaning jobs when you could do security. It pays better."

Wonder shrugged. "I like cleaning. The warehouses are unoccupied, and I find it very peaceful to work with no one around."

"Why are they empty?"

"I think they are up for sale or something. Some have signs outside that say for sale or available for lease. All I know is that the maintenance company was hired to keep them clean, and they in turn hired me to do the job."

"It makes sense that if the owners want to sell them, they need to keep the buildings presentable in case a buyer shows up."

"And that's my job."

As they reached Natasha's car, the waitress clicked the doors open. "Thank you for walking me to my car."

"No problem." Wonder waited for her to get inside and lock the doors.

Natasha opened the window and leaned out. "Good night. I'll see you tomorrow."

"Drive carefully."

"I always do. I'm a mother."

Wonder waited for the car to leave the parking lot before heading back. As she opened the back door, a couple walked down the corridor on their way out, the girl leaning against the guy and giggling at something he had said.

She held the door open for them.

"Thank you." The girl smiled at her.

"You're welcome."

As the guy brushed past her, Wonder got a weird feeling, and apparently so did he, because he stared at her for a moment before returning his attention to the girl.

It was probably nothing.

Sometimes men stared at her.

Wonder hoped it was because they found her attractive and not because she was a big woman, who was dressed in a black T-shirt that had the words Club Nirvana and bouncer printed in large white letters on its front.

But that was wishful thinking.

Men preferred dainty little women who they could feel powerful next to. Someone like Wonder, who could lift a guy up and throw him across the room, threatened their masculinity.

The feeling of unease intensified the further she got away from the back door. Ignoring it, Wonder kept walking, but as she passed the bathrooms, the prickling sensation flared into a full red alert. She had to turn around and double check that everything was alright.

Or not, as her instincts kept insisting.

It was probably nothing. The recent murders were making her edgy.

She was just going to take a peek and make sure that the couple drove away safely. The guy looked like someone who could take care of himself, but if the murderer put a gun to his head, he would be just as helpless as the girl.

Her hand hovering over her holster, Wonder closed the back door soundlessly behind her and looked around. The couple was nowhere to be seen, but a throaty moan betrayed their location.

Should she leave them alone and go back?

Couples necking in the back alley was nothing new. People did that all the time. Sometimes, she could tell by the sounds that more than necking was going on, but Wonder had never gone to investigate before.

Even though that kind of activity was considered an offense in the eyes of the law when conducted in public, it was none of her business what two consenting adults were doing out there. She was not a policewoman, only a bouncer. Her job was to break up fights and get rid of undesirables.

Except, this time she had a bad feeling that refused to go away.

Treading silently, she walked to the corner and peered into the alley. It was dark, but Wonder had excellent night vision, and what she saw shocked her.

The man had fangs, and they were embedded deep in his partner's throat. Except, the girl's expression wasn't one of fear or pain, it was ecstasy.

It should have surprised Wonder, but for some reason it didn't. On some subconscious level, she knew that the bite was pleasurable.

The absurd thought made her shake her head. From the sounds the woman was making it was pretty obvious that she was climaxing. No foreknowledge required. Evidently, fangs were not the male's only body part that was deep inside the female's.

Still, the sight of fangs should've rattled her way more than it had. Instead, Wonder experienced two totally inappropriate sensations—arousal and envy.

She wanted that.

Not like this, not propped against a brick wall in a back alley, and not with that male, but she craved the sensation of a bite, which was insane.

A killer's bite.

Except, she was an immortal and would've healed instead of bleeding to death. Maybe that was why it excited her? Some dark desire for something that was deadly to humans but not to her?

She was losing her freaking mind.

This wasn't arousing or sexy. What she was witnessing was attempted murder. This was the killer who had been biting women and leaving them to bleed to death.

Were vampires real?

Immortals, not vampires, her subconscious whispered.

After watching *Twilight*, she had dreamt about vampires, but instead of sucking blood like in the movie, in the dream the fangs delivered venom, and only the males had fangs. They also hissed like snakes before biting. Maybe that could explain her weird reaction to what she was witnessing, especially since the dream females had reacted just like the woman in the alley.

With one difference, those females were immortal. They had walked away with smiles on their faces instead of ending up dead in some back alley.

Up until tonight, Wonder had convinced herself that it had been a silly dream, and that it was all a product of her imagination, same as her being immortal. But the proof to the contrary was right there in front of her eyes.

Those fangs were not long teeth, and that male was not human.

He wasn't a vampire either. He was an immortal male about to murder a human girl.

Not tonight, though. Not on her watch.

As the woman crumpled to the ground with twin rivulets of blood streaking down her neck, Wonder pulled out her Taser gun and aimed.

6

ANANDUR

*a*s Anandur waited for Jackson to finish restocking the vending machine, he leaned against a café table and crossed his arms over his chest. "It's like a ghost town in here."

"Sad, but true."

"You might want to cut back on what you're putting in there."

"Why?"

"There aren't enough customers left to eat it all, and I would hate to see good food go to waste. You'll have to trash what's left at the end of the day, and it will be plenty."

Most of the clan members who had called the keep their home had moved to the new village. The building's café, which had been their favorite place to grab a bite and hang out, was practically deserted. Eventually, it too would get rented out to humans, which would suck, because the Guardians wanted to continue living in the keep.

Currently, they rotated between the keep and the village, but there was no guarantee that this arrangement would last.

Out of the six floors formerly occupied by the clan, only one remained, reserved for the rotating Guardians. The rest of the apartments had been rented out to humans, including the two luxury penthouses. First, Amanda's and then Kian's.

That sucked too. It had been a bad idea to rent those two out.

In some weird way, it felt like a failure, like giving away something that should've stayed in the family. Those should have been retained for whenever Kian or Amanda had business in the city and didn't want to commute from the village. As a Guardian, Anandur considered the safety and comfort of Annani's children more important than what those penthouses were bringing in rent money.

Except, ever since the clan had started their rescue operations, money was tight.

Anandur wasn't a frivolous spender by any stretch of the imagination, but if it were up to him, he wouldn't have done it.

Maybe it was just his aversion to change. Too much of it had been happening lately. None of it was bad, but his life was not the same. Hell, he felt as if he was living someone else's.

It started with the separation from Brundar.

After centuries of cohabiting with his brother, Anandur had moved out to give Brundar and Callie the privacy and intimacy they needed as a mated couple.

But it was more than that.

Before Callie, Anandur had always looked after Brundar, making sure his brother was doing okay, or as okay as Brundar had been capable of before Callie had healed him.

Now, Anandur was suffering from what felt a lot like empty nest syndrome. His kid brother was all grown up, living his own life with his mate.

Anandur was no longer needed.

It was a miracle that he was thanking the Fates every day. But instead of feeling unburdened, he felt as if an essential part of him had been rendered useless. A void was created that was begging to be filled with a new purpose.

Then everyone had moved into the new village, and the few apartments still reserved for Guardians in the keep were managed like hotel rooms, including a maid service that came over twice a week to clean, and change sheets and towels and other stuff like that.

A human maid service, no less.

Not that there was such a thing as an immortal maid service. Still, everyone could clean up after themselves, or not. It was their choice. After all, they had done perfectly well without a cleaning service before.

Well, to be frank, that wasn't entirely true. From time to time, Okidu had cleaned up Anandur and Brundar's apartment, but that was before the butler had gotten too busy for that. There was only so much even a tireless biomechanical marvel could do in the span of twenty-four hours.

Jackson stuffed the last slot and closed the machine's back door. "I filled it up yesterday, same as the day before, and everything was gone by morning, even the egg sandwiches, which are the least popular. It seems like your Guardians have big appetites."

Anandur's eyes followed the big box of pastries Jackson pushed with his foot to the next vending machine. That was what he was waiting for.

There was nothing as mouthwatering as the smell of freshly-baked goods.

"I can't believe that the twenty Guardians on rotation in the keep are responsible for picking clean both machines."

Jackson pulled out a key and opened the back door to the pastry machine. "They are too lazy to make anything for themselves or go out to a restaurant or even a fast food joint. They eat every meal here, breakfast, lunch, and dinner. Pretty damn pathetic. If you want my opinion, you guys should pitch in and hire a chef to prepare proper meals for you."

"But that would put you out of business, buddy."

Jackson sighed as he started restocking the pastries. "You think I want to do this?" He motioned at the machines. "I wish I could move to the village as well. I want to leave Nathalie's old café to Ruth and manage the new one up there."

"So why don't you?"

"I can't. Eva is still refusing to move because of bloody Nick, which means that my Tessa can't move yet either. They run the detective agency from the house they all share. Well, except for Sharon who moved in with Robert and is schlepping back and forth. I don't want my Tessa to lose two hours a day on the commute. Which means that for the time being I still have to live in the dump above Fernando's Café instead of a nice new house in the village."

Stubborn woman. Eva was getting huge, which meant that her baby was coming soon. She should be living up there already, where it was safe.

"How far along is she?"

Jackson looked up. "Seven and a half months? Maybe eight? I don't know. Ask one of the ladies. They are all keeping tabs."

Anandur grimaced. "What ladies? There are only guys here, and I'm on rotation for another week."

When the last pastry had gone into the machine, Jackson closed the back door and pushed up to his feet. "Aren't you Kian's personal bodyguard? What happens if he needs to go somewhere?"

Anandur punched the numbers for a Danish and stuck his credit card into the slot. "Right now, retraining the old Guardians is more important to him. They need a lot of work." He collected the wrapped pastry. "The last time any of them fought with weapons we were still using swords."

"You should've told me you wanted a Danish, I would have left one out for you."

"Nah. This is your livelihood, and I'm not a mooch."

"Let me at least get you a coffee."

"Only if you're having one too. I hate sitting here all by my lonesome."

Jackson glanced at his watch. "Ruth is opening Fernando's up today, so I can spare a few minutes."

"Are you still keeping the old name? I thought you'd changed it to Nathalie's Café."

"We call it that, but the sign over the door still says Fernando's Café. Nathalie would never agree to change it. The café is like a monument to her stepdad's legacy."

Anandur sat at the table, took the wrapper off the Danish, and bit into it. The thing was so good that he closed his eyes and moaned. It wasn't as if anyone other than Jackson could see him having a love affair with a pastry. And if they did, screw them. Anandur didn't care.

It was hard to believe Vlad was the baker. It was true that the kid was using Fernando's old recipes, but not everyone could pick up a recipe and know what to do with it. The kid had talent.

Jackson came back with two coffees and put them on

the table. "It's so bloody annoying. Nick and Ruth are acting like a couple from the fifties. Because of them, I'm stuck here in the city while Carol is doing her best to run the café in the village. It's too much for her to handle on her own."

"Can't she hire some help?"

"No takers. You know how spoiled most of the immortals are. No one wants that kind of work."

Anandur had been entertaining thoughts of kicking Carol's training up a notch and getting her to adopt a more merciless attitude. At the rate she was going, she would never be ready to take on a spying mission of any kind, let alone infiltrate the Brotherhood's camp. But as long as she was stuck running the village café by herself, that option was not on the table. He would have to wait for Jackson to take over, which meant Nick needed to step up his game.

"Can't you give Nick a kick in the ass and get him moving?"

"You think I haven't tried?" Jackson pushed his long bangs back. "It was such a dumb idea to introduce those two. I should've hooked him up with someone else."

"Are they in love or not?"

Jackson sighed. "Yeah, they are. But I don't understand what they are waiting for. It's not like they need to get married to have sex, for Fate's sake."

"Are they even attracted to each other?"

"Are you kidding me? I'm sure Nick is jacking off at least five times a night."

"What about Ruth?"

"She is attracted to him, that's for sure. But she is in no hurry, even though she knows everyone is waiting for her to do it. She says she wants to take her time and get to know Nick first."

"That's not unreasonable."

Jackson grimaced. "Maybe for a teenage virgin in the fifties it would've been reasonable to wait for so long, but not for a grown woman in today's world. No one waits months before hooking up anymore. I can understand waiting for the third date, but no more than that, for a normal couple that is. There might be some religious restrictions or other crap like that. These two started dating seriously right after Eva and Bhathian's wedding. That was three freaking months ago."

Anandur scratched his beard. "What does Eva think about that?"

"She says to give them their space, and that rushing them might ruin things for them."

"Smart woman. Not everyone marches to the same beat."

"I guess theirs is glacial."

Anandur stuffed the rest of the Danish into his mouth, then washed it down with what was left of his coffee. "Thank you for keeping me company." He pushed to his feet.

"Anytime, dude." Jackson offered his hand. "I'm here every morning at five-thirty."

Anandur shook his hand and pulled him in for a bro embrace. "Hang in there, kid. Everything is going to turn out okay." He clapped the guy's back before letting him go.

Jackson picked up his empty boxes off the floor. "You're an optimist."

"Yes, I am."

7

LOSHAM

*S*ipping his morning coffee while lounging on the living room couch, Losham waited for Rami to come back with his newspaper. It was an old-fashioned habit in the era of internet, but he was a very old immortal.

It was important to him to have his finger on the pulse of humanity and be apprised of which way public opinion was blowing. A quick scan through the headlines and the editorials sufficed.

Rami walked into the living room with the newspaper folded under his arm, and his laptop clutched in his hand.

"Would you like the newspaper first or the report, sir?" his assistant asked.

"The report."

"Naturally, sir. Would you like me to print you a copy before we begin?"

"No need. Just tell me the highlights." Assistants were meant to save time. There was no need for Losham to read over every detail. Rami was smart enough to figure out what required his attention and what did not.

"Of course." Rami bowed.

"Let's do it out in the garden. Bring out a good bottle of whiskey and a bowl of nuts."

"Yes, sir."

As Losham glanced at the view through the open patio doors, he could see the entire San Francisco Bay including the magnificent Golden Gate Bridge.

The house had been a splurge, which he'd justified as being a good investment. But the truth was that he just wanted it, and it had not been offered for rent. The structure itself wasn't big, or even opulent, but it was enough for him and his assistant, and Losham had furnished it lavishly.

Besides, its best feature was the garden and the view from it.

Losham was spending most of his time out there while managing the various operations his father had put him in charge of. If it were up to him, Losham would have never returned to the island, but his father demanded updates in person.

It was as good as it was going to get. Other than the once-a-month trips to the island, Losham enjoyed freedom away from Navuh's tight control.

Unfortunately, trip number five was coming up soon.

"Would there be anything else?" Rami asked as he returned from setting up the table outside.

Losham rose to his feet and waved a hand at the garden. "What more could we ask for?"

Rami smiled and inclined his head.

His assistant was having the time of his life away from the island and its strict rules against any deviation from the norm. Here, there was no need for Rami to hide his preferences while out on the town, only when dealing with the warriors Losham was in charge of, and the selection of possible partners was nearly limitless. Young men flocked to the city, and not only for work.

Still, there were enough heterosexual men around to keep Losham's club turning healthy profits. In fact, the SF club was the most profitable in the chain, especially ever since he had brought in paid service providers.

That part of the operation he was not proud of. Not because he didn't approve, but because it was beneath him to act as a glorified pimp.

Except, he'd discovered that the operation wasn't as simple as he had expected, and he couldn't leave it to someone else yet. Trafficking inside the borders of a progressive, democratic country needed to be done carefully and discreetly, and there were many moving parts to coordinate.

Abducting girls and immediately shipping them to the island was a straightforward operation. Training them and putting them to work within the borders of the United States required much more sophistication.

"Okay, Rami. What do you have for me?"

"Should I start with the drug trade or the human flesh trade?" Rami asked with a straight face.

Losham sighed. How far he had fallen. From the lofty position of strategizing wars and political maneuvering, he had been reduced to dealing with the ugly sludge of humanity.

Nevertheless, this degrading step was necessary to refill the Brotherhood's coffers as quickly as possible so they could move on to the next stage of his plan: catching up to the clan's technological level and leapfrogging over it.

"Let's start with the drug trade. It still makes much more money than the other one."

"Indeed, sir. And the warriors are quite happy doing it since you offered them a small cut in the profits."

Losham grimaced. "Apparently not all of them are satisfied. Did you find out who is responsible for the recent killings?"

Once it had been decided to abandon the hunt for Guardians, at least for the time being, the warriors had been instructed to stop killing human women. They were free to frequent the clubs at their leisure, but the idea was to maintain a presence, not to lure in Guardians. Naturally, if the occasional immortal civilian were encountered, they were free to do with him as they pleased.

The men had seemed happy when the order had been rescinded. The Brotherhood held females in low regard but acknowledged their value as breeders. Killing them was considered a waste of resources.

As expected, the warriors had obeyed.

But then two recent cases had been reported in the news of females who had been left to bleed to death from twin puncture wounds to the neck. Apparently, one of the warriors had gotten a taste for it and didn't want to quit.

"You said it wasn't a priority, sir."

It wasn't. In fact, an occasional murder might be just what was needed to keep the clan wasting resources on shoring up their defenses.

"No, you're right, it is not. I'm just curious who is doing it and why."

Even if the Brotherhood benefited from the killer's insubordination, it still needed to be dealt with.

8

KIAN

"*I* don't like it," Anandur grumbled. "Having the Guardian meeting outdoors is a security problem. The fact that we are in the village and there are no humans around doesn't mean we should broadcast our business to everyone."

"Take a seat, Anandur." Kian pointed to a chair. "We are not out in the open. This is a private enclave of the administration building that is occupied only by council members and Guardians. Besides, nothing on the agenda for today is confidential."

Turner stretched his arms and then crossed them behind his head and tilted his face toward the sun. "It's a beautiful day. It would be a shame to waste a couple of hours indoors when we can have the meeting in this lovely garden."

The transformation the guy had undergone was profound. And it wasn't only physical. Turner's face looked younger but also more relaxed, and he smiled more often which further softened his features. The difference in height wasn't all that significant. He was still short compared to Kian, but Turner was very happy about the inch and a half he'd gained.

The guy was also back in fantastic shape. After waking up from his coma with atrophied muscles, it must've been one hell of an effort to regain what he'd lost and to add more.

Turner never did anything half-assed.

The most notable change, however, was the mop of blond hair on his previously bald head. The guy was really enjoying his new hair, and the fact that it was fast growing had allowed him to try a new style every week.

Kian wondered if Turner would still feel the same in a couple of centuries. Fast growing hair was a pain in the butt. Who had the time to deal with all the haircuts?

Onegus pulled a stack of papers out of his briefcase and handed everyone a page. "Those are just the main points. I emailed you the rest, but I know some of you never read your emails." He glared at Arwel.

Kian scanned the page before putting it on the table. "Let's start at the top. The monastery. What's the status with that?"

Onegus folded the page into a small square and tucked it inside his shirt pocket. "The place is ready. Ingrid is putting in the finishing touches on the interior design. It's not fancy, since the emphasis was on comfort, durability, and low cost, but it looks good. The girls are going to love their little rooms."

Taking into account Vanessa's input, the bedrooms of the reconstructed monastery had been reconfigured to allow single occupancy and provide privacy, which meant that everything had been scaled down and there was not much room to put in anything other than a single bed, a compact desk and a chair.

"I want to see it." Kian turned to his assistant. "Shai, put it on my schedule."

The guy lifted a brow. "I'm afraid that it will have to wait for next year. Your schedule is full for the coming months."

Kian waved a hand. "Move things around."

"Where to?"

Amanda put down her paper cup, probably filled with coffee from one of the building's vending machines, and crossed her arms over her chest. "You can take Syssi with you and call it a date."

That was actually not a bad idea. After realizing that unless it was on his schedule, he and Syssi were never going to go out like a normal couple, Kian had told Shai to mark off two time-blocks a week for personal time.

"Make it so, Shai. This Saturday."

"Yes, boss."

"Next item, although it is not on the agenda. How is the retraining of the old Guardians going?"

"They are ready," Brundar said. "After they have gained some field experience, and we've had a chance to evaluate their performance, we can transfer command of the units to the most capable members."

Currently, they were divided into six units, each commanded by one of the Guardians from the original group.

"Can I start scheduling them for raids?" Turner asked.

Brundar nodded. "Start them on small operations."

"Naturally."

"Next item," Kian said. "The reported Doomer sighting."

"Yes." Onegus pulled out his laptop and flipped it open. "A civilian emailed us, claiming to have encountered Doomers in a San Francisco nightclub."

"How did he get away?" Arwel asked.

"He claims that he recognized who they were before they noticed him and made a hasty exit."

"Is it possible the guy was paranoid and only thought he saw Doomers?" Yamanu asked.

"Could be." Kian tapped his fingers on the printed page. "But I think we should investigate. With the old Guardians ready for action, we have the manpower to scope the clubs in the area. If Doomers are back on the night scene, I need to reinstate the prohibition on clubs."

"I'll go," Anandur volunteered. "If you can spare me, that is. I don't think it's a good idea to deploy a large force before determining if the report is valid. First, I'll question the civilian and check if there is anything to it. If there is, Onegus can then send reinforcements to scope the clubs." He crossed his arms over his chest. "All in the spirit of saving money, right, boss?"

"Spoken like a true tightwad," Yamanu said.

That earned him a flick to the back of the head. "Watch out, weirdo."

"Who are you calling a weirdo?" Widening his pale blue eyes, Yamanu leaned toward Anandur and stared into his.

The big oaf lifted his hands to block the sight and turned his head sideways. "Not the eyes, please, not the eyes!" Anandur cried in mock horror.

"Idiots," Kri mumbled.

Stifling a laugh, Kian drummed his fingers on the table to get everyone's attention. "Agreed. Take one of the new Guardians with you." He turned to Brundar. "I'm sure you'd rather stay here, right?"

Before Callie, the brothers had been inseparable. They had lived together and had gone on missions together, but now that Brundar had found his true love, things were changing. The Guardian preferred to stay close to home, which he no longer shared with his brother.

Anandur was putting a happy face on it, but the big guy looked a little lost and much less upbeat than usual. Maybe a trip to San Francisco was just the change in atmosphere he needed.

"I'll take Magnus." Anandur cast a quick glance at his brother. "That is if you're sure you don't want to come."

Brundar arched a brow. "What do you think?"

With a sigh, Anandur leaned back in his chair and crossed his arms over his chest. "Magnus it is."

9

WONDER

Present day.

"I brought you new books." Wonder pushed the worn-out paperbacks through the bars of Grud's cage.

Her prisoner didn't answer, but he took the books and added them to the growing stack by his mattress.

"It's Jules Verne, your favorite."

Grud shrugged. "Are you expecting me to thank you?"

He had a point.

It had been months since she had caught the immortals and locked them inside their cages. Wonder hadn't let any of them out yet, not even once.

In the movies she'd seen, jailed prisoners didn't spend their entire time locked up in their cells. They went out to the exercise yard and were given work to do.

It was unusually cruel to keep hers in perpetual lockdown.

In a moment of weakness, she'd even bought reinforced handcuffs with the intention of taking them out one at a time and letting them stretch their legs by walking around the warehouse. But it was just too dangerous.

The men were immortal, like her, and as such were probably incredibly strong. She could not afford to take the risk. Unlike a real jail, hers had only one jailer and no backup in case a prisoner misbehaved.

When the murders had stopped after she had caught Mordan, Wonder had assumed that she had the entire murderous ring contained. For months there had been nothing, and then three weeks ago another murder had been committed in precisely the same way. Yesterday, a second body had been found.

There was another murderer out there, and Wonder just knew that she was going to find him the same as she'd found those three.

It seemed as if this was her fate all along, and that everything that had happened to her led her to this place. Her incredible strength, the fighting moves that came to her as naturally as if she was born a warrior, the security position she'd been given at the club, it had all been for a reason.

There was one ingredient missing, though. Wonder wanted none of that. Fate had messed up by choosing her for the job. If it were up to her, Wonder would have put on a nice dress, let her hair down, and worked as a teacher, or a librarian, or any other job that was as far removed from violence as possible and didn't require her to get her hands dirty—literally and figuratively.

But that was not the ticket she'd drawn.

Somehow the murderer would end up in her back alley, and she would immediately sense his otherness.

With Grud, she hadn't known what to look for yet, and

it had taken her brushing against him to trigger her senses. With the other two, she had known what to expect—a male who would trigger that very particular sense of alarm.

"What about me?" Shaveh asked.

"I have comics for you." She shoved a stack of five through the slot in the bottom of his cage.

Sometimes she wondered if the guy knew how to read at all. He had never opened any of the books she had brought him, but he liked flipping through magazines and looking at the pictures, and he liked comics.

Mordan enjoyed crossword puzzles and Sudoku, even though he sucked at both. But at least he was trying to keep his gray matter from rotting away.

Out of the three, Grud was the only one with a brain, and he did most of the thinking and talking for them. In the beginning, he kept trying to convince her to let them go but had eventually given up. Now that the murders had resumed, he was at it again.

"Has there been another murder?" Grud asked.

She nodded. "Yeah. They found another body last night."

He got up and grabbed the bars of his cage. "You see? I told you the killer was out there, not in here, and that you're keeping innocent men locked up."

She put her hands on her hips. "Right, and I also imagined the three of you with your fangs inside your victims' throats."

Grud shook his head. "I've told you a hundred times already. All immortal males bite during sex. The biting is for pleasure, not to kill, not females anyway. It goes against everything we believe in. We can't overdose a woman even if we wanted to. It doesn't work like that."

Supposedly, the only time an immortal male used his

fangs and venom to do harm was in a fight with another immortal male.

Shaveh and Mordan supported Grud's claim, but Wonder didn't believe any of them. They were either lying or telling her half-truths. After all, in each case she'd seen the woman crumple to the ground like a discarded rag doll. She had been the one to seal the puncture wounds with her saliva, not the male who'd caused them. Though to be fair, they couldn't do much after getting Tasered.

Except, if any of the three had been indeed just having sex, and if biting was an integral part of it, he would've sealed the holes instead of letting his partner drop to the ground with a bleeding neck.

Still, even though she was quite certain of their guilt, she'd figured that even prisoners on death row were granted some privileges.

"Here is your Sudoku, Mordan." She shoved the little booklet inside his cage.

"I need a new pencil," he said as he collected it from the floor.

"I'll get you one."

"You are so kind," Grud grumbled sarcastically.

Well, what did he want her to do?

For murderers, they were treated quite well, for the simple reason that Wonder had a soft heart and could not stand to see even the worst of scum suffer in subhuman conditions.

That was why she brought them books so they would have something to do other than stare at the walls, and why she had gone to the Salvation Army store and had bought them a bunch of fresh clothes and blankets. She even hosed down their cages daily and, upon Grud's request, their bodies every other day.

Not to mention the food she cooked for them, even

though it was mostly rice and beans. With her modest means, that was the best she could do to keep three grown males fed.

As it was, Wonder felt like a fool for doing so much for three killers of innocent women. Not that they had actually killed anyone, but that was because she had intervened. Otherwise, these women would have died just like those in the newspapers.

The thing was, her conviction that they were indeed killers wasn't absolute, especially since Grud did everything he could to sow seeds of doubt in her mind, claiming that he would have sealed the female's wounds a moment later.

And now, with the new murders, her doubts were growing.

As someone who had never had sex with an immortal, or a human for that matter, Wonder didn't have enough information about the process, and Grud could have told her anything he wanted. She had no way of verifying it.

But even if she was sure of their guilt beyond a shadow of a doubt, Wonder could not have acted differently. Cruelty was not in her nature.

What was she going to do with them?

Was she forever stuck taking care of the three?

The sad truth was that Wonder was starting to think of them as hers. Not like pets, but like distant family members that she disliked and yet felt responsible for.

After all, as far as she knew, her tribe consisted of only four members.

Four immortals among billions of humans.

10

ANANDUR

"Who is going to ask the questions?" Magnus asked as Anandur parked the car next to the civilian's home.

"I am. You're a rookie."

"I beg your pardon?"

Anandur killed the engine. "You've been out of commission for so long, and things have changed so much, that even after the retraining you're not ready to go solo. You might know how to handle a gun and a semi-automatic now, but you still don't know how to talk to a civilian. People have gotten incredibly touchy. If you want to get any answers, you need to handle them with care. Follow my lead, listen and learn."

Magnus shook his head and opened the passenger door. "I think I can still handle basic interrogation."

"Maybe of a Doomer, but not a civilian."

"Suit yourself." Magnus slammed the door shut. "Sorry about that. Didn't mean to."

Magnus had a bit of a temper problem. Nothing severe enough to disqualify him from the force, but definitely something he needed to work on. The ability to keep a cool head was a prerequisite for a Guardian.

The slamming must've alerted the civilian. He opened the door a crack but left the chain on. As if a paltry security measure like that could keep a Guardian out, or any immortal for that matter.

"Anandur, right?" he asked.

"Hello, Vincent." Anandur smiled to reassure the guy. "Thank you for agreeing to see us. I'm Anandur, and this is my partner Magnus."

Vincent eyed Magnus suspiciously. "I don't remember seeing him at Eva's wedding. I would've remembered him. He looks like that actor."

"I was on duty at the keep." Magnus climbed the two steps up to the guy's front door. "And this is new." He smoothed his hand over the goatee. "You might have recognized me without it. I remember seeing you at the other weddings. I'm one of the new Guardians, or old ones. Depends on how you want to look at it."

"Oh, yeah. That's awesome. You have the clan's gratitude. Or at least mine. I have a lot of respect for Guardians." Vincent released the chain and opened the door. "Come in. Forgive me for being overly cautious, but I'm still quite shaken after that encounter with the Doomers."

They followed him inside.

Vincent pointed to the couch. "Take a seat. Can I offer you something to drink?"

"Scotch?" Magnus asked.

"I'm sorry, but I don't have anything alcoholic. I meant coffee or tea or water."

Magnus eyed the guy as if he'd sprouted horns on his head. "What's wrong with you, mate?"

Vincent shrugged. "I like to keep sharp."

"Of course." Anandur lifted a hand to stop Magnus from continuing that line of conversation and inadvertently offending the guy. "You're a programmer, right?"

"Yes."

"Your mind is your work tool. Naturally, you can't allow yourself to compromise it."

Vincent's shoulders relaxed. "Exactly. Can I bring you some water?"

"No, thank you. Please sit down with us for a few minutes. This won't take long."

"Okay." Vincent took the armchair, sitting on its very edge.

His eyes darting nervously from side to side; the guy was definitely twitchy. Perhaps he was indeed paranoid like Yamanu had suggested? Or maybe he was just scared?

Civilians were terrified of Doomers, as they should be.

"Tell me about the incident."

"I already put everything in the email. You have the name of the club, the date I visited it, and the exact time I encountered the Doomers. What else is there? I didn't stay to chat with them."

"How can you be so sure they were indeed Doomers?"

Vincent crossed his legs, his foot going from side to side like the tail on an agitated cat. "I'm very sensitive to the presence of other immortal males. Like right now with the two of you, my neck is all tingly, and I have an uncomfortable feeling in the pit of my stomach. That's why I live alone and have no plans to move into the village."

That was an unusual reaction. Anandur had never heard of a male with a problem like that.

All immortal males had a built in alarm system, alerting them to the presence of another immortal male. But it was very subtle and easy to miss if one did not pay attention. Usually, once it was ascertained that an immortal or immortals were nonthreatening, the sensation dissipated completely.

"Doesn't it go away after a few moments of exposure?" Magnus asked.

"Not for me. My alarm system is broken. It doesn't have an off switch. It is also stronger than normal. I felt you the moment you parked the car in front of my house."

"I was sure it was the noise of the door slamming that alerted you," Anandur said.

"No." Vincent shook his head. "I was in the kitchen when I felt you, and I was heading for the door when I heard the door slam."

Anandur and Magnus exchanged glances.

This was a very useful talent. The question was how it could be best utilized. The guy seemed too anxious and stressed to accompany them on club tours.

Then again, it never hurt to ask. "We could use someone like you on the force. From what you are telling me, it seems you can detect Doomers from afar. It's a huge advantage."

Vincent chuckled. "I hope you're not suggesting I join the Guardian force. You could not have picked a worse candidate. I'm like a Chihuahua—I can bark when I sense danger, but only when I'm at a safe distance."

The guy's self-deprecating comment made Anandur uncomfortable. Men in general and immortal males in particular tried to at least appear brave. Anandur didn't know how to respond to someone who had no problem admitting cowardice.

"That's an interesting idea." Magnus smoothed his hand over his goatee. "Maybe we can train dogs to sniff out immortals. I read somewhere that dogs can detect illness and even differentiate between the various types of cancer.

If they can do that, they should be able to tell the difference between humans and immortals."

Anandur turned to his partner. "Magnus, you're a genius. How come no one has thought of that before?"

"You can't bring dogs into clubs," Vincent said.

Anandur scratched his curly mop. The idea was too good to pass up because of a technicality. "What about those tiny dogs girls carry in their purses?"

Magnus shook his head. "Those are so inbred that they can't be trained. But you can bring a seeing eye dog everywhere. A Guardian could pretend to be blind and walk in with a dog."

Right, as if that was going to fly. Anandur had been to plenty of clubs, and he hadn't seen even one blind person in any of them.

"I need to think it through. First, we need to check if dogs can indeed be trained to detect immortals. Once that is established, we can figure out how to utilize them best."

11

NICK

"Good morning, beautiful." Nick kissed Ruthie's cheek. "Is the breakfast rush over?"

The café wasn't packed, but that didn't mean a thing.

From experience, he knew that it worked in waves. He'd read an article claiming that all minds were connected on a subconscious level, which could explain that otherwise inexplicable behavior.

"It looks like it. But in case this is just a lull, grab a barstool before the next wave hits, and there is no place to sit."

"You're so wise, baby." He kissed her cheek again then pulled out a stool at the counter.

Ruth was starting to gain confidence at running the place. She had even made some changes with Jackson's blessing. The cash register had been moved to the corner, and the pastries went into baskets and onto a shelf he'd helped Jackson mount on the wall. All of that maneuvering cleared room for more seating at the counter.

Her next project was to get rid of the booths and get

more tables and chairs. The only problem with the idea was that the city required another bathroom when occupancy went above a specific number.

It meant either remodeling the downstairs, or freeing the second floor bathroom for customer use.

The problem with that was that Jackson still lived in the upstairs apartment. The guy had mentioned something about moving to a new place once some obstacle was overcome, but he hadn't elaborated. Whatever that was, Nick hoped it would get resolved soon, so Ruthie could implement her plan.

He loved seeing her gain confidence in her managerial skills, and with people in general. She was much less timid now than when he'd first met her. In three short months, his girl had gone from someone who'd never worked before to a manager with a good head for business.

Jackson was talking about leaving her in charge and opening a new place, but every time Nick had asked him about it, the guy wiggled out of giving him a straight answer.

As if Nick had any interest in stealing Jackson's idea for a new location.

Running a bakery café was the last thing he wanted to do. Talk about boring. Not to mention dealing with customers and having to smile all day.

No thank you.

"Your usual?" she asked.

"Yep, you know me. I'm a loyal kind of guy. Once I find something I love, I stick to it." He winked.

Ruth blushed and looked away, pretending to get busy with typing in his order on her tablet. It was another innovation she'd incorporated. There was also a tablet in the kitchen, displaying the orders for the girl she'd hired to prepare the sandwiches.

"Like glue," he added. "So you better get used to the idea of having me around. Because I'm not going anywhere."

Ruth waved a hand. "Stop it," she whispered. "You're embarrassing me in front of the customers."

"I don't care."

She was so shy, getting all flustered every time he complimented her or told her that he loved her. But instead of discouraging him, her blushes and protests only spurred him on.

Maybe if he kept it up for long enough, she would finally believe him. And maybe when she believed him, she would finally be ready to take their relationship to the next step.

Everyone thought they were being ridiculous, and that their courtship period was taking way too long. But Nick didn't give a damn what everyone else thought.

He loved Ruth, and if she needed to take things slow, he was fine with that. Well, as fine as any guy his age could be with getting no further than kissing.

Nick had a feeling that Ruthie was a virgin like him, but unlike him, she was intimidated by the idea of having sex.

To be frank, though, he was a little intimidated too.

Watching as much porn as he did, he knew all there was to know, but only in theory. After all, porn wasn't real sex, not even those clips that were supposedly of real couples. He wasn't fooled. It was all staged.

The thing was, pressing the issue might get him dumped. It was better to wait until Ruthie was ready and not risk losing her. He would be devastated if that happened.

Hell, Nick was afraid he would never recover.

And it wasn't as if he was paranoid or anything. She wasn't as invested in their relationship as he was. Something was holding her back. Hopefully it wasn't about him not being good enough, or lacking something she needed or wanted.

If she would only open up and talk to him about it, he would do his damnedest to become whoever she wanted him to be.

"Here you are, Nicki, your favorite sandwich. Double-decker roast beef." She put the plate in front of him. "Enjoy."

RUTH

"*H*i, Ruth." Tying her apron, Sylvia gave her a quick hug. "Sorry I'm late. Traffic was bad. Do you want me to take over the cappuccino machine?"

"Let me finish with these cups and then it's all yours." Ruth frothed the milk for the four cups of cappuccino she had lined up.

Being called Ruth instead of Mom was taking some getting used to. For years, it was just the two of them, and they had either been alone in the house or around other immortals. There had been no need to hide the fact that Sylvia was her daughter.

Now they told everyone they were sisters.

When the cappuccinos were ready, Ruth put them on a tray and handed it to Lori, one of her new hires. "Here is your order."

"Thanks." The girl took the tray and headed for the last booth on the right. It was the same one Nick used to sit in until he'd gathered enough courage to ask her out.

He was such a sweet boy, so patient and so gentle. But

even an angel like him would eventually get tired of waiting.

Unless he was as terrified of intimacy as she was.

Jackson had hinted Nick was still a virgin.

"I'm going to try and make a leaf again." Sylvia started frothing more milk. "It drives me crazy that I haven't mastered it yet. Every Starbucks barista can do it, and I can't? It's unacceptable."

Her girl had always been competitive.

Ruth was so proud of Sylvia's achievements, and so disappointed that her daughter insisted on helping out in the café. This wasn't a job for a highly educated woman like her.

"You're wasting your time here, Sylvia. I told you that. A woman with two undergrad degrees and a master's on the way, shouldn't be making coffee and waiting tables. There are better jobs out there."

Sylvia waved a hand. "I study for the sake of studying, not because I want to get a job at some fancy office. I couldn't even if I wanted to because places like that require a full-time commitment. Besides, I like it here, and I like helping you out."

That was the problem.

Sylvia didn't need the money. Her share in the clan's profits was enough to cover all of her expenses, and the clan was also paying for the tuition. The only reason she was spending three hours a day helping during the lunch rush, was to help her mother.

Her daughter was afraid for her.

"You can help out your boyfriend, like you did before." At least that had required some skill.

"Roni doesn't need me for anything other than holding his hand, and he needs that hand to keep hacking away on the keyboard. And anyway, spending too much time together is unhealthy for a relationship, not to mention Roni's output at work."

From experience, Ruth knew that there was no point in arguing with Sylvia. The girl was stubborn and would just keep going until Ruth folded.

"Two more cappuccinos," Lori said. "One with skim milk, and the other one with soy."

"Got it." Sylvia reached under the counter and pulled out a new carton of soymilk.

"It's impossible to make shapes with soy. Don't even try."

"I've seen it done. But until I can do it with whole milk, there is no point in trying it with anything else. Even skim milk."

Ruth leaned against the counter and crossed her arms over her chest. "All that matters is that the coffee tastes good, and ours is the best in the area."

"It's the best in the entire freaking city." Sylvia finished frothing the soymilk and poured it into the cup.

"How are things going with Nick?"

It was a question her daughter had been asking every day and receiving the same answer.

"Great."

"Great as in things going on as usual, or great as in things moving forward?"

Ruth felt her ears heat up. "You shouldn't be asking me that, Sylvia. It's not your place."

Her daughter puffed out a breath and turned around, mimicking Ruth's arms across the chest pose.

"The thing is, you don't get those questions from every freaking family member because people are afraid to hurt your feelings. But I do."

"You can tell them that's none of their business. What a bunch of relentless busybodies. I'm now convinced more than ever that I don't want to move into the new development."

The clan was already behaving like a hive. It had been bad enough when their population had been divided between the keep and private residences. Now, with everyone moving into the village, it would be intolerable.

Ruth was a private person, and she put too high a value on her privacy to become another worker bee.

"It's a shame. I'm sure Nick would love to move into a brand new house with you. Living and working with Eva has its advantages, but it also has its disadvantages. And if you ask me, it's a weird arrangement. She thinks of her employees as her children, but they are not hers, and they are not children. He should be living with you. It doesn't even need to be in the new place. He would love it if you invited him to live with you in your house."

He sure would.

But Ruth wouldn't.

The idea terrified her, not because she didn't love him, but because she did. She loved his quirky sense of humor, and his inappropriate jokes and his big heart. That was why she didn't want to ruin the good thing they had going on by moving on to the next step. The attraction was there as well, but there was a big difference between that and actual sex. In her experience, things fell apart at that stage.

Sylvia would never understand, nor would any other immortal female, but Ruth wasn't like them. The question that kept bouncing around her head, though, was whether she'd been born different or had her miserable experience shaped her attitude.

Probably both.

She was a virgin when she met Sylvia's father, which was very unusual for an immortal female in her early thirties. Hell, it was unusual for a human that age. But she'd always been socially awkward and stayed away from people as much as she could.

Ruth had met Ashton at the supermarket. He was charming and outgoing, all the things she was not, and she'd fallen for him in no time at all, or so she'd thought at the time. She had definitely not fallen in love with his lovemaking, if it could've even been called that.

What a nightmare that had been.

He'd basically date-raped her. Except, Ruth wasn't sure if what he had done qualified as rape. After all, she hadn't fought him off. She hadn't even said no. But she hadn't said yes either.

Some naive part of her had hoped that he wouldn't want to hurt her, and that he would realize that she wasn't ready and needed more time. But Ashton was a selfish man, and she had been in love with the idea of love, not him.

How could she have loved him if his hands on her repulsed her, and nothing he had done to her had felt pleasurable?

He'd told her he loved her, and she'd been so starved for affection that she'd kept coming back for more despite the prohibition on having an ongoing relationship with a human. And for what? So she could suffer silently while hoping it would get better?

Eventually, it did. Less fear and less pain had made it more tolerable.

Still, Ruth couldn't understand why the other immortal females were so obsessed with sex. Were they all masochists?

And what about human females?

She'd read sweet romances filled with tender lovemaking scenes and could relate to none of it. Maybe she was just different. Perhaps she was defective in some way.

If she were a brave soul, she would have sought a different partner to see if it was her fault or not. But once Ruth had discovered she was pregnant with Sylvia, none of that mattered anymore.

As a mother, her number one priority was to protect her child. And as an immortal female, it had been her duty to keep her conception secret from the father, or sperm donor as the other immortal females referred to the humans who fathered their children.

It had to be done that way even if the human male had been perfect in every way, which Ashton hadn't been. Not even close.

Ruth had broken things off with Sylvia's father before he could suspect the pregnancy and try to lay claim to her unborn daughter. She'd never seen him since, neither did she want to, nor had she been intimate with anyone else.

Living inside her books and her own imagination was much safer than risking another disappointment. She'd been content to keep things the way they were and had had no desire to upset her comfortable routine.

But then Nick had stormed into her life, awakening her sleeping heart and her dormant desires along with the demons she'd worked so hard to bury.

13

GRUD

*A*s soon as the woman left, Grud walked over to the grate covering the refuse gutter and pulled.

It had taken him many days to loosen the bolts securing it to the concrete. He'd had to be careful, making sure that the floor looked as intact as possible so Wonder wouldn't notice what he'd done.

Taking the grate with him, he walked back to his mattress, sat down, and started working on the metal rods.

"Why are you wasting your time on it?" Shaveh asked. "The gutter is too shallow for you to fit in. Work on the gate instead."

That was what his two jail mates had been doing since day one.

But unlike the two morons, Grud was smart. He'd reached the conclusion that the cages had been built to hold gorillas or orangutans a long time ago. Supposedly, the big apes were ten times stronger than the average human man, which meant that they were about twice as strong as an immortal male. Not that he knew that for a fact. Maybe immortal males were only three times stronger than humans. It didn't change the fact, though, that there was no way for them to break free from cages designed for the powerful apes.

For a long time, Wonder had refused to tell them anything about where they were and what the cages had been used for before. Grud had thought she didn't know, like she didn't know a lot of other things. He was an uneducated soldier, but compared to her he felt like a scholar. It was amazing how little Wonder knew about anything, especially since he didn't think she was dumb.

Eventually, though, she'd revealed that the facility had been used for testing drugs on apes. Later, it had been outlawed or something, and the place had been shut down.

Grud had shared the information with the two, explaining that they could work from now until eternity and not succeed in bending even one bar. But if they wanted to waste their efforts, it was their business. He was getting out of there, and once he was free, he would consider coming back for them.

Maybe, he wasn't sure about that part.

"What are you planning to do with the grate?" Mordan asked.

There was no harm in sharing his idea. "I'm trying to pry one of the slats free, so I can use it as a tool to dig a hole in the back wall."

Shaveh grabbed onto his cage's bars and poked his nose into Grud's. "Do you think it leads to the outside?"

The guy was a moron.

"We are in a basement, so obviously it can't lead to the outside. But it leads to another room in the facility."

"What if there are more cages on the other side?" Mordan asked.

The guy was slightly smarter than Shaveh.

"That's possible. But I'm betting on it being just a

regular room with a regular door designed to keep humans out that I can break down easily."

"How do you know there is a room on the other side and not dirt?" Shaveh asked.

"If you put your ear to the back wall and listen, you can hear Wonder's footsteps when she leaves."

"Oh." Shaveh seemed satisfied with the answer.

Mordan threaded his arm through the gap between the bars and waved a hand. "What are you going to do with the rubble? Where are you going to hide the blocks?"

Grud sighed. "I don't have a tool yet, and you worry about the debris? I'll crumble the blocks and dump them in the gutter."

"It will get clogged, and we will be stuck with shit piling up." Finally, Shaveh had something smart to add.

Turning to look at the guy, Grud shrugged. "If I crumble it enough, the little pieces will get washed away when Wonder hoses the cages down. And in any case, there will not be that much rubble. All I need is a hole large enough to fit through."

"How are you going to hide the hole until it's ready?" Mordan asked.

Grud pointed to the stack of books by his bed. "I'm going to move this against the back wall. That's why I've been asking her for more and more books."

Mordan laughed. "So that's why you're suddenly interested in reading. I thought you wanted to impress the woman, because you only pretended to read while she was here."

Well, that too. She was softening toward him. But Grud couldn't count on her lowering her guard enough to let him out of the cage. Still, that could be a backup plan in case the first one failed.

He picked up a book and lifted it to Mordan's dangling

hand. "Start reading out loud. I need to know what the book is about if I want to strike up a conversation with her."

Mordan threaded the book through the gap and started flipping through the pages. "You still think you can soften her up?"

"If I can loosen an iron grate, I might be able to loosen Wonder's will."

"What about us?" Shaveh asked. "How are we getting out? Will you come back for us?"

"Of course."

Maybe.

14

ANANDUR

"Will it take you much longer to get ready?" Anandur asked Magnus as they returned to their hotel room.

The guy fussed with his appearance like a teenage girl.

"Blow me." Dressed in grey boxers, black socks, and a black button-down, the guy pulled out the ironing board from the closet and put his slacks on it.

Well, that was his answer. Ironing pants took time. Anandur plopped on the couch and clicked the dumb box on.

"Aren't you going to get changed?" Magnus asked.

"Nah. What I have on is fine."

"You're going to a club, not to toss out the garbage."

Anandur switched to another channel. "My clothes are clean, free of stains, and don't smell. It's good enough."

"You'll be the only one wearing a T-shirt and Levi's. You're going to stick out." The iron hissed as it released steam over Magnus's pants.

"I'm six foot six with a mop of red curls on my head and

on my puss. You think a fancy shirt is going to help me blend in?"

"You've got a point." Magnus flipped the pants upside down and kept ironing. "You should consider giving that hair of yours a trim. And shorten the beard too. I can take you to a good stylist."

Wonderful. The guy was fresh off the boat, so to speak, and he knew a stylist already. It was good Magnus could kick ass with the best of them. Otherwise Anandur would have wondered about his aptitude for a Guardian job.

"Next time you go for your Brazilian blow-out, take me with you," Anandur mimicked a valley-girl. "We can get matching hairdos."

Magnus waved a dismissive hand. "Forget I ever mentioned it. Let's go." He pulled on his slacks and then threaded a fancy belt through the loops.

The thing probably cost more than Anandur's entire wardrobe.

"What do you think of Vincent's story?" Magnus asked as they got in the car.

"I believe him. Unless he's lying about his hypersensitivity to immortal males. Though I can't imagine why."

Reaching for the car's GPS, Anandur typed in the club address Vincent had provided.

"Maybe he's using it as an excuse not to move into the village."

Anandur pulled out from the hotel's parking lot and merged into traffic. "He doesn't need an excuse. Kian gave an exemption to several programmers, and Vincent is one of them. His work cannot be done online. It's classified."

"One of those, eh? What is he working on, anti-nuke missiles?"

"I don't know. Everything to do with leaking technology to humans belongs in William's domain. I'm sure

Kian gets updates, but I doubt he pays attention enough to know which programmer is working on what."

"Fascinating subject, but not for old-timers like us." Magnus sighed. "I still don't know how to navigate Facebook, let alone do any coding. The current generation is better at these kinds of jobs."

"Mark wasn't much younger than you." Anandur's good mood soured as he was reminded of the programmer's murder. "He was the best we had."

"Right. I didn't know he was that old."

With thoughts of Mark and his death at the hands of Doomers putting Anandur in a reflective mood, he spent the rest of the drive in silence, while Magnus stared out the window, probably busy with his own existential musings.

Supposedly, Mark wasn't really gone, since he'd made a reappearance as a ghost or spirit, talking inside Nathalie's head. But even though Nathalie could not have known the things she'd claimed Mark had told her, Anandur was still doubtful. No one knew what happened on the other side of the veil, or even if the veil or the beyond existed.

Being a romantic and believing in the power of love didn't make Anandur a patsy who believed in everything he was told.

"You have arrived. Your destination is on your right," the automated female voice announced.

"She sounds sexy," Magnus said as Anandur parked the car.

"You're desperate, buddy. Get yourself a woman tonight."

Magnus grinned. "I plan on it as soon as we are done with the investigation."

"Same here." Anandur nodded at the bouncer blocking the entrance.

The dude, who was about as wide as he was tall and not

because he was fat, frowned at Anandur but smiled politely at Magnus.

"Welcome to Club Nirvana, gentlemen." He opened the door for them.

"You see why it pays to dress up?" Magnus said as they entered.

"Nah, he probably thought you're that actor."

"You think?" Magnus smoothed his hand over his goatee.

Anandur shook his head. "Let's ask the barman a few questions."

With a slight bow, Magnus waved a hand. "Lead the way."

The barman wasn't much help. "Sorry, but I don't remember anything out of the ordinary happening on that day."

"Any suspicious characters?" Anandur asked.

The guy huffed. "Look around you, dude. Everyone looks suspicious." He leaned closer. "But you know what? Often those who don't look it are the worst, like the creeps who slip roofies into girls' drinks."

"Ain't that the truth." Anandur tapped his hand on the bar. "Two whiskys for me and my friend. No ice."

"What kind?" The barman threw a menu on the counter.

"No need. I'm sure you carry Chivas."

"We do."

"Any point in asking the servers if they saw anything?"

The guy shook his head. "It was a relatively quiet week. There are always a few guys who get drunk, but that's normal."

Despite the barman's assurances, Anandur exercised due diligence. After finishing his drink, he talked with each of the servers. They confirmed what the barman had said.

It had been a quiet week.

"Well, my friend." Magnus rubbed his hands. "It's time to find us some willing lassies."

"Absolutely." Anandur clapped the guy on the back. "Good luck."

"No luck needed, but I have a favor to ask." Magnus raked his fingers through his longish hair. "Do you mind if I use our hotel room? I'm not into back-alley romps."

"No problem." Anandur fished out the car keys from his pocket and handed them to Magnus. "I'll use Lyft."

"Not Uber?"

"Nah, their customer service sucks."

15

WONDER

*W*onder pulled out several rolls of toilet paper and two packets of toilet-seat covers from the storage room and headed for the ladies' room. It was no longer her job to restock it with the necessities, or make sure that there was no mess left unattended, but old habits refused to die. When she noticed that the bathroom was low on supplies, she just did it. It would've been silly to call the new cleaner for something that took her a few moments to do.

Tony had hired a guy as her replacement, which meant that while Jerry did his job, the ladies' bathroom would have been closed and a huge line of impatient women would've formed, shifting from foot to foot and complaining about the wait.

Besides, she was bored. No fights had broken out tonight, and she was tired of standing by the back door and keeping it open for people going out. She was a bouncer, not a doorwoman.

Once Wonder was done with the bathroom, she headed over to the parking lot. Ever since she had caught Grud, she had made it a point to patrol the area several times a night, paying particular attention to the back alley.

Human males were often almost as bad as the three immortals she'd caught. Not that she had encountered any with murderous intentions, but there were quite a few who had gotten too handsy with girls who were either not willing or too drunk to know what they were doing.

She waved at Jerry who was on his way to the men's room. "Hi, Jerry, I already took care of the ladies' room."

"Thanks, but you shouldn't have. Tony will think I'm not doing my job."

"Nah. The ladies' room is nothing compared to the men's room. No one will think you're slacking if you keep that place clean." What Wonder had wanted to say was pigsty instead of place, but she wasn't sure it was the right phrase to use.

Her command of the English language was good, and she had mastered the Californian accent to perfection, but some phrases and expressions still gave her trouble. They were called idioms. She'd looked it up on the used laptop she'd purchased.

Mrs. Rashid was so happy when Wonder emailed her for the first time. Since then, they had been communicating almost daily.

"Yeah." Jerry sighed. "I think after enduring that, my place in heaven is secure. I already paid my penance."

She had no idea what he was talking about.

It had something to do with a religion, but there were too many of them to remember what each one preached. They all believed in one god, though—an entity no one had ever seen.

Obviously, that entity had nothing to do with the gods her imagination had concocted. Those were flesh and blood.

Sometimes, she would have vivid dreams about a different world and a different reality, where humans, gods, and immortals coexisted and intermingled on a regular basis. The problem was that she remembered very little of it upon waking.

Smiling, as she usually did when people told her things she didn't know how to respond to, Wonder waved her hand. "See you later, Jerry. I'm going to check the parking lot."

"Be careful."

She patted her Taser gun. "I have protection." Not that she needed it against humans, but it had proven useful with immortals.

Those males were strong, and she didn't know if she could subdue one with her bare hands like she did with humans.

Pushing the back door open, she stepped out and inhaled the fresh air. That was another benefit of patrolling the parking lot. Several times a night, she got to get out of the club's stifling interior with its amalgamation of smells, and just breathe.

As always, she headed first toward the alley between the club and the building to its right, where she had caught most of the offenders, human and immortal. And as always, she had to force herself to keep going despite a strong feeling of apprehension. It wasn't that she was afraid for herself and her safety, but because she didn't look forward to the confrontations.

Except, it was her job.

Sort of.

Wonder hadn't been hired to police what happened outside the club, especially when it was done discreetly and didn't cause a disturbance, but Wonder knew that she was the only defense the women had against overeager human males and immortals with murderous intentions.

That was what made it her job.

Thankfully, other than a couple of cats and several rats of the four-legged kind, the alley was deserted tonight.

Wonder sighed in relief, leaned against the club's back wall, and got ready to get bored.

She observed a couple exit the club and head straight for their car. She chatted with a guy who went out to smoke. Then she watched, with a bit of envy, a bunch of noisy girls spill out the back door and stand around, chatting excitedly for a few minutes before parting with hugs and kisses and promises of meeting again soon.

The girls seemed so carefree and cheerful. She was about the same age as them, but for some reason she felt ancient in comparison. Her driver's license said that she was twenty-two, but that was just a guess. She could be a little younger or much older than that.

Wonder was about to step inside when another couple came out, the woman laughing at something her exceptionally tall redheaded boyfriend had said.

Smiling, he lifted her hand and kissed the back of it, which caused the woman to giggle again.

The guy had a nice smile. Open. Friendly.

As the breeze picked up, Wonder caught his smell. It wasn't one of those complicated perfume scents many of the men wore, but a simple one, clean and masculine.

As if sensing she was watching him, he turned to look at her over the top of his girlfriend's head, then frowned.

What was his problem? Was he upset that she was looking at him?

Then his eyes traveled down and stopped at her chest.

So he was one of those rude guys who shamelessly ogled women.

Narrowing her eyes, Wonder crossed her arms over her chest.

But when he lifted his head, smiled, and gave her a two-fingered salute, she realized he hadn't been looking at her chest but at what was written on her T-shirt—the club's name and the word bouncer.

Was he a bouncer too? Or maybe a policeman?

As it turned out, he was neither.

When the couple walked by her, Wonder felt the small hairs on the back of her neck tingle.

She was sensing his otherness.

The guy was an immortal.

Another killer like the three she had already caught.

A profound sense of disappointment washed over her. The guy had seemed so nice.

It was like Baron the bartender used to say, most often the worst of scum didn't look like the villains in movies, but like guys a girl would consider going on a date with. That was how they lured their victims in.

Well, not tonight, and not on her watch.

The redhead was going down.

16

ANANDUR

*T*he bouncer was a knockout.

If she weren't so damn young, and if Anandur hadn't left the club with another woman, he would have hit on that Amazon beauty like a freighter and charmed the pants off of her.

The first thing he'd noticed was her height. She was tall and solidly built, which a guy his size appreciated in a woman, and she was also generously endowed, which he liked too. A lot. But her most striking feature was her jade eyes. The unique color and the intensity of her gaze were so entrancing that Anandur had a hard time looking away.

And she was a bouncer—a fellow law enforcer of sorts.

Offering her a two-fingered salute, Anandur forced a smile and returned his attention to the woman he had invited for a quickie.

Damn it.

After seeing the bouncer, his appetite for what-was-her name had vanished. Was it Rosie? Shame on him, he should at least know the first name of a woman he was about to fuck into an orgasm or two.

But he couldn't back down now. He'd promised her a good time, and Anandur always kept his promises.

If only the bouncer were a bit older, he could've closed his eyes and pretended that it was her instead of Rosie or whatever her name was, but he had a rule about girls twenty-one and younger, and that included fantasizing about them.

He would feel like a damn pedophile if he imagined shagging the pretty bouncer against the wall.

According to the law of the land, she was most likely legal. After all, no one would have hired a girl under eighteen for a bouncer job. In fact, she probably had to be twenty-one to work in a club that served alcohol. But she wasn't legal according to his rule.

It might have not seemed like it to his buddies, but Anandur had standards. They were just different than those of his fellow Guardians. Even for a casual shag, he preferred a pleasant personality to good looks, and life experience to a youthful face. Size mattered too.

No dainty little things for him.

Even though he was always mindful of his size and his strength and tried to be as gentle as he could, he didn't want to risk hurting a girl unintentionally.

"Oh, Darren," the woman whispered as he cupped her breast through her shirt.

"It's Anandur, sweetheart." He pushed her shirt up and her bra down.

"Sorry about that." She giggled. "I'm a little tipsy."

"It's okay, darling. I don't mind." Especially since he couldn't remember her name no matter how much he strained his noggin.

Whatever, it wasn't important. He could get away with using endearments.

"Oh, yes!" The woman moaned as he latched onto her

nipple.

Thumbing the other one, Anandur closed his eyes, but as soon as he did, he saw the bouncer's intense gaze boring down into his soul. It was like the image of those jade eyes had been burned into his retinas, and no amount of willpower was going to eradicate it.

Fuck.

Just this once, he would allow himself to fantasize being with the young bouncer. Otherwise, he would have to go back on his promise to Rosie because this was the only way he could do right by the woman he'd propositioned.

After all, going back on his word was a much worse offense than a little harmless fantasy, right?

Damn it. This had nothing to do with right or wrong. He was just looking for an excuse to bend his own rules. Even if the bouncer were older, thinking about her while with another was a rotten thing to do.

Opening his eyes, Anandur pushed the woman's pants down and cupped her sex.

She moaned, gyrating her hips to get the friction she needed.

Already turned on by his sexy talk and roaming hands on the dance floor, Rosie climaxed as soon as he drove two fingers inside her.

Good girl. He loved it when nearly no foreplay was needed. Shagging random strangers was a necessity, as was reaching climax and biting, but it didn't mean he wanted to prolong the act.

The last time Anandur had taken his time was with Lana, at first because it had been his job to get her talking about Alex, and later because he'd grown fond of her. That had been the closest he'd ever come to having a romantic relationship with a woman.

Funny how everyone thought he was such a big romantic. He was just a guy who liked a good love story with a happy ending. Regrettably, though, reality precluded him from being part of one.

All he had were countless encounters like this one.

It was time to wrap things up. He needed to put the woman under a thrall before penetrating her without the protection she believed was necessary but wasn't. As an immortal male, he didn't carry or transmit diseases, and the chances of him getting her pregnant were practically nonexistent.

Having done so thousands of times before, it required very little concentration on his part. He could do it on autopilot, which was lucky because his ability to navigate his own mind, let alone his partner's, was compromised. Blocking thoughts of the bouncer was putting a strain on his mental powers, which weren't the strongest to begin with. Even with all his faculties intact, his mind-manipulating ability was mediocre at best.

As he freed his shaft and drove it home, the woman groaned in pleasure, which meant that his thrall had worked, or maybe that she was too out of it to notice he had entered her bareback.

When she climaxed again, Anandur wasn't anywhere near orgasming, but he knew he would be the moment he bit her. That was the way his body was programmed, and for once he was thankful for it. With his promise fulfilled, he would escort the woman back to the club, and then get the hell out of there.

17

WONDER

*H*er sneakers soundless on the pavement, Wonder crept toward the back alley, well aware that the male might hear her despite her best efforts at a stealthy approach. Immortals had superior senses.

Luckily, the woman was making enough noise to drown out a stomping elephant.

Hiding behind the corner of the building, Wonder listened, peeking only occasionally to check for the appearance of fangs. The guy wasn't making any sounds, but the woman more than compensated with her throaty moans and groans.

At least it sounded like she was having a good time, which hadn't been the case with the victims of the other three Wonder had caught.

The girls they had been with started out like the woman in the alley, but their enjoyment had been short-lived, and the sounds of pleasure had quickly turned to sounds of distress. Those hadn't lasted long either. With a thrall, the immortals had silenced their protests and then bitten them right away.

This guy was taking his time with the woman. Perhaps he wasn't like the others, and this was consensual sex between adults, one of whom happened to be an immortal male, and the other a human female who seemed to be in her mid-thirties or older.

Nevertheless, Wonder needed to make sure no harm was done to the woman.

Except, listening to the sounds of passion wrested a most inappropriate response out of her.

Just as it had happened when she'd caught Grud, witnessing the encounter aroused her. But this time it was much worse. That first time her arousal had been mild, more of a curiosity really. This time it gripped her full force.

It was so wrong.

She should not feel that way at a potential murder scene. In fact, she shouldn't get excited at all while spying on other people's intimate moments.

It was creepy.

What did Natasha call someone who acted like that? A Peeping Tom?

Yeah, Wonder was exactly like that Tom person, whoever he was.

Except, what choice did she have?

She couldn't leave without making sure that nothing nefarious was going on, and she couldn't Taser the redhead's ass without proper cause either.

Wonder was stuck listening to another woman orgasming and trying to imagine how it felt. She didn't know whether she'd ever had sex before her memory loss, let alone if she'd enjoyed it. For all intents and purposes, she was a virgin.

It was torture.

Upon hearing the woman climax again, Wonder peeked

from behind the corner, not because there was cause for alarm, but because she wanted to see the expressions on the couple's faces. Would they look euphoric? Ecstatic? Replete?

The woman's expression was exactly what she had imagined it would be, but the male's was not.

With his fangs fully extended, he looked terrifying.

Gods, she'd been so stupid thinking this was just about pleasure. Apparently, sex between an immortal male and a human female was always deadly to the human.

It was so incredibly evil.

If the males couldn't refrain from biting, they should stick to their own species. Immortal females could handle it. Maybe they even enjoyed it.

If there were communities of immortals out there, then for sure they had laws against killing innocents. The three she'd caught before, and now this one, were probably rene-gades, outcasts, marauders who preyed on human females.

She was doing the world a favor by eliminating these predators.

Wonder pulled out her gun, aimed, and fired.

As the male collapsed in a twitching heap on the ground, the woman screamed. Unlike the other three, she wasn't as out of it because she hadn't been bitten yet. The poor thing thought someone was attacking her lover.

Wonder was on her in a blink of an eye, pushing a hard thrall into her brain to silence her up. It was a hatchet job that would leave a big hole in the woman's memory, but Wonder didn't have the luxury of taking her time with a delicate erase.

When she was done, she helped the dazed woman to hurriedly straighten her clothes and sent her back to the club.

The big redhead was still twitching like crazy, but he

was fighting it with all his might. "Sorry about that, but you left me no choice," she said before lifting her arm and slamming the butt of her Taser gun on the back of his head.

Lights out, buddy.

Except, it wouldn't last long. Immortals recovered rapidly. Taking her pocket knife out, she quickly cut off his clothes, took off his shoes and socks and then stuffed everything under the dumpster for later retrieval. With a grunt, she hefted the big guy over her shoulder and carried him to her car.

He must weigh over two hundred and fifty pounds, all of it solid muscle. If this one woke up before she locked him in a cage, she would be in big trouble. Wonder suspected that her strength was no match for his.

As she had done with the others, Wonder opened the trunk, dumped him inside, and delivered another blow to the back of his head. That should do it until she reached the facility and locked him in a cage. The place was only five minutes' drive away. She could dump him and be back at the club before anyone noticed she was gone.

18

RUTH

"You don't have to do this," Ruth said as Nick grabbed a rag and started wiping a table.

Done with the first one, he tackled the next. "The faster this is done, the sooner I can get you out of here. And where is Jackson? Isn't he supposed to be here at closing time and help you guys clean up?"

"Jackson opened up this morning, so it's my turn to close up. He and Tessa went to the movies." Ruth took down an empty basket off the shelf and shook it upside down over the plastic tub she'd put on the counter.

"Which one?"

"*Incredibles 2.*" Ruth chuckled. "I think that they are a little too old for animated movies, but what do I know?"

Rag in hand, Nick straightened. "Are you kidding me? The first *Incredibles* was one of the best animated movies ever. Don't tell me you didn't see it."

Of course she had. Sylvia was a teenager when it had come out, and the two of them went to see it as soon as it did.

"I saw it. It was fun. I especially liked the baby, Jack-Jack."

"Don't you want to see the sequel?"

She took another basket off the shelf. "Usually the sequel is not as good as the original."

"Not this time, baby. Critics and audiences love it." He tucked the rag under his belt and sauntered closer. "Come on." He pulled her into his arms. "What say you? We can go see it tonight."

"Yeah, sure. If you really want to." She pushed on his chest and turned around to take another basket off the shelf.

Nick remained in the same spot. "Why do you always do that? Does my breath stink?"

Shit. "No, it's not that. I just want to be done with the cleanup so we can go."

Nick blew into his palm. "Are you sure it's not my breath? I ate all the leftover potato salad, and it tasted kind of funny."

He was adorable, really. Was he doing it for her? To get her off the hook? Or had he regretted putting her on the spot and was trying to cover it up?

In either case, it was sweet of him, and Ruth felt like an ass for pushing him away. It was an instinctive response. She had no control over it.

"Can you check show times while I finish cleaning the baskets?" she asked to change the subject.

"Sure." Nick pulled out his phone. "How about IMAX at ten-fifteen?" he asked after a couple of moments. "Or is that too late for you? I know you have to get up early."

"It's fine." Ruth didn't need more than four hours' sleep. It was pretty standard for an immortal, but for a human it was on the extreme end of the spectrum.

Nick leaned against the counter and crossed his feet at the ankles. "That leaves us almost two hours to snog." He winked at her as if he meant it as a joke.

Except, Ruth had a feeling it was his way of letting her decide if she wanted to take him seriously or not.

They kissed a lot, and it was more than pleasant, but she could never really relax into it because she was stressing about him wanting more. It was a nasty cycle that she was getting sick of but didn't know how to stop.

Maybe the best thing was to just let it happen.

Forcing a smile, she pointed at the back of the café. "That's a good spot for snogging. Why don't you take a seat, and I'll see if the girls are done in the kitchen and send them home."

A big grin split his handsome boyish face. "I'll be waiting right over there." He pointed at the last booth.

They were only going to kiss, that's all. Her stomach had no reason to do flips and her mouth had no business getting dry.

Locking up the back door after saying goodbye to her two employees, Ruth took a deep breath, removed her apron, and hung it on the peg next to the door.

Except, she wasn't ready to go back to Nick yet. Instead, she ducked into the bathroom. Looking in the mirror, she didn't like the anxious eyes staring back at her. She didn't want to be that mouse of a woman.

She wanted to be a tigress.

Grrr, she growled at the mirror and swiped her fingers as if they were claws, then giggled at her own silliness. Letting her hair out of the tight braid she wore during work, she finger-combed it to fall in soft waves down her shoulders.

Nick liked to run his fingers through her hair, and his

touch was always gentle. She had no reason to fear intimacy with him. He was nothing like Ashton.

"Okay, I can do this," she told the mirror.

Maybe this time she could do more than kissing. Perhaps she could take his hand and lead it to her breast. Nick wasn't going to do it unless she initiated.

Damn it, she wasn't that forward.

On the other hand, her timidity was what had gotten her in trouble in the first place. If she weren't such a pushover, who had waited for the guy to take the initiative, she might have made better choices and been enjoying intimacy for all those years instead of cowering away from it.

That's what happened to people who were reactive instead of proactive. They didn't get what they wanted. Others got what they wanted from them. She'd repeated those same words of wisdom to her daughter countless times. Apparently, Sylvia had listened, growing up to become an assertive woman who knew what she wanted and went for it no matter what.

It was time for Ruth to follow her own advice.

A lot had changed in her life lately. She'd made impressive progress if she said so herself. From someone who'd hardly ever left her house, she'd turned into a businesswoman who didn't suck too badly at managing other people.

The two human girls she'd hired had no problem listening to her and doing what she told them, which frankly had surprised her. Ruth had expected to encounter resistance and backtalk like she had with Sylvia. But apparently, mother-daughter relationships were different. There were a lot of layers to them. Besides, not many people were as stubborn as Sylvia. Her employees didn't argue with her at all.

If she could conquer one fear, she could conquer another.

Right?

19

NICK

*W*as it his imagination or did Ruthie seem a little different tonight?

Her kisses were a bit less reserved, and she had even initiated a few. Maybe she was ready for more?

Damn, he wished he knew for sure. The last thing he wanted was to make a wrong move and lose her. Should he ask?

Instead, he let his hand trail up her ribcage, but stopped right below her breast. He'd tried it a couple of times before, but she'd always pushed his hand away.

This time she allowed it to remain where it was, but to say that she looked like she wanted it was a stretch. Her breathing was shallow, but not because she was hot for him. It was more like she was terrified of making a move.

Maybe if he admitted that he was a virgin too, she would be less anxious.

He cupped her cheeks. "Are you scared, Ruthie?"

She nodded. "A little."

"Why? Is it because it's all new to you? It's all new to me too."

Her eyes softened, and she lifted her hand to his cheek. "Oh, Nicki, it's so brave of you to admit that. I'm so proud of you."

Now she sounded as if she was his teacher or his mother and he didn't like it one bit. "That's not exactly what I wanted to hear."

"I know. I'm sorry. I should've leveled with you a long time ago." She lowered her eyes.

"What is it?"

"When I told you I wanted to take my time, it wasn't because I'm a virgin."

She sighed. "I've been with one guy, years ago, and it wasn't good. Since then I haven't dated anyone until you. You're sweet and kind and I love you, but I'm scared that it will be horrible again, and that you'll leave me because I can't enjoy sex." She let out a puff of air. "I can't believe I finally had the guts to say this."

Nick frowned. Ruthie wasn't much older than him, if at all. Except, since she refused to tell him her age, she must be at least a little older. In either case, whatever had happened to her must have been when she was a teenager. Had some older guy taken advantage of her?

The thought of anyone hurting Ruth made him furious. "Where is that son of a bitch? I'm going to kill him!"

She smiled a sad little smile. "I don't know, and I don't care. I want to bury that in the past and start afresh as if it never happened. Unfortunately, I can't help that panicky feeling I get every time I think you want more than kisses."

He took her hand and kissed the back of it. "Did I ever do anything that was unpleasant to you?"

Ruth shook her head. "No. But I can't relax enough to enjoy even our kisses. I never feel safe. I know it's crazy, and I want you to know it's not your fault in any way. You're a sweetheart."

Nick was at a loss. Not only did he lack experience with girls, but he also wasn't all that good with people in general. He had the tendency to say the wrong things at the wrong time and was probably the last person to come up with a way to help Ruthie.

"Is there anything I can do?"

"You're doing it. You're patient with me, and you don't get mad at me for taking my time, and you love me anyway. I could not have asked for more."

"I wish I could do more. But I don't know what. Maybe you should talk with someone who knows? Like Jackson's mom? She is a therapist. I'm sure Jackson can get you a discount."

"I thought about it, but the idea of confiding in a stranger scares me. I don't like talking with people, and especially not about my problems."

"I could go with you, you know," he offered. "Hold your hand and stuff like that."

"That's sweet. I'll think about it."

Which meant she wouldn't do it. By now he knew Ruth well enough to be sure of that. Maybe there was another way?

Looking down at their joined hands, Nick decided to take a chance. "I want to ask you something that might embarrass you, and maybe make you think less of me..."

"Nothing would make me think less of you, Nicki. I love you, you must know that."

He nodded. "Did you ever watch porn?" He cringed before daring to look at her.

"No, why do you ask?"

"Well, I watch a lot. And I think that, maybe, if you could see people having fun doing it, you'd be less scared. There are some very nicely done movies with romance and everything. You know, the kind girls enjoy."

Ruth shook her head. "I don't know. I would probably be too embarrassed to watch."

Nick let out a relieved breath. She hadn't called him a pervert, and she hadn't said it was disgusting either. "We can watch for a few minutes, and if you don't like it, we can stop. I'll look for a nice one with lots of romance."

"Okay," she whispered and then blushed. "I guess I can watch for a few minutes."

ANANDUR

*a*nandur woke up with a bitching headache. The first thing he became aware of was that he was cold. The second was the reason for it.

He was naked, and he was lying on a thin mattress inside a cage.

"You're awake," an unfamiliar male voice said.

"What the hell?" Anandur sat up and rubbed at his temples. "Where am I?"

The male chuckled. "You said it. This is hell. Welcome to Wonder's hotel. Included in your stay are one meal of rice and beans a day and a cold hose-down shower every other day."

Anandur rubbed the back of his head where there was a large bump. Someone had knocked him out using a blunt object. With the headache he was nursing, it took him a few moments to notice that the small hairs on his neck were prickling like crazy.

His neighbor, or rather neighbors, were all immortals.

He glanced left and then right, looking at the males' faces, all three regarding him with suspicion and hostility.

Doomers.

What the hell was he doing caged up with three of his enemies? Thankfully, each had his own cage. Being locked in the same one with three Doomers would have probably meant his imminent demise.

Whoever had locked him up, apparently wanted to keep him alive. But who could consider both the clan and the Brotherhood as their enemies?

As far as he knew, there was no third faction of immortals. Except maybe for Navuh's youngest son who'd supposedly defected with his entire platoon during the Second World War. That one could've considered both the Brotherhood and the clan as a threat.

Still, even if it were him, it didn't make sense for the guy to start capturing immortal males.

Unless Navuh's son was building an army and this was his recruiting tactic.

Right. Talk about a trip down the absurd lane.

"How did I get here?" Anandur asked.

"Same as us. The immortal female."

"What female? What are you talking about?"

All Anandur remembered was taking a woman out to the back alley, getting busy with her, and then boom! Someone had Tasered his ass.

"The bouncer!" The image of her jade eyes popped into his head. "It was her!"

"That's right, brother. The pretty bouncer captured all of us."

Brother.

The Doomer thought Anandur was another member of the Brotherhood, a most beneficial misconception. He'd play along until he knew more about what was going on.

The Brotherhood had thousands of warriors, so obviously not everyone knew each other, but a six foot six inch redhead was too conspicuous to blend in.

Still, Anandur had spent enough time talking with Dalhu to be able to bullshit his way through it.

Then another thought hit him. There was only one way the Doomer could have known that the bouncer was an immortal female. He must've scented her arousal. Aside from the subtle difference in scents between an aroused human female and an immortal one, there was no other way to distinguish between them.

Well, there were two other signs, but they weren't as conclusive as the smell.

There was the glowing eyes effect when experiencing extreme emotion, but it could be mimicked by a human female wearing contact lenses, reflecting light from a particular angle. The superior strength could be explained by bodybuilding. Some human women were into that.

"I'm Grud." The guy threaded his arm through the cage's bars.

Anandur turned and shook it. "I'm Dur." His Scottish name was so old that it was doubtful anyone would recognize its origins, but Dur sounded more like a Doomer's name.

"But maybe I should get dressed before further introductions are made." Damn, he shouldn't talk like that if he wanted to sound like a Doomer. Rich vocabulary was not part of their training.

Grud eyed him suspiciously, then switched to the Doomers' dialect. *"The clothes will be small on you, brother."*

"I know," Anandur replied in English. He understood enough of it to respond appropriately, but he didn't speak it fluently enough to fool the Doomer. "But it's better than being butt naked." He reached for the small pile of old clothes next to the mattress.

Thankfully, they were clean. Otherwise, Anandur would have had a real problem. It wasn't that he was a germaphobe, but he had a strong aversion to body odors.

Grud chuckled. "You said it. But you're lucky. She kept us naked for a long time before getting us clothes. Maybe she thought you weren't good looking enough and wanted to cover you up quickly."

Anandur pulled on the training pants. They fit around his middle but reached only mid-calf.

Could have been worse.

"Maybe she thought I was too good-looking and that is why she wanted me to cover up. Seeing me naked was making her horny."

One of the others jumped up, grabbed one of the upper horizontal bars of his cage and started doing chin-ups. "Dream on, redhead. If she has the hots for anyone, it's for me."

"That's Mordan," Grud said. "The size of his biceps is in inverse proportion to the size of his brain."

"Showoff," Mordan said between one chin-up and the next. "You just want to impress the new guy with all those fancy English words you read in the books that Wonder gave you."

"At least I'm not a dumbass like you. I'm learning something. You read these books to me and learn nothing."

Anandur stifled a snort. Doomers and books didn't belong in the same sentence. Apparently, it took extreme conditions of having nothing else to do to force them to read. Even Dalhu, who was much smarter than the average Doomer and had escaped the Brotherhood a long time ago, didn't do much reading.

Not that Anandur was such an avid reader himself. He used to borrow Brundar's books on warfare and battle strategy, but he no longer shared an apartment with his brother. His new roomie was into espionage fiction. Maybe he should have Magnus recommend one of those to him.

"I'm Shaveh," the third Doomer introduced himself. "I don't remember seeing you at the island."

Anandur waved a hand. "I've been working undercover for years."

Grud pushed his nose through the bars. "On what?"

"It's classified."

"Who am I going to tell? It's not like we are ever getting out of here. We've been here for months. The female will never let us go."

"How do you know she is an immortal?" Anandur pulled on the worn-out T-shirt the woman had left for him.

Shaveh huffed. "What other female can pick up a grown man, carry him over her shoulder, and dump him in a cage?"

"A firefighter." Anandur lifted a finger. "A bodybuilder." He lifted another. "A trained soldier." He lifted a third. "Nowadays, human females do a lot of things they didn't do before."

"Wonder said she was an immortal," Grud said. "And she knew who and what we were."

"Is she from the clan?" Anandur knew she wasn't.

"No, she doesn't know where she comes from. She knows nothing. It's like she was born all grown up. She keeps asking us things about immortals."

"What did you tell her?"

Grud paled. "I told her about the island. I hoped she would let us go if I did. It's not a big deal. You know she can't force its location out of us. It's not like we can tell her where it is when we don't know it ourselves."

"True. So that's why she took us? To get info about other immortals?"

Mordan let go of the cage's top horizontal bar and jumped down. "She took us to save the women. Only later she figured out that we might be able to tell her things too."

Save the women?

A moment later it all clicked into place.

Perhaps these Doomers were responsible for the killings earlier that year, and the bouncer thought Anandur was about to do the same to the woman he'd taken to the back alley.

Maybe she was someone like Eva—a Dormant carrier of immortal genes who'd been induced by accident. Maybe a chance encounter with an immortal male had caused her to transition without either of them realizing it. And just like Eva, she knew nothing about immortals, their fangs, or what they did with them during sex.

Seeing a male with his fangs embedded in a woman's neck, she'd naturally concluded that he was responsible for the reported murders. The women had been left to bleed to death from twin puncture wounds to their necks.

In his case though, he hadn't even had the chance to bite his partner before his nervous system had gotten fried. The bouncer must've reacted as soon as he'd flashed his fangs.

The Doomers might be innocent as well, but he doubted that. The way Mordan had phrased it, it hadn't sounded like they were the victims. These Doomers were most likely responsible for at least some of those deaths.

He should find out. The trick was to phrase his question in a way that wouldn't give him away. "You were part of that unit, eh?"

Grud nodded. "We followed orders. You know how it is. Sometimes a warrior has to do things he doesn't want to. It wasn't a pleasant assignment. But we are not civilians who can do whatever we want."

Damn.

The bad news was that he was sharing space with murderers. The good news was that he might get a lot of inside information out of them.

21

RUTH

"It was a fun movie," Ruth said as they left the theater.

Naturally, Nick hadn't gotten some of the parenting jokes. While she'd been cracking up and tearing from laughter, he'd regarded her with raised brows.

Ruth had laughed the hardest when Mr. Incredible tried helping his son with math. His complaints about how even that had changed since he'd been in school reminded her of her own frustration while helping Sylvia with homework.

Nick opened the passenger door for her. "Who was your favorite character?"

"Jack-Jack, of course. And yours?"

"Mr. Incredible. It was cool how he was trying to be a good dad, kept messing up, but he never gave up."

They hadn't talked much about their families. Ruth avoided the subject for obvious reasons, and it seemed like Nick didn't like talking about his.

Should she ask?

Wasn't that something a girlfriend should do?

"What about your father? You never talk about him."

Nick shrugged. "I was adopted, and then my parents got divorced. I lived with my mom, but then she got married again, and her new husband made me feel like I was a nuisance. So I moved in with my father for a couple of years, but he was even worse. It was one thing for the stepdad to dislike me; it was another to feel unwanted by the one who was supposed to act like my father. I moved out as soon as I finished high school, which I did at sixteen. I was already making good money using my tech skills, and my parents had no problem signing all the paperwork that was necessary for my independence."

Poor Nick. He'd been on his own since a very young age. "I'm sorry to hear that."

"Nah, it's all good. Eva found me and offered me a job and a home."

Ruth looked out the window. Nick didn't have his own place, and she hadn't invited him to hers yet. They'd been meeting in the café and going out to movies or walks on the beach, and on Sundays, they surfed if the weather was good. Inviting Nick to her house would have suggested things she hadn't been ready for.

They'd been dating like a couple of teenagers who still lived with their parents, not like the adults they were. Well, Nick was living with his boss, but Eva was treating him more like a son than an employee.

Perhaps it was time Ruth invited Nick for dinner at her place and cooked him some of her specialties, spoiled him the only way she knew how.

Except, suddenly she felt impatient, or rather resolute. Yes, definitely resolute.

"Are you tired?" she asked.

"Not really, but you must be beat. It's after midnight, and you've been awake since what? Five in the morning?"

"Seven. Jackson opened up today. And I'm not tired at all."

He cast her a sidelong glance. "What do you have in mind?"

Ruth rearranged her purse in her lap, clutching it with the fingers of both hands. "I was thinking that maybe instead of dropping me off at home, you could come in and we could watch that stuff you suggested. I have Netflix."

Turning toward her with a shocked expression on his face, Nick also turned the steering wheel in her direction, getting the car into the oncoming traffic lane.

"Watch out!" she cried out as headlights rushed toward them.

"Oh, shit!" Nick yanked the wheel the other way, getting the car back into its lane.

A hand over her racing heart, Ruth slumped in her seat. "That was a close call."

"Yeah, it was." He exhaled a long breath through his mouth. "You can't spring stuff like that on me while I'm driving."

"I'm sorry."

"Don't be. I'm glad you're taking me up on my offer. I just didn't expect you to do it so soon."

Ruth chuckled. "I guess the two of us march to a different beat. Everyone else thinks we are nuts."

He put his hand on her knee. "Screw them. I don't care what everyone thinks. It's me and you, babe, and what works for us. We write our own rules."

"And those rules are?"

"Simple. Ruthie gets what Ruthie wants, when and how she wants it."

"What about what Nicki wants?"

"Nicki wants to make Ruthie happy. And whatever makes his Ruthie happy, makes him happy."

He was so sweet that it was hard to believe he was for real. Was it because he was still a virgin? But he wasn't naive, not if he watched porn.

"Nicki must be frustrated by now."

"Why are we talking about ourselves in the third person?"

"You started it."

"I did, didn't I? I guess it's easier to talk about difficult subjects that way."

Ruth nodded. "It was hard for me to ask, but I'm glad I did."

"Me too."

"I can't promise anything, though. I just want to watch."

"That's okay."

It couldn't be. Despite her attempts to pretend as if she hadn't noticed, it was impossible not to see that her poor Nicki was sporting a perpetual hard-on. "How are you managing to be so patient? You're a young guy in your prime. You must be going out of your mind."

Nick smirked. "As long as we are having a frank conversation, I guess it's okay to tell you how I manage. I jerk off about five times a day."

Ruth blushed. She'd suspected as much. There was no other reason for a guy to watch porn. But five times a day? Nick was a human, not an immortal.

According to Sylvia, immortal males, meaning her Roni, had incredible stamina and needed practically no recovery time.

"Isn't it a bit much?"

He shrugged. "I have a sexy girlfriend who wants to take her time. What else am I going to do?"

"And you're sure that you're not mad at said girlfriend for dragging things out like that?"

"I'm sure."

"How come?"

He squeezed her knee. "Because I love her, silly."

22

WONDER

"You should go home," Natasha said. "You look like you're coming down with something."

Wonder rubbed her temples, pretending a headache. "I'll ask Tony if it's okay with him. If not, I'll take those brown pills you gave me the last time I had a headache and stay."

"You mean Advil?"

"Yeah, those." She'd never taken them, just pretended she had to stop Natasha's nagging.

Pulling out the key to her locker from her back pocket, Natasha patted her arm. "Why not take them now? I'll go get them for you."

"Thank you."

Wonder wasn't a good actress, not even passable. Every emotion she felt was displayed on her face for everyone to see. When she'd returned to the club after dumping her fourth prisoner at the facility, people had kept asking her what was wrong and if she was feeling all right.

Since she couldn't hide what was clearly written on her face, the only thing she could do was give them a different explanation for it, one that sounded reasonable to humans —like a headache, or a stomach ache.

By now, she should've been more experienced, and her fourth rescue operation shouldn't have left her as shaken as her first one, and yet it had disturbed her more than the others.

Maybe the reason for that was the guilt eating at her.

The rescued woman, Rosalie, was still hanging around the club, looking drunk although she hadn't been drinking much.

Her dazed expression and uncoordinated body movements were no doubt the result of Wonder's hatchet job of removing her memories. The chunk she had taken from the woman's head was too big. What if Rosalie never recovered? What if the damage was permanent?

Had she done the same to the other women she'd rescued?

Probably not.

The others had still been euphoric from the bite when Wonder had Tasered their partners, so they hadn't screamed, and she'd had time to do a decent job with their memories.

However, they had also gone home immediately after the incident, so she had no way of knowing how they had been affected and how long it had lasted.

"Hey, Wonder." Tony walked out of his office at the back of the club. "Natasha told me you have a headache. It's okay if you want to go home."

What she wanted was to head to the facility and interrogate her latest captured immortal.

"Are you sure? I can take Advil and stay until closing."

He waved a hand. "Go home, Wonder. It's quiet here tonight."

"Thank you. I think sleep would do me good."

He clapped her on the back. "It's the best medicine. I wish I could sleep more than six hours a night. But I can't. I wake up to take a piss and that's it. I'm awake."

"I'm sorry to hear that." Was that the right response? She hoped so.

Wonder's go-to phrases were either that she was glad to hear that, or conversely that she was sorry to hear that, depending on whether someone told her a good thing or bad. Listening to the conversations in the club, she was learning new phrases every day, but she still wasn't confident enough to use them. What if she said the wrong thing?

Tony waved a hand. "I'm getting old, that's all. Good night, Wonder."

"You too."

As she headed for the back door, Natasha intercepted her. "Here, take two." She shook the pills out of the container into her palm.

"Thanks. I'm going home to sleep."

"Take those now. You'll sleep better."

"I'll take them at home." Wonder didn't know if she was supposed to chew the pills or swallow them. Better not to do it in front of Natasha.

"Good night. I hope you feel better tomorrow."

"Yeah, me too. Good night, Natasha. And thanks for the pills."

"Don't mention it."

"I won't."

By the amused look on Natasha's face, that hadn't been the right response.

Oh, well. She was doing her best.

Wonder sighed in relief as she stepped out into the parking lot. She hated lying, especially to good people like Tony and Natasha.

Pushing the two small pills into her pocket, she walked over to the dumpster and pulled out the redhead's clothes and shoes. Tucking the bundle under her arm, she got in her car and put it on the passenger seat next to her. Before she headed to the facility, she needed to dispose of everything next to a different club. If there were any tracking devices hidden inside the items, or if his comrades used dogs to sniff him out, this would throw them off her trail.

Unlike what she had told her boss, Wonder had a long night ahead of her, and it would be long hours before she went to sleep.

After she disposed of the clothes, she still needed to interrogate her newest prisoner.

On a gut level, she knew that he just couldn't be like the other three. The vibe she'd gotten from him was completely different. It was clean, for lack of a better word.

It wasn't about his actual cleanliness, although he'd smelled good, it was more about who he was inside. Or maybe she just wanted him to be different than the others because she was attracted to him, which was a weird response in itself.

Since waking up from her coma, Wonder hadn't felt that for any particular male, and if she had before, she didn't remember it. There was no shortage of good-looking guys in the club, and on occasion, their eyes lingered on her face or on her body or both.

Usually, they lingered on her breasts.

But their appreciative looks had done nothing for her. She'd sometimes found herself aroused by a sexually charged scene in a movie or a book, and a few times when watching couples on the dance floor—especially those who seemed to be completely absorbed in each other to the exclusion of everything and everyone else. But it was never the guy himself who'd produced that reaction in her, just the situation and imagining herself doing something similar with her future boyfriend if she ever had one.

And yet, one smile from a male who had taken another woman to the back alley had gotten Wonder all hot and bothered.

Maybe she had a thing for redheads.

Or maybe she liked very tall, heavily-muscled guys. Or men with great smiles. Or those who smelled really good.

Ugh. She liked everything about that guy except for who and what he was, which she wasn't exactly clear on either.

Why would immortal males kill human females? How could they do it? Was it about the sex?

She could understand one guy going crazy, but several?

After spending enough time with Grud, Mordan, and Shaveh, she knew they weren't insane. They were simple men, soldiers who did what they were ordered to. But she doubted anyone had ordered them to kill random women. Who could benefit from that?

Not that any of them had admitted to murderous intentions. They were still claiming it had been just sex, and that she'd misunderstood the situation.

Right. She might have been born practically yesterday, but she wasn't stupid. Their intent had been clear.

Maybe they were suffering from group insanity?

Perhaps there was a mental disease that affected immortal males and was contagious like the human flu?

It was just as crazy of an idea as the one of an organization wishing to create panic and ordering the killings.

Did it matter, though?

What kind of males followed unconscionable orders?

Wonder would rather die herself than murder an innocent victim.

Some orders were meant to be disobeyed.

Perhaps she should curb her curiosity and wait until

morning before questioning her new prisoner. As agitated, anxious, and confused as she still was, Wonder was in no shape to conduct an interrogation. For it to be effective, a clear head and a calm attitude were required, and at the moment she had neither.

Maybe Tony was right about sleep being the best medicine.

After a restful night, she would be in a better mental state to deal with the redhead and his charming smile.

23

RUTH

*W*hile Nick surfed the net on Ruth's laptop, searching for the movie he had in mind, she popped a bag of microwave popcorn, grabbed two cans of beer, and returned to the living room.

"Isn't it illegal to watch porn?" She put the beers on the coffee table and sat on the couch with the popcorn bowl in her lap. "Can I get arrested for that? You know that everything you do on the internet has a record no matter how hard you try to hide it."

Nick waved a hand. "Nah, regular porn is fine. Unless you want to run for office one day, that is. Then they will dig out every potentially embarrassing thing you've ever done. I bet you that devices like Alexa and Siri and Google Assistant that are sitting around people's homes looking all innocent, secretly record their farts."

Ruth giggled. The idea was ridiculous, but there was no doubt that people's lives were becoming less and less private. Technology was a double-edged sword, especially for immortals. They were the ones who'd been pushing it forward for centuries, but they were also the ones who required the most privacy. No immortal would let any of the devices Nick had mentioned into their homes, and their phones were clan issue to ensure private communication.

Still, there were laptops and tablets, and not everyone was as careful as her and hooked them up to the clan's private servers. Ruth for one was diligent about it, even though her surfing was limited to searching for new recipes and online shopping.

Pretty innocent activity.

Until now.

If anyone other than bots monitored clan members' activity on the net, and that person saw her searching for porn, she was going to die from embarrassment.

"Found it. It's an old one, so ignore the sideburns and the less than perfect bodies and faces. This was done before the era of plastic surgery fixing every little imperfection. On the plus side, the boobs are mostly real." Nick snorted. "Meaning that not all of them are plus sized."

He hadn't been kidding. By the clothes and hairstyles, the movie was from the late eighties or early nineties. "Is that why you're watching movies that are probably older than you?"

He sat next to her on the couch and wrapped his arm around her shoulders. "I watch them because back then they were done well, with high production values and good lighting and editing. There was no free stuff on the internet yet, so people could make money selling those movies. But the main reason I like them is that there is a love story in addition to the sex. Sex on its own is boring. Nowadays every idiot with a cellphone camera can make a porn flick."

She nestled closer to him. "I wouldn't know. I've never watched any of it."

"Girls watch too, you know. It's not only us guys."

Yeah, but not women her age who grew up when it was not as prevalent. Maybe Sylvia watched, but Ruth was not going to ask her if she did. To this date, she still hid her racy romance novels from her daughter. Some of the covers were scandalous.

"What are you smiling about?" Nick asked. "Do you like the movie so far?"

The actor playing the professor was far from handsome, but he had a sexy voice. It was deep and had an almost musical quality to it, soothing and titillating at the same time. The naughty student was pretty, not gorgeous, but she had long toned legs, which she was crossing and uncrossing, flashing the professor glimpses of her pink panties.

Evidently, the thong hadn't been a thing yet.

So far so good, at least they were not getting right to it, and there was some buildup. But that was not why she was smiling. Should she tell Nick about her novels?

He was brave, admitting to watching porn. She shouldn't pretend to be a prude who'd never done anything of the sort.

"I read romance novels."

"That's nice."

Obviously, he didn't know those came in a wide variety of hotness level. "Some of them are very racy."

The woman on the small computer screen got up and sauntered toward the professor, who was leaning against his desk with his arms crossed over his chest and a very visible bulge in his pants.

"Oh yeah?" Nick looked at her instead of watching the screen. "Define very racy."

The woman walked in between the professor's spread thighs, loosened his tie, and started unbuttoning his shirt.

At the same time, he put his hands under her tiny miniskirt and pushed it up, exposing her panty-covered bottom to the camera.

"Take this scene, for example." Ruth pointed at the screen. "And imagine it described in words."

As the professor squeezed the student's bottom, she put her hands on his very hairy chest and kissed him. Apparently waxing for men hadn't been a thing either.

"Wow, I bet it's hot. Can I read one?"

Over her dead body. Which would be never since she was an immortal.

"No."

The couple on the screen was still kissing when the professor pushed the girl's panties down her thighs, and the camera zoomed in on her shapely bottom. The actor's hands were big, even though he wasn't a tall guy, and one of his hands was enough to cover both of the girl's butt cheeks.

When he pushed a finger inside her wetness, the camera zoomed in even closer, proving that the girl's moans and gyrating hips were not just an act. The actress was turned on. Perhaps the two were a couple in real life?

However, even if that was the case, Ruth couldn't understand how the actress could get aroused in front of a camera crew and all the other people on the set. Maybe she was an exhibitionist? That must've been it.

One thing Ruth was sure of, watching was definitely not the same as reading.

A book was pure fantasy, and Ruth could enjoy it even though she didn't believe in the flowery descriptions of fabulous sex the heroines were enjoying. But there was no doubt that the woman on the screen was experiencing pleasure. She wasn't faking the look of pure ecstasy on her face as her lover fingered her into an explosive orgasm.

Remaining unaffected was impossible. Ruth couldn't help but respond. Her nipples hardened, and tingling started between her legs. Could she ever experience such a level of pleasure?

His hand resting just below her breast, Nick whispered in her ear, "Can I touch you?"

"Yes," she answered breathlessly.

24

NICK

*S*he'd said yes.

Nick swallowed hard. He was about to touch a woman's breast for the first time.

Ruth's breast.

If not for the two times he'd already jerked off that day, he would've embarrassed himself by coming in his pants.

His hand trembling, Nick cupped the soft mound as gently as he could, barely applying any pressure as he waited for Ruth to respond so he would know whether his touch pleased her or not.

If it did, would she let him put his mouth on the peak hardening under his palm? Or was it too soon for that?

Her eyes still on the screen, Ruth put her hand over his and pressed it to her chest.

Nick had no idea what to do next. "Does it feel good?" he whispered in her ear.

"Yes." She glanced down at his other hand resting on her knee, took it in hers, and put it on her other breast. "That's even better."

He was a hair away from busting a load.

Not going to happen. Clenching his teeth, Nick willed his dick to behave.

From the corner of his eye, he saw the guy on the screen taking the woman's T-shirt off, then popping the clasp of her bra. Ample breasts spilled into the actor's large hands, and he leaned forward to suck one turgid nipple into his mouth.

As Ruth sucked in a breath, the hard peaks under Nick's palms got even harder. Did she want him to do what the guy on the screen was doing?

Except, Nick was afraid to make a move and break the spell. She seemed so entranced. What if once the connection was severed she wouldn't allow it again?

His dilemma was solved when she clasped one of his hands and pushed it under her shirt. Ruth had a bra on, but getting so close to touching her bare breast was hot as fuck.

"God, Ruthie, I think I'm going to blow."

She turned her glazed-over eyes away from the screen and smiled. "I don't mind."

That was a relief, and a green light. Was he one lucky son of a bitch or what?

"Can I take your shirt off?" he asked with a little more confidence.

Instead of answering, she pushed his hands away, grabbed the bottom of her shirt and pulled it over her head. Sitting in her blue skirt and white bra, she turned to the movie again.

The guy was sucking on the girl's nipples, taking turns with each one.

As Ruth watched with her lips slightly parted and her breaths coming out fast and shallow, even a guy with zero experience could figure out that she wanted what the actress was getting.

Except, she didn't know what was coming next. Nick did.

In a few minutes, the professor was going to push the student face down on his desk, pull his pants down, and whip out his huge dick. The guy hadn't been a famous porn star because of his good looks.

The thing was, Nick had never expected to get so far into the movie. Who would have suspected that Ruthie would enjoy watching porn that much?

He'd thought she would get uncomfortable and tell him to pause the movie as soon as things heated up. She hadn't been supposed to reach the big dick scene.

Given her past experience, Ruth might freak out.

Should he warn her?

First thing first, though. He needed his mouth on those perky nubs that were just begging for it.

Releasing the back clasp had seemed so easy when the actor had done it, but the thing refused to open for Nick. As he kept fumbling with it like the newbie he was, Ruth reached back and did it with a dexterous two-finger pinch.

"Thank you," he mumbled into her ear.

One hell of a sexy lover he was. They should put him in the hall of fame with all the other all-time losers.

Ruth didn't seem to mind, though. Smiling shyly and blushing furiously, she let the shoulder straps slide down slowly, prolonging the reveal.

When the cups fell off, and her beautiful, perky breasts were bared to him, she looked down and then turned her face to the screen, but she was still watching him from the corner of her eye.

His Ruthie was so brave. Overcoming her shyness wasn't easy for her. He needed to step up his game and take over before her determination faltered and she closed up again.

On the screen, the actress was already down on the desk, with her bottom and everything in between on display. Any moment now, the big dick was coming out, threatening to ruin Ruth's sexed-up mood.

It was time for a distraction.

With a light pull on her hand and push on her chest, he had her lying on her back.

Ruth tensed up. "What are you doing?"

It was better to tell her the truth than try to come up with an excuse that might scare her even more. "Distracting you. The guy on the screen is about to whip out his monster dick. I don't want you to see it."

"Why not?"

"Because when you finally get to see mine, you might be disappointed." There was nothing like self-deprecating humor to defuse a tense moment. "Not that you're going to see it today. I'm still shy."

The tension left Ruth's shoulders, and she giggled nervously, then cupped his cheeks and looked at him with tender eyes. "You haven't disappointed me yet. I don't think you ever will."

"Oh, I will, there is no doubt about it. But I hope you love me enough to forgive my fumbling attempts at sexiness."

"You're doing fine. Better than fine. I'm lying here with my boobies on display, and I'm not even nervous. I feel safe with you."

She hadn't felt that way a moment ago when he'd pushed her down to her back. But if she was feeling safe now, he was doing something good.

By the sounds of slapping flesh and the throaty moans in the background, the couple in the movie was going at it full speed ahead.

Ruth turned to look at the screen.

"Close your eyes," he said.

"Why?" She was still trying to watch even though he grabbed her chin and turned her face toward him.

"Still the same reason—the big schlong. Besides, I'm going to feast on those sweet nipples of yours, and I want your full attention on me." He licked his lips.

25

KIAN

"We have a situation." Onegus walked into Kian's office. "Magnus called. Anandur is missing."

"What do you mean he's missing?"

Onegus plopped onto one of the chairs facing Kian's desk. "Last evening, after he and Anandur questioned the civilian, they went to investigate the club where he'd encountered the Doomers. When they were done with questioning the owner and the employees, they separated to pursue some company for the night. Magnus took the car and brought his lady to their hotel room. Anandur stayed behind. He told Magnus that he would use a service to get back. He didn't."

"Maybe he spent the night at the woman's place?"

"When Magnus woke up this morning and saw Anandur wasn't back, he called his number, and when he didn't answer, he called William and asked him to track Anandur's phone signal. He found his clothes and everything else he had on him in the dumpster of a different club. Not the one they'd visited."

That was bad news. Anandur was one of their best fighters. Whoever had captured him wasn't some random thug out to rob a wallet.

"That's not all," Onegus continued. "The clothes were cut off him. There was no blood on them, so it wasn't done in a fight. Someone just wanted to get him naked in the fastest way possible."

"To ensure he didn't have any tracking devices on him."

"Exactly."

"Damn!" Kian pounded his fist on the desk. "We should have implanted everyone with trackers."

"Wouldn't have worked. Our bodies would have rejected those same as they reject tattoos."

Yeah, that was a problem.

Their bodies' self-repair mechanism prohibited any internal manipulations. Changing hair color and applying nail polish were okay, but that was about it. No tattoos and no piercing.

"Assemble the Guardians. You're going to search for him. I don't care if you have to thrall everyone in that club to tell you everything they saw last night, or if you have to comb the entire city to find him."

Onegus lifted a brow. "All of the Guardians?"

"As many as you can spare without compromising the safety of the village. We have to assume the worst and get into a defensive mode. I'll take care of security here, while you head the search team, unless Brundar wants to do that. Did you call him?"

"No. I came to you first."

"I'll talk to him. In the meantime, have all our pilots ready the aircrafts for takeoff and assemble the Guardians in the training center for a quick briefing before departure. Okidu will drive the bus to our airstrip."

"Yes, boss." Onegus saluted him, not even trying to hide his grimace.

Fuck. Kian was once again falling back on old habits and micromanaging everything. The chief Guardian hadn't needed to be told what to do. For the past year, Kian had been getting better at letting others do their jobs. But in times of stress, he couldn't overcome his tendency to take over and make all the decisions.

Even the phone call to Brundar could've been handled by Onegus.

Except, Anandur and Brundar were more like brothers to Kian than bodyguards or even friends.

Like it or not, it was his job to deliver the bad news, and he needed to do it in person, not over the phone.

Damn, he dreaded what it would do to Brundar. The guy had been doing so well since Callie had entered his life. Kian feared that Anandur's disappearance would ruin all that progress. The brothers had been inseparable for centuries.

Brundar was going to lose his shit big time. But he was going to do it Brundar style, which meant getting cold and emotionless and retreating into the hard shell he called the zone—Brundar's most deadly state.

Pulling out his phone, Kian selected the Guardian's number. "I need to see you in my office. Stat."

"On my way."

26

WONDER

*A*s Wonder stood outside the door to her improvised jail, she contemplated whether she should go in right away, or stay outside and listen to the conversation between her prisoners.

There was no rush. She had plenty of time until her shift at the club began, and her cleaning jobs could wait.

The management company that had hired her didn't expect her to clean more than one warehouse a day. Except, she could easily manage three, which meant that her schedule was flexible. She could skip today and do a couple tomorrow.

Besides, no one had come to inspect her work yet. In case someone did, she kept the other warehouses just as spotless as this one, praying daily that no one would show up where she kept her prisoners. It would be hard to explain the four men she'd locked in cages.

So far she'd been lucky, but that didn't mean that her luck wouldn't run out eventually.

Not that there was anything she could do about it other than cross her fingers and hope for the best. Wonder didn't understand what crossing her fingers had to do with luck, but according to Natasha, it was supposed to help.

Right. Whatever. Maybe there was truth to the superstition.

Wonder sighed, then cringed and slapped a hand over her mouth. She'd forgotten about keeping quiet. The men might have heard her. The door she was standing outside of was thick, strong enough to hold the primates for whom the cages inside had been built. It was another barrier in case one of the big apes got free.

Poor apes. She'd found an old brochure that explained the kind of experiments that had been conducted in the facility. The tests themselves hadn't bothered her as much as the fact that some of those animals had spent their entire lives in that basement.

The irony wasn't lost on her. She was doing the same to her prisoners.

Wonder allowed herself a soft sigh. The men inside were talking, the sounds of their harsh voices were sure to drown hers out.

"Dur," Grud said. "Can't you tell us something about that supposedly classified mission of yours? I'm dying of boredom. I could use a good story."

So her fourth prisoner's name was Dur. It sounded guttural, like Grud and Mordan. It seemed that he was one of them after all.

"Nope. I already told you I can't. The Brotherhood invested a lot of resources into this mission. If I let even one word out, I can say goodbye to my head, and I'm quite fond of it. I would like to keep it attached to my neck."

Shaveh snorted. "Yeah, I get what you're saying."

Her hopes of him being different were slowly evaporating. He was obviously part of the same organization as the others.

"You must've been doing it for years," Grud said. "I'm two hundred and sixty-two years old, but I don't remember ever seeing you at the new base or the old one. I doubt I would've missed a redhead your size."

And the doubts were back. The others didn't recognize him. Maybe he was just pretending to be one of them?

But why?

Most likely to gain their sympathy. In case the other three were plotting to somehow break free, which they were probably doing every waking moment, Dur wanted to be included in the escape plan.

That was what she would have done in a similar situation. But what did she know? Probably less than the average school kid. Her entire life experience was more or less nine months long.

"As I said, I do undercover work. I'm a mole. The Brotherhood planted me when I was still a teenager. I wasn't always this big."

For a moment, Wonder puzzled over the meaning of a mole. Wasn't it a skin blemish? It could also be a small rat-type animal.

"Where? In the American government?" Mordan asked.

"That's classified. If I told you, I would have to kill you." Dur chuckled.

Oh, so that's what a mole was. She'd heard that phrase in a spy movie.

Dur was a spy.

And that was why he'd seemed so different from the others. This guy grew up in the United States, absorbing the culture and the easygoing attitude. His charm was probably a well-honed tool as well. Very useful for a spy.

The one in the movie she'd seen was also handsome and charming, with a disarming smile that had all the women drooling after him.

No wonder she'd been fooled by that. He probably fooled a lot of people with that good-guy act.

Well, now that she knew who and what she was dealing with, there was no reason to remain standing on the other side of the door.

Courage. Wonder closed her eyes and took a deep breath. It was going to be hard to pretend that Dur had no effect on her, but she had to be strong.

His charm was fake.

Everything about him was fake. She should remember that when he flashed her that smile of his again.

"Good morning," Wonder said as she pushed the door open. "I hope you had a good night's sleep." Crap, she needed to sound tough, not polite. "Not that I care if you did or did not."

Dur grabbed the bars of his cage. "Why am I here?"

"Why? You're asking me why?" Wonder put her hands on her hips.

"Yes, I am. You Tasered me, hit me over the head, and locked me in a cage. So you need to explain why the hell you did that."

In the other cage, Grud shook his head. "I told you she wouldn't listen."

Dur waved a dismissive hand at his jail mate. "Shut up, Grud."

With a shrug, Grud went to sit on his mattress.

"I'm not with them," Dur said and pointed at the other three.

"Really? So last night you weren't trying to kill that woman?"

"Of course not. Do you know anything about how immortal males have sex?"

Did he think she was dumb and was trying to sell her the same bullshit story Grud had told her?

Wonder crossed her arms over her chest. "He told me." She pointed at Grud. "But I don't believe him. Fangs are meant for attack and defense, not sex. I read about the mating habits of animals who have them, and none of them bite their partners."

Dur shook his head. "You are right. But we are not animals. We are people with special abilities. An immortal male can use his fangs in combat, that's true, but also in sex. The venom bite is most pleasurable to the female." His lips lifted in a seductive smile. "Human or immortal, but especially to the immortal ones. You should try it sometime."

She lifted her chin and huffed. "And you're no doubt offering to show me." She waved a hand at his neighbors. "Take a ticket and stand in line, but don't expect your turn to arrive anytime soon. Or ever. The four of you are murderers. As far as I'm concerned, you can rot in these cages for eternity."

Dur pinned her with a hard stare. "So you appointed yourself as an enforcer, a judge, and an executioner, all while having no definite proof."

If there was even a shred of truth in what they had been telling her about their sexual practices, then he might be right about that. She had determined their intent to kill by the show of fangs and blood running freely from their victims' necks. But if that was a regular part of sex for them, then intent was open to interpretation.

Dur must have seen the doubt in her eyes and pressed on. "Can you live with yourself while knowing that you might have sentenced innocent men to eternal misery? Are you willing to take care of us forever?"

She didn't answer, glaring at him instead. The same questions haunted her nightly, but there was no solution to her predicament. She was stuck taking care of four vile creatures.

Except, she still wasn't sure about Dur's culpability. She had struck before he had the chance to bite the woman. Unlike the victims of the other three, Rosalie had seemed to enjoy herself, at least that was what the sounds she'd been making had suggested.

"I bet you don't own this place. What did you do? Break into an abandoned building? Are you trespassing?"

For some reason, she didn't want him to think she was doing anything criminal. "I have a key. I'm in charge of taking care of this facility."

"Then what will happen when whoever owns this place comes to inspect it? Have you thought about that?"

He wasn't telling her anything she didn't know already. She couldn't hold them in those cages forever.

"I don't think so," he said.

As Dur crossed his arms over his impressive chest, Wonder couldn't help but stare at his bulging biceps. With no quick comeback at the ready, she stood there like a fool, locking stares with the guy.

"They tell me your name is Wonder," he said in a much softer tone. "My name is Dur."

27

ANANDUR

*G*rud was right about her knowing nothing about immortals.

The girl was in way over her head. Rescuing the first woman, Wonder must've acted on instinct. When she had rescued the other two, she'd already had a theory about what was going on but not the why.

According to Grud, he'd told her very little about who Doomers were, and none about their global mission. As a simple soldier, he probably didn't know the big picture himself. The Brotherhood's leadership didn't share much with the warriors. They were brainwashed by propaganda to believe whatever their leaders wanted them to believe.

Grud didn't seem stupid, but like the others, his education was probably limited to basic arithmetic, reading, and writing. Doomers were not encouraged to read and broaden their horizons. The opposite was true. They were discouraged from it.

She huffed. "I'm not going to say nice to meet you."

Like the teenager she no doubt was, Wonder was

getting defensive, which was good. It meant that he had gotten under her skin.

It was time to turn on the charm.

"I've never heard of anyone named Wonder. Is that the name your parents gave you?"

"No."

Smiling, he poked his nose between the bars. "Just no? Come on, it's not a national secret. What is your real name, the one you were born with?"

With her arms still crossed over her chest, her rebellious expression turned sad. But just for a moment. "None of your business."

He shrugged and went to sit on the mattress. "You don't answer my questions, and I don't answer yours. He turned to Shaveh. "Can you pass me one of Grud's books? If that's okay with you, Grud, that is."

The guy was smart enough to cooperate. "Which one do you want? I have a lot of Jules Verne. He was a French dude who was kind of a prophet who wrote about future technology and stuff."

Anandur stifled a chuckle. "Any of his books will do just fine."

Wonder watched the exchange with a raised brow. "You like reading?"

"So it would seem."

"What do you usually read?"

Anandur contemplated telling her that it was none of her business, but that wouldn't get him what he wanted.

"I like science fiction. Old Jules is fine, but I would rather read something by Frank Herbert. Dune is a favorite of mine." He'd seen the movie, and supposedly the storyline followed the book's faithfully. If needed, he could bullshit his way talking about it.

"I didn't read it. I'll see if I can find anything written by him for you."

"Where do you get your books?"

"People donate them to the shelter." Wonder reddened as soon as the words left her mouth.

Evidently, she hadn't planned on letting them know she lived in one. It was a perfect opportunity for him to help her out and score a few points with her.

"It's nice of you to volunteer at a shelter. I'm sure the people there appreciate your help."

"Yes." She eyed him suspiciously.

"What kind of shelter is it?"

He had her cornered. She could obviously lie, but he had a feeling she was the type who would feel bad about responding to his kindness with a falsehood.

"It's a shelter for refugees. These people arrive with nothing, and they need temporary housing until they can find a job and have money to pay for a place of their own."

She was a refugee?

From where?

Wonder sounded like every other American girl her age. Except, immortals had an excellent mimicking ability, and absorbed new languages, including the proper accents, with ease. Even the three Doomers, who had spent most of their lives on their island speaking their own language, spoke fluent American English. Naturally, if one paid attention, there were subtle tells, like incorrectly used phrases and idioms. But the men were careful to avoid such pitfalls.

"Do you like volunteering there?"

She shrugged.

Good. It seemed Wonder didn't like lying and preferred saying nothing at all.

After a long moment of silence, he asked, "Aren't you going to question me?"

"That's what I'm here for, but I doubt you'll answer any of my questions truthfully."

Anandur rose to his feet and walked over to his cage's gate. "That depends."

"On what?"

He glanced at the three Doomers watching and listening intently to every word.

"Privacy. If we could talk in private, I could tell you many interesting things."

"As if I'm going to fall for that trick. You want me to take you out of your cage so you can attack me. Not going to happen."

"You can Taser me again. Not that I'm looking forward to that shit. It was hell. And while I'm immobilized, you can put handcuffs on me. Just get the reinforced ones because I can snap the chain on regular handcuffs." Maybe telling her that he could get out of the standard kind that police used would make her trust him more.

Wonder looked up and down his body, then shook her head. "You can overpower me even with handcuffs on."

"Not if my arms are behind my back, and you put another set on my ankles. I'm good, but not that good." It wasn't true. He and the other Guardians had learned numerous techniques for overpowering an opponent even when chained like that.

But Anandur wasn't going to try and get free even though he knew the people back home were worried about him. By now, Brundar was probably freaking out and had mobilized the entire Guardian force to search for him.

It wasn't about him being selfish and wanting to get close to her, although she was just as alluring as he'd remembered. Hell, who was he kidding. Wonder was an

137

immortal female, and she was a badass. If he'd desired her before, he was practically salivating now. Not that he was going to do anything about it. She was still way too young for him.

Maybe in a few years...

And although he was curious to find out everything he could about her, and had about a thousand questions he wanted to ask her, it wasn't even about that.

The thing was, in order to get free and make the call to his brother, he would need to gain Wonder's trust first, and if he betrayed it, he would never get it back.

The only way out of this situation was to convince her to let him help her.

Wonder was all alone in the world, and she needed the clan. She also needed help dealing with the Doomers she'd captured.

Uncrossing her arms, she turned to leave. "I'll think about it."

"That's all I'm asking for. That and some food. I'm starving."

Wonder's eyes widened. "Oh, shit, I forgot the rice on the stove. I'll be right back with your lunch." She ran out.

BRUNDAR

*A*nandur was missing. Brundar couldn't wrap his head around that. Throughout his life, his brother had been his rock.

Anandur was invincible.

That something might have happened to him was inconceivable. If not for the cut up clothes Magnus had found in the dumpster, Brundar would have thought Anandur was pulling one of his idiotic pranks. The guy would do just about anything to get a laugh out of people.

His brother was a clown, and most of the time he annoyed the crap out of Brundar. Hell, sometimes it seemed as if he derived perverse pleasure from getting a rise out of him.

Forget seemed. He did.

Though right now, Brundar would have given anything to have the big oaf tease him with his half-baked bad jokes and dumb stories that only he found funny.

Brundar would've even laughed, just to throw Anandur off. His brother would have been too stunned for words.

They had played the same game for centuries, both

comfortable in their roles. The clown and the undertaker, the romantic and the cyborg.

"I packed your bag," Callie said as she entered the kitchen, her eyes misted with unshed tears and her chin quivering.

She loved Anandur too.

It wasn't just gratitude for him saving her life and Brundar's from her crazy ex. Callie loved Anandur because it was impossible not to.

Everybody loved his brother.

And so did Brundar, even though he hadn't said the words since he was twelve. Anandur knew. He didn't need to be told.

"Come here." He pulled her into his arms. "I'm going to find him."

"I know you are. You are going to move heaven and earth and not leave a stone unturned until you do."

"You said it, love."

"Just promise me one thing."

"Anything." He kissed the top of her head.

Callie looked up. "Don't slip back into that zone of yours. I'm afraid you won't find your way back."

"I can promise you anything but that. I need the zone to find Anandur. Without it, I'm a worthless emotional mess."

"Don't say that because it's not true."

He arched a brow. "Oh, yeah?"

"You're too tidy and organized to ever be a mess." She waved a hand. "And as for emotional? Tell it to anyone who knows you, and they'd laugh for hours. The most they'd believe about you is that you're slightly perturbed."

She was trying to cheer him up, much in the same way his brother had done throughout their lives.

Brundar frowned as he tried to grasp at the tendril of thought that this realization had prodded.

He was like a black hole, his dark disposition like a void that sucked the energy out of the people who cared about him. They must feel compelled to manufacture more cheer and positive attitude in the hopes of filling his darkness with some of their light.

How the hell had Anandur done it for so long?

It must've been exhausting. Had his brother resented him for it?

Forcing a smile, Brundar hooked a finger under his mate's chin and lifted her face for a kiss.

Sweet, sweet, Callie. She was his medicine, his salvation. Before she had entered his life and healed the wounds that Anandur had been trying to fix for centuries, Brundar hadn't been a man, he'd been a weapon.

Unfortunately, to save his brother, he needed to become that cold-hearted tool once again.

Wrapping his arms tighter around Callie, he pressed his cheek to hers and rocked her. "I can never get lost again, love. I'll always find my way back to you."

29

WONDER

"*H*ow is your head?" Natasha asked.

It took Wonder a long moment to remember the fake headache she'd complained about yesterday. "Much better. Thank you."

"Did you take the Advil?"

The pills were probably still in the pocket of the pants she'd worn the day before. She should fish them out before doing laundry. "Yes. Thank you."

"Whenever I have a headache, I don't even try to fight it and take something for it right away. If I go to sleep with one, I wake up with a full-blown migraine. So why fight it, right?"

"Right." Wonder smiled and nodded as if she had been listening to Natasha's prattle.

After leaving the facility and the dilemma Dur presented, she'd gone on to tackle one of her warehouses in the hopes of reaching a decision while immersing herself in physical work. Cleaning always helped clear her mind, especially when there was no one there to disturb her.

"I'll let you get back to your patrolling," Natasha said. "Tony is giving me the evil eye for standing around and chatting instead of taking orders. I'll catch you later." She patted Wonder's arm.

It was such a hard decision. On the one hand, Wonder didn't trust Dur. On the other hand, she had a feeling he could tell her much more than the others. As a spy, he must've been higher up in their organization and should know more than the simple soldiers.

Wonder was desperate for more information about who she was. Maybe if she knew more about immortals, something would nudge her memory.

Was it worth the risk, though? What if he killed her?

Immortals could die if their wounds were severe enough. It only made sense that no living creature could survive decapitation or removal of the heart, or being blown to pieces. The rapid healing could repair only so much damage. She was quite sure that growing a new head or a new heart was beyond the scope of her ability to regenerate.

Just another piece of information Dur could confirm for her. Grud and the other two played it dumb, saying they didn't know.

Right. They weren't even good liars.

Grud's eyes always darted sideways when he lied, while Shaveh's voice rose in pitch. Mordan looked down.

It was sad to think that the people she knew best were murderers who she held as prisoners. These men were the closest thing she had to friends.

Natasha was nice, but she was a married human woman who had two small kids and no time to hang out and just chill. Besides, pretending to be a normal human was draining. At least her prisoners were immortals, and Wonder didn't have to hide what she was from them.

"Hey, Wonder!" Tony waved her down. "Could you step into my office for a moment?"

Her gut clenched. Why did he want to talk to her? Had she been too preoccupied and not noticed something she should have done? Did he think she was neglecting her duties?

Wonder needed that job. The cleaning gig didn't pay enough to cover her future rent. Apartments in San Francisco were insanely expensive, and living in a shelter was a temporary solution. Eventually, they would tell her she needed to move out and make room for newcomers.

When she peered into the office, Tony wasn't alone.

Two men were sitting in front of his desk. One was a gorgeous blond with a long ponytail who looked like a statue of an angel, not only because he was so beautiful, but because he didn't move a muscle. The other one was also a good-looking man, with a neatly trimmed goatee and shoulder-length dark hair, but he was not as striking as the blond.

The moment Wonder stepped inside, the small hairs on the back of her neck started tingling.

Oh, no! These two were immortals, and they were probably looking for their missing friends.

She plastered a shy smile on her face and turned to Tony. "Could you give me a moment? I was on my way to the ladies' room."

With the way her heart was pounding against her ribcage, the immortals would hear it and know that she was scared. Not to mention that fear produced a strong odor they would be able to smell.

Wonder needed a few moments to collect herself and come up with a plan.

Tony waved a hand. "No problem. Take your time. I'll

call Baron in first. These gentlemen are with the police. They need to question everyone who worked here last night."

Police my ass.

"Sure, no problem. I'll be right back."

In the bathroom, Wonder walked up to the woman standing in front of the mirror. With a quick peek under the dividers, she confirmed that the two of them were alone. "Do you have perfume?" She imbued her words with a light thrall.

"Yes, I do."

"Can I borrow it?"

The woman reached inside her purse and handed Wonder a small bottle.

"Thank you. You can leave now."

The woman turned on her heel and walked out.

As soon as the door closed behind her, Wonder turned to the mirror and started to spray herself, first the hair, and then all over her T-shirt. When she was done, she tucked the small bottle in her back pocket and walked over to the paper towel dispenser.

Pulling down a long swathe, she bunched it up and started cleaning. First the counter, then the mirrors, and lastly the five faucets and soap dispensers.

Much calmer and composed, she straightened her shoulders and walked out.

Okay, you can do it.

Baron was still answering the fake detectives' questions when she knocked on Tony's door.

"Come in, Wonder." He waved her in.

"Let me know when you find your friend," Baron said as he got up. "He seemed like such a nice fellow."

"He is," the blond said.

"Take a seat, Wonder." Tony motioned to the chair Baron had vacated.

She sat on the very edge.

"This is Wonder. She is in charge of keeping the ladies from tearing out each other's hair when a fight breaks out, and she also monitors the back exit, the parking lot, and the alley between the club and the next building over. There is a lot of action going on out there, if you know what I mean."

The one with the goatee nodded. "I'm Detective Magnus McBain," he said as he offered her his hand for a handshake.

Still impersonating a statue, the blond didn't move or say anything.

"I'm Wonder Rush." She smiled. "Please don't make fun of my name." She was willing to say anything to cover her discomfort.

Magnus smiled back. "I wouldn't dream of it. Wonder is such a lovely name."

"I get teased a lot because of it."

He chuckled. "I can imagine. Can you answer a few questions for us, Wonder?"

"As best as I can."

He leaned toward her, his piercing brown eyes staring right into hers. "Last night, my friend and I came to ask a few questions. I don't remember seeing you around."

"As Tony has told you, I'm usually in the back, monitoring the hallway with the bathrooms and the back exit. I'm not in the club proper unless there is girl trouble on the dance floor and I'm called to break up a fight."

"I went out through the back exit to the parking lot, but I didn't see you there either. I would've remembered a pretty girl like you."

As usual, the compliment embarrassed her into a

burning blush, which was most fortunate at the moment. It was a great cover-up.

"I must've been in the ladies' bathroom or in the storage room. I make sure to restock it several times a night because if Jerry has to do it, he's our cleaner, he has to put an out of use sign on the door and a huge line of antsy ladies forms outside. When I do it, it saves everyone a lot of headaches and keeps the customers happy. As a woman, I know how important a clean bathroom is. If I go into a store and the bathroom is gross, I never go there again."

Magnus's eyes were glazing over halfway through her monologue. Good, let him think she was a dumb blabbermouth.

"That's a very commendable attitude for an employee. If I were your boss, I would give you a raise." He winked at Tony.

"In time," Tony said.

Magnus returned his attention to Wonder. "When we were done with what we came for, I went back to our hotel room, and my friend stayed to unwind after the long day we had. I wonder if you've seen him. He is hard to miss." Magnus lifted a hand. "Six foot six inches and a head full of red curls. Red hair, red beard, red mustache."

"I've seen him." It was better to tell as much truth as possible. "I was patrolling the parking lot when the guy you're describing stepped out the back door. He had a lady with him, and they headed to the back alley."

"Can you describe the lady?"

Wonder could feel the blond's eyes on her. That one was creepy, so cold she could practically feel the chill emanating from him. She had the irrational urge to wrap her arms around herself as protection against the icy waves he was emitting.

Were they playing good cop/bad cop? If they were, it

was working. Magnus was easy to talk to. The other one made her squirm.

Taking a deep breath, Wonder pretended to think it over. "Yeah. She was tall, but not as tall as me. I would say about five foot eight or nine. She was in her early or mid-thirties, had light brown hair that reached about here." Wonder pointed to her bicep.

"Anything else?"

She shrugged. "That's all I remember. And also that she was a little drunk."

"Did you see them come back in?"

"I didn't stay outside while they were busy doing you know what. Later, I saw the woman in the club, but not your friend. I remember thinking that it wasn't nice of him to split right after what they... you know." She felt herself blush again.

Perfect.

Sometimes it was good to look young, naive, and stupid. People would never expect her to do what she'd done.

"When did the woman go home? Are you sure they didn't meet outside later on?"

Wonder shrugged. "They might have after I'd gone home. When I left, the woman was still in the club."

Magnus arched a brow. "Your shift ends before closing time?"

"I had a bad headache, and Tony let me go home early."

"So as far as you know my friend could've returned after you went home."

"He might have. You should ask those who stayed until closing. I'm sure they'd have noticed if a big guy like him walked back in."

Magnus reached into his pocket and handed her a business card. "If you remember anything else, please give me a call. Our friend has gone missing, and we're worried about him."

He sounded so sincerely concerned about his friend that Wonder's gut clenched with guilt.

"I sure will." She tucked the card in her pocket, right next to the perfume she'd taken from the woman. "Good luck with finding your friend," she said as she pushed to her feet.

"Thank you."

As she walked out of Tony's office, Wonder forced herself to pace her strides. The ladies' bathroom was just a few feet away, and she headed right for the nearest stall.

The moment she closed the door behind her, Wonder put her hands on her thighs and let out a long breath.

Hopefully, she'd pulled it off.

Lowering the lid, she sat on it and replayed the entire back and forth conversation with Magnus in her head.

A few pieces of information stood out. First of all, Magnus and Dur had been on assignment at the club, asking questions. It was very likely that they had been looking for the other three she had taken. But then Magnus had asked her only about his redheaded friend and not about the other three.

Perhaps Dur had been telling the truth, and he really was not associated with them. It didn't matter if all four belonged to the same military organization. If Dur had been part of a different unit or department or whatever those were called, then he was not responsible for the activities of Grud's unit. Not unless he was their commander or someone even higher up who had given the despicable orders.

Except, if he were, Grud and the others would have known him. They didn't.

And what if his spy activities were not on behalf of their organization but against it?

Now, that was an interesting thought. The problem was that there was no way to prove it or disprove it.

Dur was her only source of information and he would say anything to get out of the cage.

30

RUTH

*a*s Ruth chopped vegetables for the dinner get-together at Sylvia and Roni's, she kept thinking about last night with Nick. She was so glad she'd finally had the nerve to try more than kissing.

The big surprise was that she'd enjoyed it. Nick had been gentle, his hands treating her body with reverence and not as an object to fulfill his own needs.

He hadn't even asked for anything in return for pleasuring her so sweetly. She hadn't orgasmed like the woman in the movie, but she'd had a good time.

It was more than that, though. The fact that she could enjoy Nick's touch and get so turned on by an erotic movie meant that she was normal, and that there was nothing wrong with her. She wasn't broken or defective.

It gave her hope that there could be more.

Much more.

Especially if Nick proved to be a Dormant.

The thing was, it was up to her to determine whether he was a Dormant or not, and she wasn't sure how to do it.

Everyone thought that once she and Nick had sex, she would know for sure.

What a bunch of baloney.

Not every immortal was obsessed with sex. Just most of them.

Ugh, there should be some kind of a sign. Some way to tell.

She loved Nick, but what did it prove? That he was a sweet guy, and that she felt less awkward around him because he was a fumbling goofball himself?

It wasn't the all-consuming, can't live without each other kind of love. She was fine with not seeing him every day. On the few occasions Nick had been gone on a job for more than a day or two, she'd missed him, but it hadn't been terrible. Ruth had filled her time the way she always had, with her hobbies and her books.

"I'm so worried about Anandur," Sylvia said as she walked into the kitchen. "No one has heard anything from him yet. I was hoping he just stayed overnight at some female's house and forgot to call. But when they found his clothing in a dumpster, that hope was busted."

Ruth felt awful. Anandur was missing, and all she could think about were her own issues. In comparison, they were so minor and unimportant.

Most of the clan didn't know about Anandur yet. Kian and the Guardians were keeping it quiet to avoid causing panic. Roni knew because he was tasked with hacking into every security camera in the area Anandur had last been seen in, and he'd told Sylvia, who'd told Ruth.

"Is Roni coming to dinner?" she asked as she pulled out the roast from the fridge.

Sylvia shook her head. "He asked me to bring it to him at the lab. Which means you should make another plate for

William. I can't take one for Roni and not for him while they are working together."

"Of course. It goes without saying. Shouldn't we cancel the dinner, though? Turner is probably working on the case too."

"He most likely is. Still, Bridget can come, and we can have a ladies' night. That could be fun."

Ruth shook her head. "I didn't think about it before, but it seems wrong to have fun while a Guardian is missing. I don't know Anandur well, but he seems like such a nice guy."

"He is. I love him. Everybody does." Sylvia wiped away a tear from under her eye.

"Oh, sweetie." Ruth pulled her daughter into her arms. "Don't cry. I'm sure they are going to find him. Our clan is strong and resourceful. You have to trust in the ability of the Guardians and everyone else who is busting their butt to bring him back."

"I wish I could do something too. My so-called unique talent is mostly useless."

Ruth patted Sylvia's back. "That's just nonsense. You're the only clan member who can affect electronics with your mind. If not for you, we wouldn't have been able to storm the monastery. Besides, your talent got you Roni. How else could you have snuck into a secure government building?"

Sylvia smiled through misty eyes. "Yay me!" She pumped her fist in the air.

"That's right." Ruth pointed a finger at her daughter's chest. "Don't you ever forget it."

For a long time, Sylvia hadn't told her how she'd met Roni. She'd kept from her the whole thing about sneaking into the government building to see him. If not for Roni blurting it out a few weeks ago, Ruth wouldn't have known to this day.

She still didn't know the reason for it. Sylvia had mumbled something about doing a favor for Andrew, but that didn't make sense. Andrew worked in the same building Roni had been under house arrest in. If he'd wanted to talk to Roni, he could have done it openly. There had been no reason for him to sneak there at night and have Sylvia fritz out the monitoring equipment.

"You still didn't tell me why you were helping to sneak Andrew in to see Roni."

"I told you. He needed Roni's help, and he couldn't ask for it during normal working hours because Roni was always watched."

Sylvia wasn't telling her the whole story. Maybe she couldn't tell her more. Perhaps she'd been sworn to secrecy, either by Andrew or by Kian.

Still, there were some things she could tell her. Not everything about her and Roni's story was confidential.

"How did you know that Roni was the one?"

"I just did." Sylvia chuckled. "I figured that if I could fall in love with a crusty, pimply, teenage virgin, it must have been fated."

"He was a virgin when you met him?"

"Yep. I took his virginity, and since then he worships me like a goddess." She winked. "Doesn't get any better than that."

Ruth put the knife down and leaned against the counter. "So let me get it straight. You figured out he was a Dormant because you liked him despite his bad attitude and his pimples and his virginity?"

"Just the first two. I had nothing against him being a virgin. That one was a point in his favor."

"Really? You didn't prefer someone more experienced?"

Sylvia shrugged. "I was twenty-five at the time, Mom. I've been with plenty of guys who were experienced. Roni was a clean slate. I liked teaching him everything and experiencing the wonder of discovery once again. It was magical."

Hmm, the wonder of discovery.

Ruth could have it with Nick. But unlike Sylvia, she would be experiencing the wonder and magic of it for the first time as well.

31

BRUNDAR

*A*s they left the club, Brundar called Callie. He'd promised her updates, but doing so with Magnus in the car meant that he had to be formal and skip the endearments. Surprisingly, it upset him. He missed her and wanted to tell her that.

"How is it going?" Callie asked.

"Nothing much for now. We have thirty-five Guardians roaming the streets, peeking inside people's heads and searching for a glimpse of Anandur. For now there isn't much else for them to do."

"What about the club?"

"They don't have surveillance equipment. Can you believe that?"

Callie sighed. "That's really bad luck."

"Luck has nothing to do with it." The conversation felt stilted because he couldn't talk freely with Magnus there. "I have to go now. I'll call you later tonight."

"Okay. Love you."

"Same here."

Magnus pulled out into the street. "I can't believe they

don't have surveillance cameras. Not inside the club or outside. Who doesn't have them these days?"

"According to Tony, the other clubs, pubs, and restaurants in the vicinity don't have them either. The wave didn't hit this area of San Francisco yet because the buildings here are so old."

Magnus shook his head. "You'd think we stepped through a portal into a different time."

They had become too dependent on technology.

What had police detectives done before the era of smartphones and the proliferation of inexpensive surveillance equipment? They'd used other methods, which old-timers like him and Magnus should have thought of right away.

"We should find that woman," Brundar said.

"We don't even have her name."

"But we have a face."

Magnus cast him a bewildered look. "How? We just talked about the lack of surveillance cameras."

"The old-fashioned way. The bouncer girl can describe the woman to a forensic artist. We can then run it through William's facial recognition program and get a name."

"That would require one hell of an artist. You're talking accuracy on the level of a photograph."

"I know a guy who can do it." Brundar pulled out his phone.

The call was answered even before the first ring ended. "Any news?" Andrew asked without preamble.

"I need you to get Tim over here. We need to find the woman Anandur was last seen with. We don't have a name, but several people in the club saw her."

There was a moment of silence. "Can't you find someone local? Tim is a prima donna. He would demand your firstborn in exchange for getting his ass to SF. And on top of that, he would want compensation for the vacation days he'll have to use, and for keeping his mouth shut."

Brundar had never met the guy in person, but he'd heard about him. None of it good, except for Tim's impressive talent.

"I want to run the portrait through William's program. It has to be photograph quality. I heard your guy is the best in the field."

"He is. But don't call him mine. It's like taking ownership of an ulcer. I'll talk to him tomorrow. What's the limit on the bribe?"

"Other than my firstborn, anything he wants."

"Will do."

Brundar disconnected the call, then pulled Tony's business card out from his pocket and dialed the number.

"Tony here," the guy answered.

"This is Detective Brad Wilson. Is your female bouncer still around?

"She should be. Why?"

"I'm bringing in a forensic artist tomorrow. I want him to draw a portrait of the woman our colleague was last seen with. I need the bouncer for a couple of hours. Can you give me her number?"

"I'll have her call you. Employee confidentiality and all that. You know how it is today. You fart upwind instead of downwind, and you get sued. I don't need trouble."

"I understand. But make sure she calls the number my partner gave you. We need it done ASAP."

"Of course. Anything we can do to help in the investigation."

Magnus cast Brundar a sidelong glance. "You could've threatened him with a subpoena. He would've given you the girl's number."

"I thought about doing that but decided against it. The

guy is cooperating. No need to antagonize him. What did you think about the bouncer?"

Magnus smoothed his hand over his ridiculous goatee. "Pretty, but too big for my taste. What was she, like six foot tall?"

"I'm not talking about her looks. She gave off a strange vibe."

"Nah, she was just nervous, and the perfume she doused herself with almost made me gag. Other than that she was just a young woman facing two police officers. Naturally, it made her anxious."

Brundar shook his head. "She knows something she isn't telling us."

"We can interrogate her again tomorrow while your guy is working on the picture. And if she resists, one of us can thrall her."

"Maybe after he's done. I need her to focus on describing the woman and not on us."

Magnus smirked. "You forgot another thing. She might have felt attracted to one of us. That would make a girl act strange, and I bet it was me. You're a pretty boy, but you're scary. I'm more approachable."

"That's why tomorrow you'll be the one asking the questions while I observe her responses."

"No problem."

WONDER

*B*y the end of her shift, Wonder had made up her mind.

Tonight, if Dur wasn't asleep when she got back to the facility, she was going to put him in handcuffs and take him to one of the empty offices. After the visit from his friends, she felt even more compelled to ask him some questions.

Things didn't add up. He didn't fit as neatly into the story she'd constructed about her other prisoners. Though maybe she was wrong about them too and had been keeping innocent males caged for months.

Except, her doubts in regards to the other three were not as bothersome as those regarding Dur. She was almost certain of their guilt. Not so about his.

The fake detectives were a problem, though. They could be following her, or they might come to the shelter in the morning and question her roommates. It would look suspicious if the girls told them that she had come in much later than usual.

Most nights the two were asleep by the time she

finished her shift at the club, but they were still new and terribly jumpy, waking up at the slightest noise. Wonder had to be very quiet not to disturb them. But tonight she was going to make some noise on purpose, so they would remember her coming in. When they went back to sleep, she would sneak out silently and go to the facility.

If she could communicate with the girls, she could've told them some story about meeting a guy late at night, but she barely knew them, and they didn't speak any English yet.

Not that it would be a problem for Magnus and his silent friend if they decided to visit the shelter. One of the many volunteers would gladly translate for them.

Hopefully, it wouldn't come to that.

Shit on a stick, as Natasha liked to say.

Wonder was probably hoping for too much. In reality, the noose was tightening around her neck. She'd been a fool to think she could keep her prisoners locked up forever.

Eventually, their friends were going to find them. Or the owners of the facility would find a buyer, and she would have to move them. The problem was that Wonder knew of no other place that could hold immortal males.

She would have two options: set them free knowing that she was releasing murderers who would go on harming other women, or she could kill them and have that on her conscience.

After all, she'd killed before.

But that had been an accident. She hadn't meant to kill her attacker, just to immobilize him.

There was no way she could execute her prisoners. As much as she detested them, except for Dur who she hadn't proven guilty yet, she had also gotten to know them.

Grud and Shaveh and Mordan didn't seem like

monsters. They weren't good people, but they weren't evil either. Not entirely.

Besides, she couldn't completely rule out the remote possibility that they were innocent. Maybe they hadn't killed anyone?

After all, she'd saved the women she'd caught them with, and there might have not been any others before that. Was the intent to murder the same as murder?

Shit on a stick and then some.

Those kinds of hard questions should be answered by people smarter than her.

As Wonder entered her room, she didn't tiptoe as she usually did. Immediately, two heads lifted off their pillows, wide brown eyes staring at her with momentary terror.

Poor girls, she felt guilty for startling them. Who knew what these two had gone through before arriving at the shelter.

"Shh, it's only me. Go back to sleep."

The girls might not have understood her, but they knew her and reacted to her voice.

One mumbled something in her language and put her head back on the pillow; the other smiled and waved, then joined her sister.

A few moments later, both were fast asleep.

Looking out the window, Wonder checked the street to make sure there were no suspicious cars parked nearby, then tiptoed out and took the stairs down to the first floor.

Outside, she scanned the street again before getting in her car, double checking that there was no one inside any of the parked cars. There wasn't. Not unless someone was hiding under the dashboard.

Still, as she drove, she kept glancing in the rearview mirror to make sure no one was following her.

Upon reaching the facility, Wonder circled around it

twice before finally parking her car across the street and not in front of the building as she usually did.

The place had an alarm, but she never activated it for obvious reasons. Using her key, she entered the lobby and headed for the stairs leading down to the basement.

The kitchenette where she cooked meals for her prisoners was on the first floor, but it was an inside room with no windows and safe to use even at night. Not like the other first floor rooms where anyone could see her if she turned on the lights. After all, she doubted anyone would believe that she'd come to clean the place at two in the morning.

Instead, she used one of the offices in the basement to store her supplies, including the handcuffs and leg restraints she'd purchased with her other prisoners in mind.

That was where she planned to interrogate Dur.

The room didn't have a reinforced door, but there was a desk with a couple of chairs she and Dur could sit on and talk.

It was a pity the basement bathroom didn't have a shower. She could have lived there rent free instead of sharing a room with two other girls. The kitchenette was enough for her needs, and she could've purchased a mattress and put it against the wall in the office she used.

It was a silly idea.

The facility would eventually get sold, and she would be missing a place to live. More critically, she would have nowhere to hold her prisoners.

A different solution was needed. If Dur and his friends were indeed not part of Grud's people, maybe she could turn to them for help.

It would be so good not to be all alone in the world, but it was also wishful thinking.

With a sigh, Wonder pulled open the filing cabinet bottom drawer and took out the restraints. She was going to find out if Dur was the answer to her problems or the end of her.

One thing she was clear on. Change was coming whether she wanted it or not.

The question was how she was going to handle it. Was she going to let it unfold passively and suffer the consequences whatever they might be, or was she going to do something about it and hopefully steer it in a better direction?

The second option was obviously preferable.

33

ANANDUR

"Go to sleep, Dur," Grud grumbled. "I'm tired."

Anandur had spent most of the evening trying to get more information out of the Doomers, but apparently, they'd had enough of his questions. Or at least Grud had, and he was the only one who seemed to actually know anything. Not that it was much.

Besides, phrasing questions to sound like they were part of a casual conversation was draining. It seemed Anandur wasn't as good of a spy as he'd believed he was. Or maybe he just lacked the proper training. Were there manuals on how to casually ask questions without sounding like an interrogator?

If there were, he should get some once this fiasco was over.

With nothing else to do, Anandur lay down on the mattress, crossed his arms under his head, and stared at the ceiling. "Toss me another book, will you? Do you have anything with detectives in it?"

"Tomorrow. Read the one I gave you already."

Grud was not in a cooperative mood.

But that wasn't the reason Anandur had learned so little. The men just didn't know much. Doomers were trained not to ask questions, or seek answers. In short, they were quite dumb—simple soldiers who did what they were told without understanding the bigger picture or even being curious about it.

If they'd been told anything, it was that Mortdh's teachings preached this and that and therefore were beyond contestation.

Turning to his side, Anandur propped himself on his forearm and reached for the book Grud had given him. But as he started flipping through the pages, he heard the door open.

He hadn't expected Wonder to return tonight.

What he also hadn't been expecting was for her to take him up on his offer, and yet she was holding handcuffs and leg restraints.

"Are you going to Taser me?" he asked, eyeing her holster.

"Only if you misbehave. Go to the back of the cage and stand against the wall."

Bossy girl.

It shouldn't have turned him on. He was not into the type of games his brother liked to play, especially not as the one being restrained. But there was something very sexy about a powerful woman with a bossy attitude.

A very beautiful, powerful woman with a bossy attitude who was also very young and naive and inexperienced and who shouldn't see him getting horny. Which was impossible to hide since the nylon pants she'd given him did nothing to conceal his hard-on.

She might change her mind about letting him out.

And that wasn't the only problem. If any of the Doomers noticed, they would have a field day at his expense, and he might lose their respect—never a good thing with people who were followers by nature. As long as they respected him, they might listen to him.

As he walked to the back of his cage, Anandur summoned the most gruesome images he could think of in the hopes of deflating the troublesome boner by the time he had to turn around. Luckily, or maybe regretfully, he'd seen enough crap in his long life to fill a library of horror movies.

"Why are you letting him out?" Grud asked. "He is no better than us."

Wonder pinned him with a hard stare. "I can do whatever I want, and I don't owe any explanations to a murderer."

That's my girl.

Right. Wonder was his jailer, nothing more.

Maybe in a few years when she got older…

Yeah, as if she was going to wait for him.

An immortal female who was not Annani's descendant was going to get snapped up faster than free ice cream at an amusement park.

Grud huffed and picked up one of his books, pretending to read. Shaveh and Mordan did the smart thing and kept their mouths shut, but the hostility in their expressions betrayed their envy.

He should thank Wonder for putting each of them in a separate cage. If they were all in one, he would not have lived long enough to see the next morning.

Wonder threw the handcuffs and leg restraints inside his cage. "Put them on and lock them."

"I assume you want my hands behind my back," he said as he picked the cuffs up.

"Obviously."

"That is going to be a bit of a challenge." Anandur sat on

the floor and put the leg restraints on, then got up and leaned his back against the neighboring cage. "Shaveh, do me a favor and lock the other one in place?"

He was taking a chance on the Doomer not shackling him to the cage's bars, but Anandur was banking on the respect the guy had for him as a member of the Brotherhood's upper echelon. Not that it would have stopped Shaveh from killing Anandur at the first opportunity, but only as long as he didn't get caught. The thing was, down here the Brotherhood or its retribution was not a factor. Thankfully, though, the cages and their jailer were.

When he heard the click, Anandur pushed away from the bars. "That was the easy part. But how are you going to remove those after we are done with our chat?"

Wonder unlocked the cage and took a step back. "Easy. I'll throw the keys in, you'll unlock the cuffs or Shaveh will do it for you, and then throw the keys back out."

"Clever," he said as he exited the cage in a shuffle.

Wonder took another step away from him. "Walk ahead of me toward the door."

"Yes, ma'am." He pretended it was more difficult for him to keep his balance than it actually was.

The safer Wonder felt around him, the more she would open up.

He stopped in front of the door. "Do you want me to open it for you?"

"No. Step back and to the side. I'll open it."

"As you wish." He did exactly as she instructed.

Wonder pulled the door open and held it, preventing it from auto closing on Anandur's face.

"Much appreciated," he said as he stepped out.

"You're welcome," Wonder answered automatically. "Keep walking," she added in a sterner voice. "It's the second door on your left."

"Yes, ma'am." Anandur's lips lifted in a smile.

Wonder was a good-natured girl pretending to be tough. Not that he had any illusions about her being soft. Her spine was made from titanium, but she was softer on the inside.

If given a chance, she would've been a giver, a pleaser. Unfortunately, life had forced her into a role she could pull off, but one she was not comfortable in.

34

GRUD

*A*s soon as Dur left with the woman, Grud pulled out the rod he had hidden under his mattress, moved the stack of books aside, and went to work.

The wall was made of cement blocks which were about sixteen inches wide and eight inches high. If he could remove four, he could probably squeeze through.

Shaveh got up and stood next to the bars separating their cages. "Why aren't you digging when Dur is here? He wants out as much as we do."

"I don't trust him." Grud kept scraping.

He wished he could attack the wall with all his strength, but that would make too much noise. He didn't know where Wonder had taken Dur. It might have been the next room over to the one he was trying to get into.

"I don't trust him either. I don't trust any of the elites. They think of us as disposable. But at this rate, it will take you forever to be done."

Grud kept scraping. "I'd rather take my time than risk our only chance of escape."

Mordan put down the puzzle booklet and sat up on his

mattress. "Grud is right. There is something fishy about Dur. I don't buy his spy story."

"Who do you think he is?" Shaveh asked. "A Guardian?" He snorted.

"He could be."

Shaveh waved a dismissive hand. "A Guardian would have never let himself get caught with his pants down." He snorted again. "Get it? His pants down?"

"Who says? They are not invincible." Mordan rose to his feet and watched Grud work from the other side. "If she got us, she could've gotten a Guardian. If you ask me, Dur is too polite and knows too many fancy words to be a brother."

"First of all, no one asked you," Grud said. "But just for your general knowledge, not all of us are raised the same. Do you think Navuh's sons are getting the same schooling as the rest of us?"

"Dur isn't Navuh's son. They are all dark-haired, and he is a redhead." Mordan jumped up, grabbing one of the horizontal bars, and started to do chin-ups.

Grud pried out a decent-sized chunk of cement block and threw it inside Shaveh's cage. "Crumble it as much as you can and then dump it down the grate."

Grud kept scraping as he talked. "Our exalted leader, Lord Navuh, could have fucked a blond or a red-haired Dormant and gotten himself a son that looked like Dur. Not that I'm saying he did. Just that he could."

For several minutes, the other two kept quiet, letting him work in peace. Then Mordan jumped down and leaned against the bars. "How are you planning on getting us out?"

"I told you, easy. I get out through the hole and go around. She never locks the door to this room."

"I meant the cages. How are you going to get us out of the cages?"

Coming back for them hadn't been part of Grud's plan, but if he didn't offer them a viable solution, they were going to tell on him. There was no way they would let him go and leave them behind.

"Unlike you morons, I observe the woman's every move when she is here. She keeps the key under the stack of papers over there." He pointed. "I saw her reach under it before she let Dur out."

"Yeah, but I saw her put it in her pocket after that," Shaveh said.

The guy would never make it as a spy, that was for sure. "No, you didn't. What you saw Wonder put in her pocket were the keys to the handcuffs. She put the cage key back under the stack of papers. Wonder likes order, if you didn't notice. She always does things in the same way."

Mordan snorted. "Stupid woman. Even with his hands behind his back, he can knock her out and take the keys. That is what I would do." He snorted again. "And then I would have me some fun."

"Who knows? Maybe that's what he is doing now?" Shaveh asked.

"If he does, I hope he comes back and gets us out after he's done with her." Mordan dropped down to the concrete floor and started doing push-ups. "I'm sick of humping the floor."

35

WONDER

*S*o far so good.

Dur was behaving perfectly, but Wonder wasn't convinced he wouldn't try something later. She was well prepared, or as well as she could be under the circumstances. She had him all tied up, kept her distance, and her right hand hovered over the holster of her Taser gun. One wrong move and she would fry his ass.

Yeah, she was fooling herself with all that tough talk, not to overcome nerves or fear, but the feelings of guilt that had assailed her as soon as Dur had left his cage. She hated to see him like that, barefoot because she hadn't given him shoes, and shuffling those bare feet because the chain was too short for a man his size.

He had very nice feet, though, and it was almost a shame to cover them with shoes.

The secondhand T-shirt she'd given him was stretched to the max over his broad chest, emphasizing every muscle, and it was also too short, riding up and exposing his midriff.

He had a very nice midriff too.

And yet, she liked the memory of him free and wearing clothes that fit him. It had been nothing fancy, just simple Levis and a plain T-shirt, but the clothes had been new and clean and the right size.

"In there?" he asked as he reached the one open door.

"Yes. Take a seat in the chair with the second pair of handcuffs attached to its back."

She waited until he was seated, then walked up behind him and attached the second pair to the chain between the ones he had on.

"I like how careful you are." He surprised her. "But this is actually a mistake. In the time it will take you to blink, I can turn together with the chair and swing it at you. It will knock you out long enough for me to take away your keys and run. If you ever take out any of the other three, I suggest you take them to an empty room with no furniture at all. Better yet, don't take them out."

Why was he telling her that?

Now that he had, however, she could imagine him doing exactly what he'd described, and he was right. It had been a stupid move.

Wonder sat in the other chair and propped her elbows on her thighs. "So what are you saying? That you can get free easily but you're not going to do it, or are you just toying with me by telling me exactly what you're about to do?"

"I'm giving you my word that I'm going to sit here like a perfect angel and talk to you. And when we are done, I'm going to go back to my cell and not give you any trouble."

"Why?"

"Because I want you to trust me. You're in way over your head, and you know it. The men you've got locked up in there are very dangerous and lack morals, or rather the morals most decent people live by. They are taught differently. If they ever get free, the first thing they are going to do is rape you and not even think that they've done something wrong."

Wonder recoiled at his blunt statement. And yet, he was probably right. After all, those young human men in Alexandria who'd attacked her hadn't been after her money. She had something else they'd wanted, and they'd thought nothing of taking it by force. But it hadn't ended well for them.

"I can defend myself. I'm stronger than I look."

He chuckled. "I bet you are. Otherwise, you wouldn't have been able to lift me up and carry me away on your shoulder. I'm a heavy bastard."

Wonder frowned. Bastard. She wasn't sure what it meant. People used it as a cuss word, but she'd never heard anyone refer to himself as one.

He smiled indulgently as if he'd understood the reason for her confusion. "It's just a figure of speech, although in my case, it's true. I don't even know who my father was."

"Did he die?"

"A long time ago."

"Oh, I'm so sorry to hear that."

"He was a human. I'm a very old immortal."

"Is your mother still alive?"

"Yes, and she is as lovely as ever."

"She is probably worried about you." The thought of a mother worried about her son tugged at her heart, but that wasn't the reason Wonder had brought it up. Maybe she could get him to talk about others in his community. Did he belong to the same group of immortals as the other three? Were all of them bad, or just some? And if he didn't, were his people better? Did they believe in freedom from oppression and discrimination and equal opportunity for all?

Wonder didn't know much about anything, but she'd been told that those principles were the foundation of democracy and a good society. If Dur's people followed those, they couldn't be too bad.

"I don't think anyone has told her that I'm missing. I haven't been gone long enough. But my brother is freaking out for sure. I bet he is combing the city for me."

Was his brother one of the two fake police detectives? Neither looked anything like Dur. Then again, they'd only asked about him, not the others.

"What about the other three? Is anyone looking for them?"

"Not likely. Their organization doesn't care about its individual cogs."

"You said theirs. Are you claiming that you are not part of it?"

For a moment, he just looked at her. "What do you think?" he finally asked.

"I don't know what to think. That's why you are here. You said that if you had privacy, you'd tell me things. So here we are. Talk."

He shook his head. "If I confide in you, I take the risk of you telling the others things I'd rather they didn't know about me. You need to share with me something that you don't want them to know either. That way both of us would have a strong motivation to keep our conversation confidential."

It made sense. "Tell me what you want to know. I might answer some questions, but not others."

"That's fair. Let's start with your name. Is it really Wonder?"

For a few moments, she debated whether to tell him the truth or not. Her memory loss wasn't something she wanted people to know about, but there was no real harm in telling Dur. It wasn't a security risk.

"Yeah. It is. I don't remember the name I was given at birth. I suffered what seems to be an irreversible memory loss. I don't know who I am, or where I came from. All I know is that I'm not human, and neither are you or the other three murderers in there."

She knew she'd hit a nerve when his eyes started glowing.

"Don't ever bundle me together with that scum." His elongated fangs made the words come out hissed.

He looked terrifying like that.

The scene of the crime had been the only time she had seen any of her four prisoners with their fangs fully extended. The other three had never done it since, so she'd assumed that fangs elongated only during sex. But apparently, in addition to arousal, strong emotions produced that reaction too.

Refusing to let him see that he was scaring her, Wonder schooled her expression as best she could. "So you're claiming that you're not with them."

"I'm not."

"I overheard you telling Grud that you are an undercover agent in their organization, and that's why they don't recognize you."

"It was a lie."

"How do I know you're not lying now?"

Dur sighed. "You threw me in a cage with my mortal enemies. What did you expect me to do?"

"Not the same cage."

"Yes, and I thank you for that. I'm a strong guy and well-trained, but there are three of them, and they are well-trained as well. I'm not sure who would've ended up dead. Me or them." He chuckled. "But that's just boasting. It would have probably been me."

Gee, the guy was blunt. But she kind of liked that about him. "Tell me more about you and your people. I assume that when you say enemies, you don't mean you personally, since those three don't even know who you are."

"First tell me why you chose Wonder as your name. Or was it chosen for you?"

She sighed. As if her name was as important as what she'd asked him. But if that got Dur talking, she saw no harm in telling him. "Both. A kid pointed at me and said Wonder Woman. I didn't know what it meant, but Wonder sounded nice to me. Then when it happened again on the same day, I thought of it as a sign. Only later I discovered I'd named myself after a cartoon character."

Dur gave her an appreciative once-over. "I can see the resemblance. You look a lot like the actress who played Wonder Woman. But you're much more beautiful. And unlike the human, you're strong for real."

Wonder felt a blush creep up her face. She wasn't used to compliments.

"What about you? Is Dur your real name?"

He chuckled. "It's Anandur. But if I told them that they might have figured out who I was."

"Why? Are you famous?"

"Anandur is a very old Scottish name," he explained. "The three in there probably have never heard of it, but it doesn't sound like one of theirs. I hope you'll remember to call me Dur in front of them."

She waved a hand. "Don't worry. I'll never do anything to compromise your safety."

"Why? Because you like me?" he teased. "Or is it just because you're afraid I'll spill the beans about your memory loss?"

She liked him, but that wasn't the answer she was going to give him. The guy was cocky enough as it was. "Neither. I'm just not sure you're guilty of what I've accused you of, and I feel responsible for you."

"I can live with that."

36

ANANDUR

*A*nandur shifted in the chair, the unnatural pose putting a strain on his arm muscles.

But it was well worth it. He was making good progress. Wonder's hand no longer hovered over her Taser gun, and her shoulders were losing their rigidity.

Ha, Brundar should have seen him in action to finally appreciate the power of charm.

His humorless brother believed in only two ways of solving conflicts—with a sword or with a knife. And if absolutely necessary—a gun.

Brundar preferred his kills up close and personal.

"Your turn." Wonder trained her intense green eyes on him, scrambling his thoughts. "Tell me about your people and how are they different from the other ones. Are there many communities of immortals scattered around the world?"

Mesmerized by her eyes, he hadn't heard the first part. To cover it up, he chuckled. "That's more than one question. I'm a simple guy. Can you repeat them one at a time?"

"Simple. Right. But whatever." She waved her hand.

"Question number one: how many communities of immortals are there?"

"There are only two known factions. Well, known to immortals that is. Humans don't know we exist, and we do everything to keep it that way. I belong to the clan, and the other three belong to the Devout Order of Mortdh Brotherhood, or Doomers for short. Other than that, we suspect that there are some lone immortals out there who are on their own and don't know that there are more people like them. Same as you."

Her beautiful eyes narrowed at him. "I might belong to the clan or to the Brotherhood and not remember any of it because something happened to me. Are the communities so small that everyone knows each other?"

"The clan is small. I know each of the members. I might not remember everyone's name, but I know their faces. So you are not one of ours for sure. And as to the Brotherhood, if you were theirs, you would've never gotten away. You wouldn't have been an immortal at all. They don't activate their females."

She frowned. "Why not? Not that I know what you're talking about in the first place. Aren't we born immortal?"

"No, we are not. Those who carry the gene are called Dormants, and they have to be activated. That's one of the many uses of the fangs and venom."

Her eyes widened. "You bite a person to activate her or his dormant genes?"

"Yes."

Her hand flew to her forehead. "Oh, wow. That puts everything in a different light. What if the other three were in the process of activating the females and not planning to kill them?"

Anandur shook his head. It was too much information

for Wonder to process all at once, and she was making a mishmash of what he'd told her.

"No, sweetheart. They weren't. Doomers don't activate their females on purpose. It might happen by accident with a Dormant that doesn't know she has the gene, but not deliberately."

"Why not?" Wonder asked again.

"Fertility rates. A Dormant female can produce as many children as a human female. When she turns immortal, her fertility rate drops to almost nothing."

"Why?"

Her why questions were like those of a young child, which in a way she was because of the memory loss. Luckily for her, Anandur was a patient guy.

"Considering our lifespans, it only makes sense that nature will want to curb our ability to proliferate. After all, we are at the very top of the food chain. If there were many of us, we would've driven all other species to extinction."

"So the Doomers want many children? Is that it?"

"Yes. They want warriors for their army. The males can't transfer the immortal genes, so their only use is as fighters. The females are used to make more warriors. They are breeding them like cattle."

"That's horrible."

"I agree. They are not good people. Or rather their leaders are not. If given a chance, some Doomers might have turned out alright. I know two who did."

She looked so sad that if Anandur weren't in chains, he would've taken her into his arms and rocked her like a baby. Not that there was a chance in hell she would've let him. The girl was putting on a tough as nails act.

"There is so much I don't know. Like what you've told me about fertility. I haven't given it much thought before, but I would like to have children one day. From what you are telling me, that might never happen for me."

"If the Fates will it, it might."

"The Fates?"

"It's also a figure of speech. I'm not a big believer, but I'm not a heretic either." He winked. "I'm hedging my bets."

"What does that mean, hedging your bets?"

He wondered whether her memory loss had been so complete that she'd had to relearn how to speak. "It means that I'm not taking chances in case the Fates are real. Did your memory loss include the use of language? Did you have to learn to talk?"

"Maybe. I don't know. Nine months ago I woke up from a coma in Egypt, but I didn't know Arabic. I learned some on my own. Then I was forced to run away, and I snuck away on board a ship. I learned basic English from a kind old lady who hid me in her cabin all the way to the States. Mrs. Rashid is a retired English teacher, and she said she'd never met anyone who'd learned a language so fast."

"That's a trait all immortals share. We learn languages fast. But why were you running? And from what? Or rather who?"

Wonder dropped her head. "I was attacked." Her voice lowered to a whisper. "I might have killed someone. It was in self-defense, but it would have been my word against his buddies. I couldn't take the chance."

Anandur felt his fangs elongate. "How many attackers were there?"

"Four."

"And you dispatched all of them? By yourself?"

She nodded.

"That's impressive for a civilian with no training."

"I knew the right moves instinctively. But I didn't

realize how strong I was. After the first went down and didn't get up, I used less force with the others. I didn't kill them."

"Good. It means that I can finish the job for you. It would bring me great satisfaction."

His vehemence had her lift her head and look at him. "Why are you experiencing such strong emotions?" She pointed at his fangs. "Does that happen every time you get angry?"

No, it didn't happen often at all. Most of the time Anandur was a chill guy. But the idea of anyone wanting to harm Wonder infuriated him. On some level, he was starting to think of her as his. So yeah, she was too young, but she must've been at least eighteen to get the bouncer job at the club, and even more likely twenty-one, which meant that she had reached her majority in every way.

Yeah, how was that for convincing himself it was okay to lust after her?

Her eyes on him, Wonder was still waiting for him to give her an answer. It was good that he had another reason for wanting to eliminate the bastards who'd attacked her. "Because they don't deserve to live. You got away, but I bet many human females were not as lucky."

37

WONDER

*S*he shouldn't enjoy Anandur's rage on her behalf so much, but she did. Wonder could've kissed him in gratitude.

Not on the mouth, that was too intimate, but on the cheek.

As a thank you.

Yeah, who was she fooling?

She'd been attracted to Anandur from the first moment she'd seen him, and the more time she was spending with him that feeling was only getting stronger.

Maybe she should return him to his cage already.

Not only because she was afraid of her own reaction to him, but because he looked in pain. It must've been very uncomfortable for him to sit with his arms pulled behind his back for so long.

The fact that she was tempted to unlock his handcuffs and rub his sore muscles was a sure sign that it was time to end this.

Except, she didn't want to.

Anandur was telling her so many new things, and she

had a feeling he hadn't even scratched the surface. They could keep talking all night and not cover it all.

"I should take you back. You look uncomfortable."

He pinned her with a pair of glowing eyes. "Did my show of fangs scare you?"

She shook her head. "The other time when you got mad at me for bundling you with the Doomers, I'll admit I was a little scared, but not this time. I actually thought it was nice. I don't know if I ever had someone to defend or avenge me before my coma, but for sure not since I've woken up. It's not that I need it. I'm not one of those dainty females who needs a strong protector. But it's just nice to know that someone cares."

"I care."

"Why?" She was starting to sound like a soundtrack stuck on a loop, but she really wanted to know why Anandur was being so nice to her.

Did he desire her?

Did she want him to?

Or was he putting on a show to make her like him and lower her guard?

Already, she was less alert than at the start of their talk. On the other hand, she believed Anandur when he said he could've overpowered her even with all the precautions she'd taken.

"I don't want you to be alone. You were probably activated by some random immortal, and for some reason reacted badly to it, falling into a coma. That's my best guess. You are resourceful, I'll give you that, but it doesn't mean that you don't need the support of a community."

Her thoughts exactly.

"And how do you suggest I join that community? And what about my prisoners? I can't release them so they can go on killing, and I can't dispose of them either."

"Why not?"

Wonder scratched her head. Good question.

When Anandur had talked about killing the rest of her attackers, she'd had no problem with the idea. His reaction and the explanation he'd given her had lifted the guilt she'd been living with since she'd killed one of them. If no one stopped them, those men would go on raping other females. The same logic should have applied to her prisoners.

The difference was that Grud, Shaveh, and Mordan hadn't attacked her, and that she'd gotten to know them. They were people to her. Her attackers had been strangers.

"I know that they probably deserve it, but I've been taking care of them for months, and I just can't."

Anandur shook his head. "A Stockholm Syndrome in reverse. That's a first. "

She had no idea what he was rambling about.

He continued, "But I have a solution for that as well."

"For that Stockholm Syndrome whatever that is?"

"Yeah, and it's quite simple. You unlock the handcuffs, give me your phone, and I call my brother. He will come here with a force of Guardians and take the prisoners off your hands."

That sounded like the solution to all her problems. It also sounded too good to be true, which meant that it probably wasn't true. It was just another ploy. "What about me? Is he going to take me as well?"

"Of course. I'm not leaving you alone here. You'll come with us."

"As what?"

Anandur sighed. "As a new member of our community. But I can see that you don't believe me."

"Let's pretend that I do. Are your people in the habit of collecting stray immortals?"

"To this day, you're the second one we ever found. And yes, the first one joined our community. In fact, she is married to a good friend of mine."

Wonder crossed her arms over her chest.

He was selling her a fairytale, and it was getting more unbelievable by the minute.

"And I guess that your friend is taking care of her and she doesn't need to do anything other than look pretty, and that they live in perfect harmony."

Anandur erupted with laughter so loud that he had trouble catching his breath.

"What's so funny?"

The laughter started again, and it was so contagious that a moment later Wonder was laughing too, even though she didn't know why.

When he finally stopped wheezing, Anandur took a deep breath. "Eva, the other immortal we found, is the owner of a private detective agency, and she is the toughest lady I know. I wouldn't want to get on her bad side, and I pity anyone who does."

For some reason, his gushing admiration irked her. She was tough too.

But Anandur wasn't done singing that female's praises. "Even the pregnancy didn't mellow her out. She is still as vicious as ever. Maybe when the baby comes, she'll take it easy."

That remark got Wonder's full attention. Hadn't he just said that fertility went way down when a Dormant turned immortal? If she'd caught him making a contradictory statement, she would know it was a lie.

"How long have they been married?"

"Not long. The wedding was a couple of months ago. But Eva was already pregnant. In the short time since the wedding, she grew a tummy the size of a watermelon."

Wonder narrowed her eyes at Anandur. "Didn't you just say that it's really hard for an immortal female to get pregnant?"

"It is. Eva and Bhathian are blessed. In fact, they've been blessed twice. This is their second child. They made the first one thirty-something years ago."

He was confusing her. But given the lifespans of immortals, it made sense that children could have been born decades or even centuries apart. Although it was strange that they'd decided to finally get married only when Eva had gotten pregnant again.

"Why did they wait so long to get married?"

Anandur shifted in his chair again. "That's a long story for another time. As much fun as I'm having talking to you, the pain in my arms is making it more and more difficult to enjoy it."

"Of course." It was so selfish of her not to pay attention to his discomfort. She hadn't even offered him a cup of water.

Tomorrow she would do better. Maybe even treat him to a beer and some snacks. As a little bribe to keep him talking, of course, not because she felt like doing something nice for him. But for Anandur to be able to drink it, he would have to have his hands cuffed in the front and not behind his back, and that was risky.

She'd think it over on the way to the shelter. Hasty decisions were never good.

Pushing up to her feet, she walked over and got behind Anandur's chair to unlock the cuffs tethering him to its back. "It was a very interesting talk, and I would've liked to continue, but we are both tired. How about we continue tomorrow?"

"Perfect."

38

BRUNDAR

*T*he presidential suite of the hotel seemed to shrink as it filled up with some thirty Guardians.

"We should've reserved one of the conference rooms," Onegus said.

Magnus crossed his arms over his chest and nodded in greeting as one more Guardian entered the room. "I tried. They need at least three days' advance notice. I figured we would be out of here by then."

"After this meeting, go to the front desk and ask to talk with the manager. Use a thrall if you need to, but get us a room." Onegus pointed at the Guardians, most of whom were standing because there was nowhere to sit.

Brundar shook his head. As if it mattered. It was an emergency operation, not a conference for fuck's sake.

When the last of the Guardians arrived, Brundar moved to stand in front of the fireplace and waited for everyone to hush.

It didn't take long. Most of the re-enlisted Guardians knew him well and had a healthy respect for him after fighting by his side in numerous battles over the centuries.

Still, he would have preferred to have the small group he'd worked with over the last several decades. They stayed behind with the rest of the re-enlisted Guardians to protect the village and the keep in case Anandur was compromised.

No one knew the exact extent of the power Navuh and his sons possessed. It was possible that one or more could use compulsion on other immortals, forcing Anandur to reveal the clan's location.

It was a worst-case scenario. Hopefully, it wouldn't come to that.

When the room turned silent, Brundar addressed his army. "The back alley Anandur was last seen in stretches for about half a mile. Five clubs, seven pubs, and twelve restaurants have either their sides or their backs to it. Which means that whoever took Anandur, which we must assume were Doomers, could have come from any of these places. I want you to concentrate on them. Go in and check who worked there for the past week, then sift through their memories for anything unusual. Doomers may speak perfectly accented American English, but they occasionally stumble and misuse words or exhibit slight behavioral anomalies. Those small details might have registered in the subconscious minds of the waiters, bartenders, bouncers, etc."

It was an invasion of privacy that wasn't normally allowed, but even Edna would agree that this was an emergency and a potential security breach.

"Any questions?" Onegus asked.

"What do we do until the pubs and clubs open?" one of the guys asked.

"Check the restaurants."

"Any other questions?" Onegus scanned the group of men. "If not, go get breakfast."

A stampede of hungry men rushed out the door.

"We should go too before they pick the trays clean," Magnus said.

People needed to eat, Brundar reminded himself. As the saying went, an army marches on its stomach. But he felt no hunger. It seemed surreal to think about food while Anandur was missing.

"Go, I'll stay and make a few phone calls."

"You need to eat, Brundar," Onegus said.

"I'm not hungry."

"It's not a suggestion. It's an order."

Damn chief. This wasn't the time to pull rank. Still, Brundar was not in the habit of disobeying orders.

"I can make phone calls from there."

Onegus clapped him on the back. "I'm glad you see reason."

As if he had a choice.

Down at the hotel's restaurant, servers were busy refilling the buffet trays, while Guardians stuffed their mouths with mountains of food.

"I bet they never saw men eat so much," Magnus said.

"Unless they've hosted football teams. Those humans can eat."

Onegus's voice had been just above a whisper, but he shouldn't have said it. The humans around them couldn't hear that, but footage from surveillance cameras could be manipulated and sound enhanced.

This was the age of technology, with cameras recording everything. Except, unfortunately, where Brundar actually needed them to.

And wasn't that a perfect example of Murphy's law.

As the three of them joined two other Guardians at a

table, Brundar pulled out his phone to ring Andrew. The guy hadn't called him about Tim yet.

Onegus shook his head. "I'm getting you a plate. Anything in particular that you want?"

"Coffee will do."

"I meant food."

Brundar waved him away. "Since when did you become my mother?"

Onegus leaned forward and got in his face. "Are we really having this conversation? All I want to hear from you are food choices."

"Whatever you're getting yourself is fine by me." He didn't intend to eat any of it anyway.

"Fine. Don't complain if there is nothing on the plate that you like. And just so we're clear, I'm going to make you eat it."

"Yes, Mother."

Onegus shook his head and turned on his heel, while Magnus stifled a chuckle and followed the chief to the buffet.

One warning look shut the other two Guardians' mouths before they had a chance to open them.

Finally. A few moments of peace and quiet.

Brundar selected Andrew's contact and dialed.

The guy picked up on the second ring. "You know it's eight in the morning and I don't go to work until nine, right?" There were some scraping noises, then heavy baby breathing, then something that sounded like "pwa."

"Did you give the phone to Phoenix?"

"Give it to her? No. She grabbed it and is chewing on it."

Brundar rolled his eyes. "Did you talk to Tim?"

"Give the phone to Daddy, sweetheart. Phones are dirty and yucky."

A moment later a piercing scream sounded. "Noooo!"

Apparently, the baby had learned a new word and was using it to express her displeasure.

"Not yet. It was too late last night, and calling him early in the morning before he's had his fifth cup of coffee is a really bad idea. He'd say no. I know you're impatient, but let me handle it the right way."

Damnation. What choice did he have?

"I'm going to make sure that there is a jet ready to fly him here as soon as he's ready."

"That's a good idea. Tim would love a ride in a private plane."

Brundar ended the call, then looked at the time. It was still too early to ring the guy with the dogs, or The Finder of Lost Things as he called his service. It was a long shot, but it was worth a try.

After all, the clothes that had been cut off Anandur's body had his brother's scent on them. It was still strong even though they'd been in the dumpster for a few hours before Magnus had found them.

39

ANANDUR

*A*s soon as Anandur woke up the next day, he was greeted by three hostile stares.

"Did you get lucky last night, Dur?" Grud asked.

Anandur ignored him, got up, and walked over to the lever that served as a faucet to release water from a plastic tube. He took a few gulps, gargled it in his mouth, then spat it out.

Fates, how he wished he had a toothbrush. Toothpaste would've been nice too, as would have been coffee and about a mountain of Okidu's waffles.

Wonder wasn't feeding them enough. One meal a day just didn't do it for him, even if he stuffed his face and ate every last grain of rice and every bean.

He took a drink from the tube and went back to his mattress.

"What's the matter? Suddenly we are not good enough to talk to?" Grud was still staring at him with murder in his eyes.

"I'm hungry," Anandur said.

Shaveh humphed. "We've been hungry for months. Didn't she feed you last night? Or did you do the feeding?"

So that was what it was about. The Doomers were jealous, thinking that he'd gotten something from Wonder they had all been coveting.

Impersonating a Doomer meant that he couldn't act like a gentleman. He needed to throw around a few crude remarks and hand gestures for them to believe he was one of them. The problem was that the words refused to leave his mouth. He wasn't one to talk disrespectfully about women, and especially not about his own magnificent Wonder Woman.

Damn it. Had he just said those words in his head?

Talk about Stockholm Syndrome. And not in reverse.

"I'm working on it."

"How is it going?" Mordan asked, his eyes blazing with curiosity rather than hatred.

"I'm making progress." Anandur waved a hand over his body. "What female can resist all this, eh?"

Grud chuckled. "That one is not going to give it up unless you take it by force."

Anandur closed his eyes and started counting sheep. This was not the time to flash fangs and glowing eyes. If he did, he would have to pretend it was the result of arousal rather than rage and talk about raping Wonder.

Wasn't going to happen.

One sheep, two sheep...

Anandur's imagination had a mind of its own and took over the scene. Suddenly, Brundar popped up on the other side of the fence the sheep were jumping over, the sheep turned into Doomers, and Brundar unsheathed two swords.

There was a lot of blood.

Anandur smiled. That was much more satisfying than counting sheep.

He felt his fangs retracting. "That's because, you, my friend, lack charm. The girl is putty in my hands."

Shaveh made a hooting sound and threaded his arm through the bars for a bro fist bump.

Grud wasn't amused. "What kind of a spy are you that you couldn't overpower the woman and get free? Each of us could've done it, and we are just ordinary warriors, not master spies."

"Aha." Anandur lifted a finger. "I didn't get free *because* I am trained as a spy, not despite it. I need to question the girl and find out where she is from, and if there are more free immortal females out there that we could get our hands on."

"Yeah!" Shaveh offered his fist again.

Grud sat back on his mattress and lifted a book. "She doesn't know anything, and she is all alone. You're not going to find any other immortal females or males. It's just her. Instead of wasting your time, do what needs to be done, and don't forget about us. After months of being locked down here we deserve some payback."

Anandur was definitely not going to forget about Grud. He was going to come back for him and tear his throat out with his fangs and then remove his black heart. The others, if they kept their mouths shut, he might still grant mercy.

But not Grud.

In order to carry out this fantasy, though, he needed Wonder to release him first.

It would be so easy to overpower her, take her phone and call Brundar. Help was practically around the corner.

But he couldn't bring himself to do that. Every time the thought entered his mind, he saw her looking at him with her big green eyes.

She was so young and so naive. Last night she started to look at him with the beginnings of trust, and a little bit of desire.

The scent had been very subtle, like that of a young immortal girl just discovering her sexuality. If Wonder were a mature immortal female, the scent would've been irresistible to him. Hell, if she were older and more experienced, her needs would've been stronger, and she wouldn't have waited for him to make a move. She would've initiated it.

Immortal females weren't shy in regards to their sexuality. They knew what they wanted and went for it.

Well, except for Ruth, but she might be the only exception.

Anandur often wondered what had happened to her. He hoped it wasn't anything close to what had been done to Brundar, but he had a feeling someone had hurt her.

Otherwise, her reluctance to make love with Nick didn't make sense. She wasn't a virgin, she had a grown daughter, and Nick was a good guy despite his quirkiness. It was evident that the two had feelings for each other, and yet Ruth still hesitated.

Wonder didn't have that deer-caught-in-the-headlights look in her eyes like Ruth. Her gaze was focused and intense, and she'd looked him straight in the eyes when they'd talked.

What a fascinating woman.

Girl.

Woman.

Her contradictions intrigued him—strength and softness, innocence and maturity, trust and caution. Somehow all of that worked, creating a perfectly balanced person even though for all intents and purposes she was a nine-month-old baby.

Well, obviously that wasn't the case. The person she was had been shaped before her catastrophic memory loss. But as far as education and worldliness, she was a baby learning everything from scratch, albeit at a much accelerated pace.

If he betrayed her, though, if he hurt her, physically or emotionally, that balance might get all out of whack and she might never find it again.

Like Ruth.

Anandur would rather let Brundar beat him to a pulp, which his brother would definitely do after learning that Anandur could've gotten free and hadn't because he'd refused to hurt his kidnapper.

40

WONDER

*H*er phone's ringing woke Wonder up way too early. With blurry eyes, she reached for it and brought it to her ear while glancing at the clock on the wall. Who could be calling her at eight-thirty in the morning?

There were only four people who had her number, Tony, Mrs. Rashid, Mrs. Rashid's daughter Serena, and the shelter's administration.

Mrs. Rashid was back in Egypt where it was the middle of the night, Serena never called, and the shelter's administration office didn't open until ten. Which left only one person.

"Hey, Tony, what's up?"

"Do you remember the detectives from yesterday?"

No longer sleepy, Wonder sat up and clutched the phone to her ear. "What about them?" Had they figured out she had taken Anandur? Were they coming for her?

"They are bringing a forensic artist to draw the picture of the woman the missing guy left with."

That was a relief. Wonder plopped back on her pillow. "And you're calling me so early because?"

"They need you to come in and describe her to him. He is going to draw her picture from what you tell him."

Wonder knew what a forensic artist did from one of her television shows. "Do I need to come in now? I just woke up."

"No, he will be at the club around three. I just wanted to let you know right away so you wouldn't make any plans. This is important."

"Yeah, I know. I'll be there."

"I'll be there too. I'm not going to leave you alone with those detectives. I know they scared you a little."

Shit, so those two were going to be there too. She'd hoped it would only be the artist.

"Thanks, Tony. I appreciate that. The one with the goatee, Magnus, he was nice, but the other one creeped me out."

Tony laughed. "Yeah, I know what you mean. I think the dude has a speech impediment, that's all. That's why he hardly talks. And when he does, he sounds like a robot."

"Maybe. I don't know. I'm just glad you're going to be there."

"No problem. See you here at three."

One of those immortals must've been Anandur's brother. It wasn't the dead serious blond, that was for sure. He didn't resemble Anandur in any way, not in looks and not in behavior.

That left the other one, Magnus with the warm brown eyes and the goatee, who had given her his business card. But he had referred to Anandur as his partner and not his brother.

Anandur had said something about his brother coming with a force of Guardians, so maybe neither of the two fake detectives was his brother. But that didn't make sense. The club was the last place Anandur had been in and should have been the first place his brother checked.

Had he lied about his brother searching for him? Had it been a ploy to gain her sympathy?

She could ask Anandur to describe his brother. If his description matched either of the two, she would have proof that he'd been telling her the truth.

And then what?

It was so tempting to believe him. Too tempting. And that made her suspicious. Or maybe just cautious.

Wonder put her head in her hands and sighed. It was quite simple, really. If Anandur truly believed that he could overpower her despite the handcuffs and leg restraints and was refraining from doing it to convince her he meant her no harm, then everything else he'd told her was probably true as well.

But maybe he didn't.

After all, she had a Taser gun and had used it on him before, rendering him immobile long enough to knock him out with a blow to the back of his head. Maybe he was wary of that.

She could test her theory.

Today, she would have him put the handcuffs on with his hands in the front and see if he tried anything. She would pretend to have relaxed her guard, but her hand would never be far away from her holster.

Even better. She was going to stop by the market and get a six-pack of beer and some snacks. It would convince him that she was falling for his manipulations.

If he were indeed trying to manipulate her. She would be very happy if her suspicions were proven wrong.

41

ANANDUR

"*I*s she coming for you this morning?" Shaveh asked between one chin-up and the next.

There wasn't much to do in the cage other than reading or training, and Anandur was too agitated to read, so he trained.

Following Mordan's example, he'd started with pushups and then both of them had moved to chin-ups. Now with Shaveh joining in, and the three of them hanging shirtless from the top horizontal bars of their cages, they must've looked like the original inhabitants of the place—big apes.

Unable to help himself, Anandur hung from the bar, and holding on with only one hand while scratching himself with the other, called out, "hook, hoo, hoo, hoo, oo, oo, oo!"

With the other two adding their own gorilla calls, the noise made the room sound like an asylum for demented apes.

Grud expressed his opinion by shaking his head.

"What's going on?" Wonder ran inside then stopped in her tracks and looked at them as if they'd lost their minds.

Anandur let go of the bar and dropped down to all fours, then loped to the cage's front and sniffed at her before pushing up and puffing out his bare chest.

"Me, Tarzan." He pointed at himself. "You, Jane." He pointed at her.

Instead of laughing, Wonder stared at his chest for a split second too long and then frowned. "Are you okay?"

He'd forgotten that she didn't have a lifetime of movies stored in her head. She had no idea who Tarzan was.

Damn. There was so much he needed to teach her. "It's a line from a movie about a man who was raised by gorillas."

"Oh." She forced a smile, her eyes darting back to his chest for a moment.

Anandur smirked. Wonder liked what she saw.

Naturally.

He was a fine male specimen if he said so himself.

True, she'd already seen him in all his naked glory, but that was back when she'd thought of him as a murderer. Her perspective had obviously changed.

Shaking her head, Wonder waved her hand in a shooing motion. "Put a shirt on and stand against the back wall."

"Yes, ma'am." He turned around and sauntered toward the mattress where he'd left his T-shirt.

Bending down to retrieve it, he paused for a second, giving Wonder a chance to have a good long look at his ass.

He had a fine ass too, if he said so himself.

Wonder didn't wait for him to stand against the back wall before throwing in the shackles. "Hands in the front this time, but I added another chain to connect the leg restraints to the handcuffs. If you do it sitting down, you don't need help putting everything on."

"Very clever." He took the bundle and sat on his mattress.

When everything was on, he pushed up to his feet and waited for Wonder to inspect him.

When she deemed him secure, she opened the cage. "You can come out now. And just so you know, the keys to your restraints are not on me, and they are not where I'm taking you. So don't get any ideas. There is no way you're getting free."

Very clever, indeed, Anandur thought as he walked out of the room with Wonder following a few steps behind him. She'd listened to what he'd told her, internalized it, and adapted her safety measures.

He was so damn proud of her.

"That was mostly for their ears," she said as she entered the office they'd used last night.

Anandur salivated as he saw the six-pack of beer on the desk. "Is that for me?"

Wonder pointed at the chair. "Take a seat. And yes. I got it for you. I don't drink alcohol." Pulling one can from the pack, she popped the lid and handed it to him. "Enjoy."

Seated, the chain connecting the cuffs to the leg restraints was long enough to allow him a good range of motion. It felt good to sit in a chair and hold a cold can in his hand.

"Thank you. I usually don't drink first thing in the morning even though I'm a Scot. But these are unusual circumstances." He lifted the can to his mouth and took several long gulps.

It was piss poor beer he would not have touched a couple of days ago, but it tasted like heaven to him now.

"Would you like some cold cuts with your beer?" Wonder lifted the lid off a prepackaged container.

"Would I ever." He reached with his hand then stopped.

"My hands are dirty." It was hard to keep clean when the only water source dispensed just drizzle, and he hadn't done even that before leaving the cage.

Wonder lifted a brow. "You're not going to eat because you don't want to touch your food with unwashed fingers?"

"I know it's strange, especially for an immortal. It's not like I'm going to get sick. But I just can't. I'm very fastidious." He chuckled. "Though that's my take on it. Most of my friends call me a neat freak."

"What's wrong with cleanliness?"

"Nothing. They just think I'm excessively concerned with it. I care about being clean and wearing clean clothes, but oddly enough not about tidiness."

"I care about both." Wonder pushed a hand inside her jean pocket and pulled out a small container of hand sanitizer. "Would that help?"

Anandur eyed the container, then shook his head. "Normally yes, but I haven't washed my hands properly for two days."

Wonder popped the cap, squirted a generous amount into her hand, then rubbed her palms vigorously. "I washed my hands several times today." She lifted a couple of turkey slices, rolled them into a cylinder, and brought it to his mouth. "Would you eat it from my fingers?"

Instead of answering, he leaned forward and took a bite. His eyes rolled back from pleasure, and he moaned, but it wasn't because the turkey was that exceptional. Eating from Wonder's hand was a big time turn-on.

He hadn't expected the strong reaction. Was it because of the intimacy that the act of feeding him implied? Or was it her proximity?

He couldn't remember ever responding so strongly to

such a small gesture. Thankfully, his chains allowed him to cross his legs and hide what the nylon pants didn't. Except, she would no doubt smell his arousal. Hopefully, though, Wonder wouldn't know how to interpret it.

Would she react to it?

He didn't know.

She was the first unattached immortal female he'd met that wasn't related to him.

When he opened his eyes, she was staring at his mouth, her lips slightly parted as if she wanted a taste of him.

If he leaned just a little closer, he could kiss her.

He must've done so involuntarily because Wonder leaned away. "Open wide." She lifted the hand holding the rest of the rolled slices.

Pretending that was the reason he'd gotten closer, Anandur tilted his head and opened his mouth so she could drop it inside.

Fates, how he wanted to catch her fingers together with the meat and suck on them. It took a monumental effort to refrain from doing so. Instead, he closed his mouth and chewed, making the appropriate sounds of pleasure.

"Is it that good, or are you that hungry?" Wonder rolled up a few more slices.

"I guess both. Or maybe it's so good because you're feeding it to me."

Wonder's olive-toned cheeks became rosy.

"You look beautiful when you blush."

She narrowed her eyes at him. "Stop it, or I'm not feeding you any more of this." She dangled the roll in front of his face.

He'd gone a bit too far and scared her.

A little self-deprecating humor would fix that. "Oh, no, please have mercy and take pity on an old romantic fool. I can't help myself." With a pout and a trembling lower lip, he steepled his fingers and batted his eyelashes.

Wonder chuckled. "You're such a clown."

"So I've been told."

WONDER

"Would you like another beer?"

"Yes, please."

"Promise to behave?"

"I do." Anandur put a hand over his heart, his other one dangling from the chain below. "For now."

Trying very hard to keep a straight face, Wonder crossed her arms over her chest. "Not good enough. If you want another beer, you need to promise to be good the rest of the morning."

"Fine. I promise, bossy lady."

She popped the lid on the can and handed it to him. "Here you go."

"Much appreciated."

Anandur was growing on her big time, and not just because of his incredible body, although that was a big part of it. He was what Natasha called a hunk.

Add to that his easy-going charm and his humor, and it was impossible to be around him for any length of time and keep a stern expression.

Yesterday at work, and later as she'd lain at night in

bed, Wonder would catch herself thinking about his smiling eyes, or his sensuous lips, or his big hands, then quickly chase those images away before they scrambled her brain completely, only to be reminded of something he'd said and smile like an idiot.

Her defenses were crumbling, and she was starting to think and act like an ordinary girl, which unfortunately she wasn't.

The man was her prisoner. Her job was to determine whether he'd been telling her the truth or charming her with his humor and his good looks and his respectful attitude towards her.

Anandur never used cuss words, not around her, and he never raised his voice either, reinforcing her first impression of him as being clean. Inside and out.

Absentmindedly, she picked up a cheese cube and brought it to his lips. The thing was small, and as he gently closed his lips around it, they brushed against her fingers, sending shivers down her spine.

Hiding her reaction, Wonder pulled her hand away, looked down at the container, and reached for more turkey slices. Rolling them up like she'd done before, she lifted her head and glanced at the man driving her crazy.

His eyes were glowing.

"Why are your eyes doing that?"

"You mean why are they glowing?"

She nodded.

"Your eyes glow too when you experience strong emotions. It's an immortal thing."

She needed to check it out in front of a mirror. She hadn't known that her eyes did that and it was a big problem.

Tony had told her that the forensic artist she was meeting later that afternoon would be accompanied by the two fake detectives. If she got overly anxious or upset, her eyes could give her away.

And she still hadn't questioned Anandur about his brother. Something she'd been meaning to do since yesterday but had gotten sidetracked by Anandur's stories and his jokes.

"Is your brother also a redhead?"

Anandur tilted his head. "Why do you want to know?"

"Just curious."

"He's not. We had two different fathers." Anandur must've seen something in her expression that prompted him to explain. "It's not unusual for my people. Since most members of our community are genetically related to each other, we must seek partners among humans. But because we have to keep our existence secret, we can't form lasting relationships with them. As a result, none of us grew up with fathers around, and siblings share only a mother."

That was so sad. "So if one of your male members fathered a child with a human, he couldn't acknowledge that child?"

Anandur nodded. "Yup. It sucks, but a child of a human female with an immortal male doesn't carry the special genes. It doesn't happen often, though. Especially now that everyone is on birth control."

"How likely is it that I'm somehow related to your community?"

"Not likely at all. We keep tabs on our people."

The pieces of the puzzle were starting to align. Anandur hadn't tried to escape and had no intention of doing so because he needed her. Not the other way around.

She was a rare find, an immortal female he was not related to. Wonder could've been as ugly as a toad, stupid, and have a nasty attitude, and still Anandur would have done everything to win her over and have her agree to come with him.

Were the other three she'd captured planning the same thing? It was possible that each of them wanted her for himself too, but they'd failed to get close to her because they lacked Anandur's natural charm and ability to get under her skin.

"What about the other faction? You said that they don't activate their female Dormants. But what about the genetic thing? Do they have the same problem your people have?"

"No, they don't. They are a patriarchal organization. Since the very beginning of the rift, they managed to capture a good number of immortal and Dormant females that were not related to each other. Their leader instituted a breeding program that serves them to this day. That's how there are so many of them and only a few of us."

Wonder narrowed her eyes at him. "It seems to me that finding an immortal female who is not related to you would be quite a catch. Wouldn't you say?"

Anandur's expression turned somber. "This is not what you think, Wonder. I like you, I won't deny it, but this is not why I'm here trying to convince you to join my people. You need us more than we need you. Trust me on that."

She crossed her arms over her chest and glared at him. "So all of your subtle and not so subtle flirtation wasn't because you wanted me, but because you're completely selfless and wanted nothing more than to help the woman who Tasered you, hit you over the head, and locked you in a cage."

Anandur shifted in his chair, the chains at his ankles rattling as he moved his legs. "You're a beautiful girl, Wonder, and I like you and admire you. I can't help my attraction to you. But you're also very young."

He lifted both hands to scratch his beard, which pulled

the chain connecting his handcuffs to the leg restraints. "Too young," he murmured.

"Too young for what?"

"For me."

Why the hell did it hurt so much to hear that? Hadn't she just realized that he'd never been interested in her personally but just in her immortality?

"I could be ancient for all you know. Immortals don't age."

"True. But there are tells. You can't be older than eighteen or nineteen, and that makes you a teenager." He grimaced as he said it.

Wonder had suspected more or less the same, but her estimate was early twenties. She'd seen teenage girls. She was nothing like them.

"So what are you saying, that you wouldn't want me even if it were on the table?"

Looking away, he scratched his beard again. "I didn't say that."

"You're confusing me."

"I'm confusing myself." He lifted a pair of serious eyes to her. "But that's not the issue here. I'm not trying to seduce you, Wonder. I just want you to realize that I'm a good guy and that you should let me out of these chains."

He shook his hands to make them rattle. "Once I make that phone call to my brother, all of your troubles will be over. You'll meet a lot of new immortals, maybe even find a young one who's more suitable for you, and not an old fart like me."

Huh, who was he kidding?

The glow in his eyes belied his statement. Anandur didn't want her to find a suitable young immortal. He wanted her for himself.

Maybe.

It was all very confusing.

Did he want her or not?

Had she imagined it or not?

Was he a good guy or not?

"I need to think about it," she said, realizing a moment later that it sounded like she wanted to find herself a young immortal. "I mean about freeing you and letting you call your brother."

"Don't take too long. You're sitting on a ticking time bomb here."

She waved a dismissive hand. "I've had the other three for months. A few more days will not make a difference."

"For some reason, I think it will."

"You're just impatient and want out of the cage. Not that I blame you, I would feel the same. But you must understand that I can't make a rash decision. It seems like it was longer, but the first time we actually talked was yesterday morning. Do you expect me to trust you after such a short period of time?"

"Yes, I do. Listen to your gut, Wonder. What does it tell you?"

"That I need to exercise caution."

GRUD

"*T*hank the great Mortdh." Grud sat back on the concrete floor and examined his handiwork.

Shaveh got up and pushed his nose through the bars. "You got one block out. Congratulations. I was starting to think you'd never get it loose."

Grud turned around and cast him a superior glance. "I don't give up easily."

"What's on the other side of the wall?" Mordan asked.

"Not dirt. But it's too dark to see if there are more cages there."

"Let's pray to Mortdh that it's not another cage room." Mordan had taken to praying over the last couple of days, saying that it was his way of helping out.

Did he think Grud was stupid?

This was Mordan's way of convincing Grud that he should not leave him behind.

Grud still wasn't sure about that. It all depended on how easy or difficult it was going to be to get out of the building, and whether he would need the other two for anything. He'd been unconscious when Wonder dropped him in the cage, and so had the others. None of them knew the building's layout or how far it was from the city.

He would need clothes and shoes and money, all easily attainable if there were any humans around to thrall. Hopefully, the building wasn't in some isolated location.

But that was putting the carriage before the horse, as the humans liked to say. The other three blocks were not going to crumble on their own.

Grud collected the debris and divided it between Shaveh and Mordan. "Now that the first one is out, it's going to be easy to take the other three blocks out. We can be out of here tonight. Tomorrow at the latest. The best time to do it is while Dur keeps the woman busy."

"What about Dur?" Shaveh asked. "Aren't we taking him with us?"

"Fuck Dur."

"Speaking of fucking. What about the woman? Weren't we supposed to have some fun with her before we left?" Shaveh thrust his hips against the bars in case someone didn't get his meaning.

Moron.

"We should take her with us," Mordan suggested. "We can keep her locked up somewhere and not tell anyone we have an immortal woman to fuck."

Shaveh snorted. "I have a better idea. We can lock her right here in one of these cages. Payback is a bitch, bitch." He snorted again.

"We can keep her naked and come to bang her whenever we want." Mordan's fangs punched down over his lip. "I'm so sick of fucking my fist and biting the blanket."

"Me too. And I'm sick of eating rice and beans," Shaveh said.

Grud contemplated their idea.

Payback could indeed be sweet, but if anyone was going to fuck Wonder, it was going to be him.

Unlike the other two, he wasn't planning on returning to the Brotherhood. As far as their commanders were concerned, the three of them were dead, so no one was looking for them. It was a rare opportunity and he would be a fool not to take advantage of it.

Grud was no fool.

He'd given it much thought and decided he no longer wished to serve anyone. He wanted to taste life as a civilian, free to do as he pleased. Money would not be a problem. He could just thrall humans to give it to him. And the bonus of owning an immortal female sounded sweeter than the promise of heaven.

Except, this would require getting rid of the other two. Not a problem. He could get them out, kill them somewhere nearby, circle back, kill Dur, and put the woman in a cage.

Naked.

He liked Mordan's suggestion.

He'd give her clothes to wear only if she behaved and cooperated. Not that he had anything against rape, bitches shouldn't say no, but he didn't like doing it exclusively. Sometimes he wanted the woman to come willingly to him.

But that wasn't a big problem either.

He'd seen it done on the island. Those who still thought they had any say about whom they spread their legs for were taught the error of their thinking in no time at all.

It wasn't hard to turn the most stubborn bitch into an obedient female. A few beatings for acting bitchy, a few rewards for spreading her legs on command, and she'd learn what was good for her very fast.

Killing Shaveh and Mordan needed some planning, though.

He would have to take them by surprise. First, he would knock them out with a fast blow to the head. A big rock would do. He could find one before coming back for them. Or maybe he could make further use of the rod he'd pried off the grate.

Once they were out, he would finish the job with his fangs and venom, treating each one to a deadly dose.

The question was whether he could produce enough venom to kill two immortals so quickly. If not, he would have to resort to cruder methods. Cutting a heart out with a dull rod was not going to be easy.

He'd use the same method on Dur and Wonder, just without finishing the woman off.

When she woke up from the knockout, she would find herself naked in a cage.

Sweet.

Payback is a bitch, bitch. He repeated Shaveh's words.

44

WONDER

*A*t five minutes to three, Wonder parked behind the club, right next to Tony's yellow Corvette. It was a cool-looking car, except for the color. The thing was so bright she was sure it could be seen from passing airplanes.

Not that Wonder had ever flown in one and knew what could be seen from up there. Mrs. Rashid had said that it was unnatural for people to be in the air like birds, but she was curious. It must feel amazing to be up in the sky and look down.

One day she was going to try it.

As an immortal, she had plenty of time to experience everything life had to offer. Just not yet. Right now she didn't have enough money or free time and was burdened with taking care of four prisoners.

Wonder sighed. Her life was complicated.

Tony's was the only other car in the parking lot, which meant that the forensic artist and the two immortals hadn't arrived yet. On second thought, though, the immortals could've parked out on the street, or since they were not locals, they might have used a taxi. The area code of the phone number on the card Magnus had given her wasn't one she recognized.

To calm herself before facing the fake detectives again, she'd spent the two preceding hours cleaning one of her warehouses. When she'd left, the floors gleamed, the windows sparkled, and every surface shone from having been dusted and then polished twice.

Wonder Woman was ready to tackle anyone, including the two immortals with all their questions and their super-sensitive noses.

Good luck with that. She smirked. The way she stank from all the cleaning products she'd used, the moment they sniffed her they were going to gag. And if anyone asked, she had a very legitimate excuse to smell like Pine-sol, ammonia, and furniture polish.

As she walked in through the back door, the sounds of conversation coming from Tony's office warned her that the men were already there. Or was it two men and one woman? She didn't remember if Tony said it was a he or a she.

Taking a deep breath, she knocked and then pushed the door open. "Good afternoon, Tony." Wonder entered her boss's office with a smile. "Detectives." She nodded toward the two immortals. "And you must be the forensic artist." She offered her hand to the short, nearly bald guy with a comb-over who was checking her out without trying to be discreet about it. "I'm Wonder."

"Tim." He cracked a big smile as he took her hand. "I don't normally shake hands, but for you, I must make an exception. Wonder, what an unusual name. It fits you, though. You inspire wonder." He waved his other hand over her body.

"I'm flattered." She smiled back. For some reason, Tim's open admiration and bold approach didn't offend her.

Maybe because he sounded sincere, or maybe because she was impressed by his guts.

The few men who found her attractive were usually too intimidated by her size, or her bouncer T-shirt, or her Taser gun, to summon the courage for casual flirting. They either ogled her from afar or covered their insecurities with crude remarks. Tim, who wasn't a young man or a handsome one, oozed natural confidence.

In her peripheral vision, she caught the blond immortal crinkling his nose and turning his face away.

Her plan was working better than expected.

Tim was still holding on to her hand. "I would love to do a portrait of you. Perhaps after I'm done with what I'm paid for, you could pose for me? It won't take long. I'm fast." He winked. "But I would love to take my time with a beauty like you."

Bold little bald guy.

Wonder stifled a smile. "I start my shift at six. If you can do both by that time, then by all means. I would love to pose for you." Not really, but she could use Tim as a shield against the immortals and their inevitable questions.

The guy had enough attitude to stand up even to those two. And since they needed him, they weren't going to do anything to antagonize the artist.

"I can't work here." Tim looked around the office. "The lighting is crap. Show me what else you got."

It was kind of funny the way Tim ran from place to place with the four of them following him around.

"This is it." He finally stopped in the kitchen. "Still crap, but not as bad as the rest of the place. You need to invest in better lighting, my friend." He clapped Tony on the back.

Her boss wasn't going to roll over and take the insults. He slapped the artist's back. "It's a nightclub. The lighting is supposed to be crappy. It's part of the atmosphere."

"I get it. Don't think that I don't. But I look at every-thing with an artist's eye, and I know what looks good and what doesn't. Your place needs work." He turned to Wonder. "Lovely young lady, please sit here." He pulled out a stool for her. "I'm going to sit right over there." He pulled another one for himself.

"Any of you gentlemen care to bring my equipment from Tony's office?" It was more of a command than a request, and yet the goateed one rushed to comply.

She'd been right about Tim. The guy's attitude was about ten times his size.

The blond leaned against the wall, crossed his arms over his chest, and trained his cold, cold eyes on her.

Creepy.

Wonder looked away, pretending to admire the commercial fridge.

"So how did you end up with a name like Wonder? Were your parents DC fans?"

"I guess." She had no idea what he was talking about.

Magnus came back with Tim's equipment and put it on the kitchen table.

"Thank you." Tim pulled out a large drawing pad and a pencil case.

"So you're not a fan?" he asked as he took out one of the pencils.

"Not a fan of what?"

"DC comics. They introduced the character of Wonder Woman."

The blond's eyes were still trained on her. A wrong answer might trigger suspicion. She'd seen the movie, maybe she could talk about that.

"I'm more of a movie girl than a comic book fan. I loved the movie. A strong superwoman, what's not to love, right?"

"My thoughts exactly." Tim waggled his brows. "Let's get to work, shall we?"

"I'm ready."

"What was the shape of the woman's face? Would you say it was oval? Or round? Or..."

For the next hour, Tim kept asking questions, and she kept answering while watching Rosalie's face take shape on Tim's drawing pad. The guy had real talent.

"I don't know how you can do it just from my descriptions, but that's Rosalie. It's her face."

The blond pushed away from the wall. "You know her name," he stated in a cold, robotic tone. "Why didn't you tell us before?"

Shit, Wonder had forgotten that she was not supposed to know Rosalie's name. It wasn't as if she could tell them that she'd picked it up from the woman's mind "It just popped into my head." She snapped her fingers. "Just like that. I didn't remember ever asking her for her name, but maybe I heard someone call her."

"That happens to me a lot," Tim said. "I'm trying to remember some actor's name and it just won't come, and then later, boom! It pops into my head. Memory is a strange thing."

She snorted. "Tell me about it."

The blond's eyes were still drilling holes in the back of her head. Was he buying it?

Tim put a few finishing touches on his creation and lifted it for her to see. "What do you think?"

"It's her. Exactly."

"Can I have it?" the blond asked.

Tim put the pad down. "Money first, buddy. I've been swindled before."

"Here." The blond took out a wad of cash and dropped it on the table. "You can count it. It's all there."

Without batting an eyelid, Tim unfolded the wad and started counting. "It's all here. Thirty-five hundred." He lifted his head and smiled at the blond. "It was nice doing business with you, my friend. Call me anytime you need an emergency portrait done. I'm your man."

"Highway robbery, that's what this is," the goateed one murmured.

The blond turned his cold eyes to his partner. "I don't give a fuck about the money. I just want to find my brother."

Wonder felt as if someone had poured a bucket of ice water over her head.

The blond was Anandur's brother? They really were nothing alike.

There was so much anger and pain in his voice, which was doubly shocking when coming from a guy who'd sounded like a robot the other times she'd heard him speak.

His nostrils flared, and he turned to look at her quite sharply. "Is there anything you want to tell me, Wonder girl?"

He must've smelled her guilt. Evidently even the strong residual scent of Pine-sol couldn't overpower it.

"Only that I hope you'll find your brother soon."

He nodded, then extended his arm toward Tim. "The portrait."

"Of course," Tim said.

Carefully tearing the page out, he rolled it into a cylinder, secured it with a rubber band, and handed it to the blond. "It's all yours."

45

NICK

"*R*uth invited you for dinner?" Sharon beamed at Nick like a proud mother. "That's awesome." She looked him over and then waved a hand. "Wear something nicer, like a dress shirt."

He looked down at the T-shirt he had on. "What's wrong with that? This is how I always dress."

Sharon put her hand on her hip and struck a pose. "Exactly. But this is not business as usual. It's a big deal, and you should treat it as such. I also suggest you get her a nice bottle of wine. And a box of chocolates. And maybe even flowers."

That seemed excessive. Not that he minded getting stuff for Ruthie, but he didn't want to appear too eager. "Are you sure? I don't want to look as if I'm trying too hard."

Sharon pointed a finger at him. "Just do as I say and don't argue. You'll thank me later."

Truth be told, Sharon had a lot of dating experience, and he had practically none because Ruth was his first girlfriend. He was taking his dating cues from movies, which wasn't the smartest thing to do.

"Fine. I'll go change."

Sharon patted his arm. "Good boy." She leaned and kissed his cheek. "Good luck tonight."

"What's happening tonight?" Eva waddled into the living room with her huge belly leading the way.

"Ruth invited Nick to dinner at her house."

A huge grin split Eva's face. "That's wonderful. Congratulations. It's about time."

Why the hell was everyone making such a big deal out of it?

"I'm going upstairs to change into another shirt."

Eva nodded. "Good thinking. You don't go to a woman's house for dinner wearing this." She grimaced as she waved her hand over his clothes. "I would suggest that you put on some dress slacks as well."

Bossy women.

Eva was his employer, which gave her the right to boss him around during work hours, but not when he was off the clock. And Sharon had no right at all.

"I draw the line at the shirt."

Eva shook her head. "Suit yourself." She waddled away toward the kitchen.

Not trusting Sharon's instructions, after changing his shirt, Nick did a quick internet search. Apparently, it was in the codebook of dating that a guy had to bring at least one of the three items she'd mentioned when invited for the first time to his girlfriend's house for dinner.

Well, why not. Anything to make Ruthie happy and put her in the right mood.

On the way to her place, he stopped at the supermarket to get the wine, and the chocolates, as well as the flowers— the biggest damn bouquet the store had to offer.

The bigger, the better, right?

The question was whether he should grab a box of condoms too, and if yes, what size.

Had he been reading the signs right? Was Ruth ready for the next step?

It had started with the night at her house and their first session of heavy necking while watching that porn movie. A brilliant move on his part if he said so himself. It had worked much better than Nick had expected. Who would've suspected that Ruthie would get so horny from watching porn?

Certainly not him.

The most he'd hoped for was getting her interested in giving necking a try. Boy, had she gone for it. She'd been like a different woman.

Then yesterday, at the café, when he'd come in for his usual breakfast and lunch, she'd kept sending coy smiles his way. He hadn't seen her in the evening because she had been invited to Sylvia's. Which, by the way, wasn't cool with him.

He should've been invited too. After all, he and Ruthie were an item.

Ruth had mumbled something about Roni inviting a guy from work, and that she was there as a cook more than a guest.

Which irked him too.

Why should Ruth cook for Roni and Sylvia?

Now he wasn't sure if Ruthie had invited him for dinner at her place because she felt bad about him not having been invited yesterday, or because she was interested in more snogging.

Or if he were incredibly lucky, maybe even more than that.

Hence the condoms.

Eh, what the hell. He grabbed several boxes, each in a different size.

As he put everything on the checkout counter, the cashier dude gave him a knowing nod, the equivalent of one bro telling another good luck. The guy swiped Nick's credit card, then put everything other than the flowers in a brown paper bag.

"Thank you." Nick took the bag and the flowers and made a hasty exit.

The cashier was a guy his age, and Nick hadn't minded the nod. But everyone standing in line behind him had no doubt guessed his plans for tonight as well.

Damn it, he should have bought the condoms at a pharmacy.

Whatever. What was done was done.

He didn't do grocery shopping at that supermarket anyway. At least he'd done one thing right.

Looking left and right to make sure the drivers of the cars parked next to him were not sitting inside them, Nick pulled the three boxes of condoms out of the bag. It wasn't as if he could walk into Ruth's house with a paper bag full of condoms.

After unwrapping the cellophane covers, he opened the boxes and pulled out one packet from each.

In the movies, guys always had a condom in their wallets, but he doubted all three packets would fit in his.

Should he try them on for size in the car?

Nah, even he wasn't that crazy.

He would have to choose one. Nick decided to bet on the large. The medium was probably too small, and thinking he needed an extra-large was a bit optimistic on his part.

But what if he messed it up and the thing tore?

Just to be safe, he stuffed two more in his back pocket.

Damn, it was so stupid of him not to think of practicing with putting on rubbers before.

46

RUTH

"Oh, my goodness! What's all that?" Ruth took the box of chocolates and the bottle of wine, leaving Nick to hold the enormous bouquet.

"Isn't it customary for a guy to get his girl flowers and the other stuff when she invites him for dinner?"

If he were embarrassed, she couldn't tell because his face was hidden behind the ginormous bouquet, and she couldn't smell his emotions either, because the smell of flowers was overwhelming.

"Follow me to the kitchen. I don't think I have a vase big enough for that."

"Too big, eh?" Nick chuckled.

Knowing her guy, he was probably biting the inside of his cheek not to add a that's-what-she-said.

Silly boy, she loved his stupid jokes, even those no one else laughed at. Crude humor was better than no humor, and Ruth had discovered that she liked to laugh.

Not that anyone knew that about her. Most of the time she was too shy to laugh out loud, opting to smirk quietly while hiding her face.

Not with Nick, though, not when they were alone. He didn't mind that her laughter sounded like that of a rabid hyena. In fact, he loved it because it made him laugh too.

"How about that?" She pulled out her biggest pot.

"Are you going to cook them or sniff them? And speaking of sniffing, what's that delicious smell? I can't see anything from behind these damn flowers."

"Give 'em." She took the bouquet, dumped it in the pot and took it to the sink to fill with water.

"You're stronger than you look," Nick said as she carried the pot to the living room. "But you should've let me do it."

Oops. Small slips like that were exactly why relationships between immortals and humans were not a good idea. It was hard to monitor every move and make sure she didn't do anything weird.

"It's all the weeding I do in my garden. You have no idea how hard it is to pull those suckers out. It's a better workout than lifting weights. " She put the pot on the floor next to the front door.

When she turned around, Nick was no longer behind her. Instead, he was in the kitchen lifting lids off the various pots and pans and peeking inside.

"You cooked enough for twelve people, Ruthie. Are you expecting more guests?"

She didn't need immortal super senses to know Nick hoped to be the only one she planned on entertaining tonight.

"No, it's just you and me."

The truth was that Ruth always cooked too much when she was nervous. It calmed her down. But this time even that hadn't been enough.

After deciding that tonight was the night she was taking Nick to her bed, she'd been a nervous wreck.

First and foremost, because if it turned out to be as bad an experience as she'd had before, it would ruin the good thing she and Nick had.

He would be so disappointed.

But she wasn't going to let it happen no matter what. If need be, she would fake an orgasm. Nick had nothing to compare her to, so he wouldn't even know the difference. She could moan and pant like the actress in that porn movie.

So what if it was dishonest.

She wasn't going to lose the best thing in her life because of her inability to enjoy intercourse. As Nick had shown her the night before last, there were plenty of other ways to enjoy intimacy. They could spend most of the time touching and caressing and licking each other for pleasure, and dedicate only a little bit of time to the act itself.

But that wasn't the only reason for her nervousness.

While watching the movie, Ruth had realized something that had confused her. The part that had turned her on the most was the one Nick had been sure would scare her off.

It hadn't been the actor's impressive size, she could've done without seeing that. Body parts didn't excite her, the situation did. When the professor took charge, pushing the student face down on the desk, that was when Ruth had nearly orgasmed.

As someone who'd had a bad experience, that should've turned her off, scared her, not turned her on. And yet, her body had reacted most unexpectedly. Maybe the difference was seeing the actress so aroused and responsive. It had been enviable.

Did she want Nick to be more assertive with her and take charge?

Ruth wasn't sure.

And if she did, could he do it?

Nick was a confident guy as far as his smarts and his skills went. So he had it in him. If she were less of a scaredy cat, he might have been less hesitant. But then she probably would've freaked out.

Confusing? You bet.

Where was the balance? How could she reconcile her need for a dominant lover and her fears?

How could she expect poor Nick to know what to do when she herself didn't know what she wanted?

Ugh, she needed help. Maybe she should find a human sex therapist, preferably in a different city, a female of course, and ask her to explain how two such conflicting feelings could coexist, and what could she do about them.

Nick came out of the kitchen, rubbing his washboard abs. "If everything tastes as good as it smells, you'll have to roll me out of here."

"Or I'll feed you more until you can't fit through the door. You'll be trapped here forever." She led him to the dining room. "Take a seat and prepare to get pampered."

Nick laughed as he shook out the napkin and put it over his lap. "Why does it sound like a threat instead of a promise?"

"Because it is." She leaned over him from behind and kissed his forehead. "I'm going to seduce you with my gourmet cooking and never let you go."

"Oh, baby, you could feed me dog food for all I care, and I wouldn't want to leave."

She slapped his bicep playfully. "If you call my famous roast dog food, I'm going to kick you out, close the door, and never invite you again."

"Oh, no!" He cupped his cheeks in mock horror. "Anything but that. I will stand outside your door and howl until you let me in." He demonstrated. Loudly.

"Stop it. The neighbors will think I have a wolf in here."

Nick smirked. "A very hungry wolf."

"Don't worry." She patted his shoulder. "If by the time you finish eating, you're not ready to admit that this was the best meal you've ever had, I'll know you're lying."

NICK

*N*ick patted his stomach. "It's the best meal I've ever had." And he wasn't lying or exaggerating. Ruth had the touch.

It was like magic. With the perfect blend of seasoning and the ideal combination of flavors, she'd transformed ordinary dishes into something special.

"Thank you." Ruth bowed her head.

He rose to his feet and started collecting the dishes. "I'll clean up."

"Let's do it together, so it will go faster." She blushed.

What was going on?

All during dinner he'd made her laugh with his ridiculous stories and his dumb jokes. Ruthie had seemed happy and relaxed. Now she looked anxious again.

Was she afraid he was going to initiate something?

The truth was that this was exactly what he'd had in mind, but if that made her so nervous, he would have to change his plans.

Regrettably.

Nick had been hoping that after tonight, he would finally be a virgin no more.

When they were done with the cleanup, Ruth took his hand and led him out, but instead of taking him to the living-room couch, she took him down the hallway to her bedroom.

No way, it was actually happening, he was going to get laid.

I'm such a moron. It's not like some random chick is doing me a favor. This is Ruthie, the girl I love.

"I think it's time," Ruth said as she looked into his eyes. "I love you, Nicki. And I know you love me."

"I do." He wrapped his arms around her and kissed her gently, running small circles on her back over and over again because he had no idea what to do next.

"You'll have to tell me what to do, Ruthie," he whispered in her ear.

She smiled up at him, but the smile didn't reach her eyes. "After watching so much porn, I thought you knew everything there was to know."

"I do. But I doubt you want me to treat you like a porn star."

She narrowed her eyes. "Why not?"

"Because, because." Suddenly he was stuttering. "Because you're not. You're shy."

She leaned her forehead on his chest. "What if I'm tired of being shy? What if I want to be confident and assertive like the girl in the movie?"

He chuckled. "That girl is probably a grandma by now."

For some reason that made her giggle.

"What's so funny?"

"Nothing. It's just hard to imagine her as an older woman." Ruth giggled again.

She was either nervous or drunk on the wine they'd had with dinner. Hell, he was nervous too.

"I have an idea," Ruth murmured into his chest. "Since we are both kind of nervous and don't know what to do. How about we role-play? We can reenact that movie." As she lifted her face to him, her lower lip was caught between her teeth.

She looked so adorable he could eat her up. Hey, maybe he would. Later, after they did the scene from the movie.

Nick liked the idea, a lot. This was familiar territory, and he knew what to do. Besides, the movie had made Ruthie horny as hell.

"Works for me. Who do you want to be, the student or the professor?"

"The professor."

He'd asked it as a joke. Ruth's choice had taken him by complete surprise. "Really?"

"But with a twist," she added with a sly smile.

"That I can't wait to hear." He sat on the bed and pulled her down onto his lap. "Tell me."

"Since you're the virgin and I'm the more experienced, older woman, I think it makes more sense for me to play the professor and you the naughty student who lusts after his bookish and yet sexy teacher."

"Perfect. Go on."

Ruthie's eyes sparkled with excitement. "I'm a divorcee who hasn't been with anyone for years. I'm practically a virgin again. I have this very sexy student I've had my eye on since the beginning of the year, but he is way too young for me. I did my best not to let him see how much he affected me, but he figured it out. He comes to my office after hours on the pretext of needing my help with a difficult subject."

Talking fast as if afraid to lose her nerve, Ruth had run

out of breath. It seemed as if she had it rehearsed. How long had she been planning the scene? Since they'd watched the movie?

"That's it. That's all I've got. Can you take it from there?" She looked at him with hopeful eyes.

"I definitely can." He glanced around her bedroom. "Do you have a room with a desk?"

A look of uncertainty crossed her eyes. "My sister's room. She moved out several months ago."

That's right. Sylvia, Ruth's sister, was living with her boyfriend now. "She wouldn't mind?"

"I'm not going to tell her. Are you?"

48

RUTH

*S*itting behind the desk in Sylvia's old room, Ruth waited for Nick's knock on the door with part apprehension and part excitement.

Somehow the role-playing made everything seem lighter. It was so different from before, and Nick was the complete opposite of Sylvia's father. With his humor and his playfulness and his gentle nature, Nick was everything the other guy hadn't been, and Ruth had a much easier time separating the two experiences in her head.

Perhaps she was going to have fun this time. Yes, that was how she needed to think. Positive attitude was half the journey to success. And who knew? Maybe after tonight she would join the other immortal females in obsessing about sex. In a good way.

Ruth chuckled. Way to get carried away.

If she survived tonight without sustaining or inflicting new emotional scars, she would count it as a huge success.

"Knock, knock," Nick said as he opened the door. "Can I come in?"

She waved a hand. "Please do. How can I help you, Nickolas?"

Nick sucked in a breath. "I've never liked my full name until I heard it coming from your luscious lips, Professor." He sauntered toward her and sat on a corner of her desk. "You can call me Nickolas whenever you want."

"That's most inappropriate behavior for a student, Nickolas. Please remove your backside from my desk."

He leaned forward, his face hovering a couple of inches away from hers. "On one condition. You change my grade from a C to an A."

Getting into the role, Ruth leaned away from him and crossed her arms over her chest. "Not going to happen, Nickolas. Please take a seat, in a chair, and tell me what you need help with."

Instead of giving her more lip, Nick dropped to the floor and knelt at her feet. "Please, Professor. You've tortured me enough."

He put his hands on her knees and pushed her pencil skirt up a little. "You come to class with those nerdy narrow skirts, and those nerdy thick glasses, and those pouty pink lips, and you scramble my brain. I have such a gargantuan crush on you."

Ruth stifled a smile. She'd never worn glasses, but she liked knee-length pencil skirts. They weren't nerdy, though.

As he slid her skirt a couple of inches higher, his warm hand on her thighs creating heat somewhere else, Nick looked up at her with puppy eyes. "Please, have mercy on me. Let me kiss you. Just one kiss." He lifted a finger.

"Well, it's highly inappropriate, but I guess one kiss would do no harm."

"Thank you." He clasped her hands and kissed both backs. "Thank you, thank you, thank you."

Ruth giggled as he lifted her off the chair and seated her on the desk. "That's better." He cupped her cheeks and kissed her softly.

She melted into him, threading her fingers into his soft, shoulder-length hair and kissing him back for all he was worth.

"Wow, teacher, that was one hell of a kiss," he said as they parted to take a breath.

He then looked at her hard nipples, their outline clearly visible through the thin fabric of her blouse. "I think the teacher likes me. I think she wants me to kiss her some more." He thumbed both nipples through her blouse. "Right here."

As Ruth nodded, he reached for the first button. "May I?"

"Yes, you may."

Fates, she loved the game they were playing, and she loved Nick for, well, being Nick.

He was playful, considerate, never took anything for granted, and yet he was assertive as well. The combination was hotter than hell and way more arousing than anything she'd read in her raunchy novels or what she saw in that porn movie.

When he was done with all the buttons, Nick parted the two halves of her blouse and pushed the sleeves down her arms.

As she shrugged the rest off, he leaned and planted a kiss in the valley between her breasts. "With such a beautiful teacher, I might never graduate." He lifted his eyes to hers. "Can I please see more of you?"

Ruth reached behind her and popped the snap of her bra open. "Just because you asked so politely, you have permission to kiss them."

Nick's grin was so wide he might as well have won the

lottery. With his hands on her back holding her gently, he lowered his head and took one nipple into his mouth, sucking and licking until Ruth pushed on his head. He then moved to the other and did the same.

The throbbing between her legs was getting so intense that she considered reaching down with her hand to relieve the pressure. Instead, she slid forward a little.

With Nick's hips wedged between her spread thighs, and her skirt bunched up at her waist, all that was between her hot center and Nick's groin were her panties and his pants. A little further, and she could rub herself against him.

As one of his hands left her back, smoothing over the dip of her waist and then resting for a moment on her tummy, Ruth held her breath.

Was he going to touch her there?

But she was still wearing the skirt, and it was in the way of his hand sliding further down.

Nick leaned away a little and glanced at her crotch, where she was sure there was a big wet spot on her panties.

Could he see it?

If he were an immortal, he could've smelled her arousal, but he was only a human, with his limited human senses.

For now.

Reaching with his finger, he touched her over her panties. "You're so wet for me, baby," he whispered. "Can I kiss you here too?"

Ruth knew he had never done this before, but neither had she. It seemed like a little too much too soon. It was such an intimate act. She couldn't imagine herself so vulnerable, so open. Maybe someday she would feel safe enough, but not today.

He saw her hesitation. "Over the panties, that's all."

That seemed safe. "Okay," she breathed.

Dropping to his knees, Nick put his hands on her inner thighs and applied gentle pressure to keep them spread.

Her legs were trembling, but Ruth didn't know whether it was from the excitement of anticipation or from apprehension.

Surely, a kiss there would feel good. All of Nick's other kisses had, and this one should be no different.

When he leaned forward, Ruth squeezed her eyes shut and held her breath. Except, she shouldn't have feared. Nick's lips feathered over her most sensitive spot with the gentlest of kisses.

"Thank you." He dropped down to his haunches and looked up at her with so much love in his eyes, that Ruth felt like tearing up.

49

NICK

*N*ick was drunk on pheromones. That was the only explanation for the sudden lightheaded-ness. Ruth's scent was literally intoxicating.

"You've slain me, Professor." He put a hand over his heart. "You've enchanted me with your womanly wiles, and now I'm forever your slave." He was only partially joking. "Do with me as you please."

Ruth smiled, the momentary tension that had gripped her when he'd suggested kissing her sweet slit all gone. He would gladly spout endless nonsense in exchange for Ruth's smiles in the nude—partial nudity as it was, but still, it was a fair exchange.

The thing was, it wasn't really nonsense. She had indeed slain him. And he wanted her to do with him as she pleased. Hopefully, what she wanted was to take him to her bed.

Sliding off the desk, Ruth rearranged her skirt and kneeled in front of him. "I love you." She wrapped her arms around his torso and buried her face in the crook of his neck, her naked chest pressed to his. "Take me to bed, Nick."

Nick, not Nickolas. Did it mean that the game was over?

Abruptly, Nick felt his confidence take a nose dive. It was safer in the game.

Maybe he could keep on playing, and Ruth would follow his lead?

He pushed up with her still in his arms, then tugged on her skirt. "I've been dreaming about taking off those tight skirts of yours the entire semester."

Ruth lifted her arms to his neck. "Then take it down, big boy."

Good, she was playing along.

The zipper went down smoothly and the skirt dropped to the floor as soon as it was all the way down.

Clad only in a pair of sexy pink panties, Ruth stepped out of the garment.

"Gorgeous, as I knew you'd be." He bent down and lifted her into his arms. "Let's find us a bed, shall we?"

Ruth put her head on his chest. "You know where it is."

"I do." He stepped out of Sylvia's old room and into Ruth's across the hallway.

As he laid her on the bed, she scooted back, propping herself against a stack of pillows. "I want to see you, Nickolas. All of you."

"Yes, ma'am." He grinned.

This part Nick would have had a problem with a couple of years back, when he wasn't as ripped as he was now. But that chubby pale geek was gone. Now he had the toned and tanned body of a surfer and was damn proud of it.

Still, he'd never undressed for a girl before.

Should he go slow? Or should he do it as fast as he could?

If his dick had any say in it, then the faster, the better. His foresight to relieve tension a couple of times earlier in the day meant that the situation wasn't desperate yet, and he wasn't going to blow the moment he freed that bad boy. But it was getting there.

Yeah, fast was better.

He kicked off his shoes while unbuttoning his shirt, dropped it to the floor and went for the zipper of his pants. The moment those dropped down, though, so did the two packets of condoms he'd shoved in the back pocket.

Ruth giggled. "You brought two? Wasn't that a little presumptuous?"

Nick collected the packets from the floor, then opened his wallet and pulled out the third. "Three. I didn't know which size would fit."

Ruth opened her arms. "Come here, Nicki."

He put the packets on her nightstand and joined her on the bed.

Chest to chest, skin to skin. He was in heaven. "This is good. I can spend eternity like this."

"Me too," she said, then pushed on his chest. "There is no need for condoms. I'm on birth control, you've never been with anyone, and the last time I did was years ago. We are both clean."

That was a relief. One less thing to fumble with.

"Tell me what to do, teacher."

She smiled. "First, take off my panties."

He did, slowly sliding them down her long legs, then sat back and ogled her body as he waited for further instructions.

"Now, take off yours."

Lifting up to a kneeling position, he hooked his thumbs in the elastic of his boxer briefs and pushed down.

His cock sprung free, and as soon as the boxers were off, he covered it with both hands, pressing it to his belly.

"Don't cover up. I want to see you. Come, lie next to me."

When he did, she reached for him. "You are very nicely made, Nickolas. Everywhere."

He had trouble breathing, let alone talking. This was the first time a hand that wasn't his was touching his shaft, and it felt amazing.

"You can touch me too. Just be gentle. I'm very sensitive down there." She parted her legs a little.

"Always." As if he would ever touch her with anything other than gentleness.

Focusing on her face, he reached with the pad of one finger, feathering it over her folds. She was so wet and so slick and completely bare. Had she waxed for him? Or had she done that laser hair removal thing?

On the one hand, Nick hoped she'd prepared especially for him, but on the other hand, waxing sounded painful. He didn't want her to do anything that caused her discomfort.

"Is that good?" he asked, although it was pretty obvious Ruth enjoyed his touch. Between the soft moans and the gyrating hips, there was little doubt left.

"Yes. Can you put a finger in me?" Ruth whispered.

She didn't need to ask twice. Again, he was slow and gentle and watched her face for the slightest grimace.

Focusing his attention on her helped him hold off too, which was one hell of an accomplishment, since her soft hand was still on his shaft, caressing it in slow up and down movements.

As his finger sunk inside her moist heat, Ruth moaned and let her legs fall apart, giving him all the access he needed.

"Good?" he asked again.

"Yes, very. Can you try adding another finger?"

She'd asked, but by the way her body had tensed all over, she was afraid of it.

Again, Nick went very slowly, watching her closely as he did.

A look of wonder crossed her eyes when his second finger slid all the way in, apparently causing no discomfort.

So far so good.

He had a surprise for her.

There were some inherent benefits to the theoretical studying of all the ways a man could pleasure a woman—meaning, watching lots of porn and reading up on the subject.

Curling both fingers inside her, he found that secret G spot everyone was talking about. It wasn't even all that hard to find.

Ruth moaned and arched her back. "Oh, Nicki, this feels wonderful."

Happier than if he'd hit gold, Nick massaged that magic spot, enjoying the throaty moans he was wresting out of Ruth.

After a few more moments, she caught his wrist to stop him. "I think I'm very close to orgasming. I want you inside me when I do." She pulled him on top of her.

The girl was really strong, she'd practically lifted him up. But who cared about that when he was finally going to receive the best gift a woman could ever give a guy?

"Take me, Nick." She spread her legs even wider, cradling him between her thighs. "I'm more than ready."

Gripping himself, he positioned his shaft at her entrance and pushed inside with just the tip. When that resulted in a throaty groan, and her grip tightening on his ass, he pushed a little more.

"Nothing hurts," Ruth whispered in an awed voice. "Everything feels amazing." She arched up, gripping his ass even tighter. "More!"

When he found himself all the way inside her, Nick wasn't sure whether he'd been the one to thrust in, or Ruth had impaled herself on his shaft.

He stilled.

If he moved, he was going to come, and he refused to let it end so soon.

This was so much better than he'd imagined.

It was as if one plus one didn't equal two, it was more like a thousand. The feeling was incomparable, the joining so complete it was way more than physical. It was metaphysical.

Love combined with sex equaled magic.

It should have been included in the list of theorems.

50

WONDER

*W*hen Wonder's shift at the club ended, she was no closer to making a decision than when it had started.

Anandur's brother looked like a dangerous man. He hadn't talked much, but the little he'd said included a cuss word. Not that it was all that unusual. People cussed all the time.

But not Anandur.

Believing that he wasn't like her other prisoners was easy because he was different in almost every way.

They were harsh, hardened soldiers, while he was full of smiles and charm. They cussed frequently, but Anandur didn't. They were crude. He was polite.

Their covetous glances gave her the creeps. Anandur's excited her.

Then there was his brother. The guy seemed harsher and more vicious than the three Doomers combined. He wasn't exactly like them, but he wasn't like Anandur either. Which made it hard to decide if there were indeed two warring factions, one good, and one evil. Anandur claimed his people were the good guys, and the Doomers were the bad guys, but was it true?

Tonight, he expected her to release him and allow him to call his brother.

Wonder still wasn't convinced that it was wise, but she'd made him a promise to give him an answer, even if it was a negative one.

"Wonder, wait up." Natasha trotted down the corridor, her purse hanging from the crook of her elbow as she tried to put on her jacket with the other one. "Walk me to my car?"

"Sure." Wonder waited by the door. "Maybe you should get pepper spray. Tamara has one that goes on her keychain."

Panting, Natasha handed Wonder the purse to hold while she shrugged the jacket on. "I thought about that but decided against it. If anyone jumps me, I'll probably panic and spray myself with it. Besides, I have two little monsters who get into everything, especially my purse. I don't want them to hurt themselves, and I'm not sure I'd remember to take it out and put it somewhere safe every time I get home."

She took her purse back. "Thanks. I heard you had an artist draw your portrait today."

Wonder waved a hand. "He is a forensic artist, and he came to draw the picture of that woman who the guy that went missing was last seen with. I had a little time left before my shift, and he offered to draw mine. He didn't finish it, though."

"Is he coming back?"

"He snapped a picture of me with his phone and said he'll use it to finish the portrait. He promised to mail me a copy."

Natasha raised a brow. "What is he going to do with the original?"

"I don't want to think about it."

"Yeah, I can imagine." Natasha laughed as she opened the car door. "Thanks for walking with me. I'll see you tomorrow."

"Good night." Wonder waited until the woman had locked the doors and turned on the engine, then headed for her own car that was parked on the other side of the lot.

A prickling sensation made her turn her head and look out onto the street. Two cars were parked on the other side of the road. One was old, and she'd seen it there before, the other one looked brand new.

This time of night all the restaurants were closed, but the Irish pub was still open. The car might have belonged to one of its customers.

Just to make sure, though, Wonder decided to do a drive by. If someone was sitting inside, she would see him.

She had a feeling it was a he and not a she—a certain dangerous-looking blond guy whose brother she held locked in a cage.

The car's interior was dark, and its windows were tinted, but Wonder had exceptional night vision. Even though she pretended to look straight ahead, she could practically feel his gaze on her.

As she continued down the road, her eyes kept darting to the rearview mirror every couple of seconds or so. When the car didn't move, she started to relax, telling herself she'd just imagined someone sitting inside it, but as she made the first turn and glanced at the mirror again, the car pulled out into the street without turning on the lights.

She was definitely being followed.

If she tried to lose him, he would know she had something to hide. Instead, Wonder did the same thing she'd done last night and drove to the shelter first.

He was good, following her from a great distance, turning at a light and then reappearing again a block or two later. If she were human, she would've not seen him, mainly since his headlights were still off.

When she arrived at the shelter, Wonder parked her car and then walked up slowly to the front door, shuffling her feet as if she were tired after a long day at work, the way she assumed a human would. Punching the numbers into the keypad, she watched the white car park about a hundred feet or so down the street.

"It's me," she whispered right as she opened the door to her room. This time her roommates didn't start the way they had last night, lifting their heads for a moment then going straight back to sleep.

Good, she never wanted to see the girls' panic-stricken eyes again.

Not making a sound, she walked up to the window and peeked out.

The white Ford was still there.

Two hours later, when it still hadn't moved, Wonder gave up. Even if he left now, she was too tired to get in the car and drive to the facility.

Anandur would have to wait for her answer till morning. Hopefully, his stubborn brother would be gone by then.

The problem was that she hadn't made up her mind yet.

Maybe a hot shower would help.

A towel and her pajamas in one hand, toiletries in the other, Wonder headed for the bathroom. For some reason, washing her hair always helped clear her head.

51

ANANDUR

"*L*over-boy is disappointed," Grud taunted.

Waiting for Wonder and her decision, Anandur had been pacing his cage for hours. First, he'd been impatient, then he'd gotten angry, and lastly, he'd begun to worry. She'd promised him an answer tonight, and Wonder didn't seem like the kind of person who broke her promises. Something must have prevented her from coming. Or someone.

Still, appearances had to be kept up, and he needed to act like a Doomer would.

"Shut up, Grud. I'm doing this for all of us. I'm trying to sweet talk her into letting me out of the chains."

"Right, as if you needed her to release you. You could've gotten free a long time ago. What's the matter, Dur, you need a female to come willingly? You don't have the stomach for good old-fashioned rape?"

Fighting for self-control, Anandur closed his eyes. "In fact, I don't. There is nothing sweeter than a willing female. But I guess an ugly bastard like you can't get it any other way."

Grud waved a hand. "The bitches love it. I give them a few minutes of hard fucking, and they get wet for me. The next time they know to come willingly. Especially after a good beating."

Shaveh snorted, saving Anandur from having to respond, which he wasn't sure he could've done without snarling. "They get wet for you because of the venom, not because you know what to do with your dick."

"And you do?" Mordan asked.

"Naturally. Never heard any complaints."

As the crude banter between the three Doomers continued, Anandur jumped up and grabbed the cage's top horizontal bar. There was nothing like physical exertion to drive away the demons and help him get the rage under control.

Fifty chin-ups or so later, he was in a better mental state. It lasted for about five minutes. Evidently, the ratio of chin-ups to calm minutes was ten to one.

Not a good ratio.

And it made the stench worse.

He stank, the Doomers stank, and it was getting to him. The irritation was growing worse by the minute, primarily since he was well aware that he wouldn't have been in this stinking situation if he were less of a fucking romantic.

None of his fellow Guardians would have chosen this course of action. They would've been out of there as soon as the first opportunity presented itself.

If Wonder continued with her indecision, he would have no choice but to knock her out, get her phone, and call Brundar.

Enough was enough.

It was one thing to rough it out when out on a mission or on the battlefield; he had done it plenty of times, but doing so voluntarily and for no good reason was another.

Tomorrow, he was going to sleep in a clean bed, after brushing his teeth and taking a two-hour-long shower. He would scrub himself clean using up an entire bar of soap, and wash the stench out of his hair with a whole bottle of shampoo. He would even use conditioner. But before that, he was going to eat half a cow's worth of steaks with a side of mashed potatoes the size of a mountain.

He was so damn hungry.

Brundar would have never been as patient.

If he had even an inkling of a suspicion that Wonder knew where Anandur was, he would have no qualms about torturing the information out of her.

Fates, he hoped that wasn't what was holding her up. He would hate to beat the shit out of his brother for trying to find him. It would be a grossly ungrateful thing to do.

But no one harmed Wonder without paying for it, not even Brundar, and not even with the best of intentions.

52

BRUNDAR

"What floor is she on?" Brundar asked as they entered the lobby of the building where Rosalie had an office.

"I forgot to ask." Magnus walked over to the board and scanned the list of names and their suite numbers.

With the help of the facial recognition software and the woman's first name, William had found out who she was.

Rosalie Sanchez was an accountant and she had her own office.

This morning Magnus had called her, introducing himself as a police detective, and scheduled an appointment.

"Found her. Third floor. Suite three hundred and two." Brundar started walking toward the elevators.

As they followed a leggy woman in a tight skirt inside, Magnus leaned over her and pressed the floor number. "Pardon me, miss," he said with an exaggerated Scottish twang.

She smiled. "What a lovely accent. Are you Australian?"

Brundar rolled his eyes. This was no time for flirting.

"Come on." He gave Magnus a shove out as they reached the third floor.

When he found the right suite number, Brundar knocked and then walked in and flashed his fake badge. "We are here to see Ms. Sanchez."

"Good morning," the receptionist greeted them. "Please take a seat. I'll let her know you're here." She picked up the phone. "Rosalie, your ten o'clock clients are here."

As the accountant opened the door and walked over, Brundar knew he had the right woman. She was Anandur's type. A sturdy build, a pretty face, and a welcoming smile.

"Detective Magnus McBain?" she asked.

"That's me." Magnus pushed to his feet and shook her hand. "This is my partner, Detective Brad Wilson."

"Can we talk in your office, Ms. Sanchez?" Brundar asked, ignoring the woman's offered hand.

Since Callie, it had gotten easier for him to touch others, but he still preferred not to.

"Yes, of course. Please come in." She motioned for them to follow her inside, and then closed the door.

"What is it all about?" Rosalie asked as the three of them sat down.

Brundar pulled out his phone and chose one of the few pictures of Anandur he had. It was good that Callie liked to snap photos and share them with him. Otherwise, he wouldn't have any.

"Do you remember this man?"

Rosalie took the phone, looked at the picture, enlarged it with her fingers, and then shook her head. "He looks vaguely familiar. But I don't remember where I've seen him."

That was odd. Anandur sucked at thralling, but even he knew how to erase the memory of the bite without erasing everything else. Unless, he'd wanted the woman to forget him completely, which wasn't like him at all.

"You were seen with my partner two nights ago at Club Nirvana," Magnus said. "You left together with him and then returned to the club alone. No one has seen or heard from my partner ever since."

As Magnus kept her occupied, Brundar peeked inside Rosalie's brain, quickly sifting through her recent memories. She'd been telling the truth, Anandur wasn't there, as well as a big chunk of other memories. Someone had done a shitty thralling job on her.

A Doomer, no doubt.

Rosalie blushed. "I seriously can't remember any of it. In fact, I don't remember much about that night at all. I was there with a friend. Maybe she remembers your partner."

"Can you give us her name and phone number?"

"Sure." She took a post-it note and wrote the information down. "Here you go. I remember getting home and feeling drunk, which was strange since I only had two drinks, and they weren't loaded. I expected to wake up with a headache, but I didn't. Could someone have slipped me a roofie?" She cast an accusatory glance at Magnus.

"If someone had, it wasn't my partner. I can assure you of that."

Brundar got up. "Thank you. We will be in touch."

"If you remember anything else, please call me." Magnus handed her his business card.

"I will. I'm so sorry I couldn't be more helpful."

"You've done your best." Magnus offered her his hand. "We will let ourselves out. Good day, Ms. Sanchez."

Brundar nodded and followed Magnus out.

"So what do you think?" Magnus asked as they stepped

out into the corridor and headed for the elevators. "Was she lying?"

"No. Someone did a piss poor job on her memories. Anandur wouldn't have erased himself completely. Someone else did it."

"Doomers?" Magnus asked as they exited the lobby.

"That's the most logical assumption. They either followed him and the woman from the club to the alley, or they happened to be there with their own catch for the night and seized the opportunity. After all, that same alley serves several clubs, pubs, and restaurants, though I doubt Doomers pick up their victims in restaurants."

Magnus shook his head. "If this is so, Anandur is screwed." He clicked the rental's doors open.

Brundar got in the passenger seat and dropped his head against the headrest.

Something in this scenario didn't add up.

As soon as the Doomers arrived at the club, Anandur would've felt them.

Brundar knew his brother well. Anandur wasn't rash, and he wasn't the type to jump into a situation. He would have never taken the woman outside.

What he would've done was get out himself and call Magnus to come back. Together they would've waited for the Doomers to exit and engaged them away from the humans.

As for getting jumped in the alley, that could've happened only if Anandur was too preoccupied with the woman. Knowing Doomers, though, they would've knocked her out as well, instead of bothering to thrall her. Capturing a Guardian was too big of a deal for them to risk taking the time to thrall Rosalie. She would have been found either unconscious or dead in that alley.

Except, what other possibilities were there?

The bouncer knew something she wasn't telling, but Brundar couldn't begin to guess what it was. He'd tried to take a peek at her memories while she'd been busy with Tim, but the girl's mind was impenetrable. She was either too cautious to lower her mental shields, or she was an immune.

Some humans couldn't be thralled. There were those whose brains were too powerful, like Turner, and there were those whose suspicious nature made them unreceptive, like Alex's Russian crew. Wonder didn't strike him as overly bright, so she must've been the second type.

On a hunch, he'd followed her last night, hoping to uncover something about her that would substantiate his suspicions, but the girl had gone home and stayed there.

After waiting for a couple of hours to see if she would get out and drive somewhere else, he'd wised up and headed for the nearest twenty-four-hour Wal-Mart. Given that there was nowhere he could have gotten a tracking device in the middle of the night, he'd done the next best thing, buying a throwaway cellphone, including activation and an extra battery pack.

Anandur would have a good laugh about it when he got back. The discount store was his go-to shop for everything destination, and for years Brundar had looked down on him for being a cheap bastard. However, there was something to be said for the convenience of finding most everything in one spot, especially late at night.

With William's help, the improvised tracker Brundar had taped under Wonder's car chassis was transmitting her location to the tail she now had.

The moment she did something suspicious Brundar would know.

"Did you get the list of places Wonder cleans during the day?" he asked.

Magnus nodded. "Yeah, I texted the addresses to Liam."

The strong smell of cleaning products she'd been covered with yesterday had been so overwhelming that Tony had felt like he needed to explain that Wonder had another day job as a cleaner for a commercial real estate maintenance company.

That was most likely what Liam would find out. But on the remote chance that there was more to her than met the eye, the Guardian should follow her until her shift at the club began. Once there, another undercover Guardian would monitor her activity and then follow her home.

After all, it wasn't as if Brundar had any other leads. At least not yet.

The guy with the dogs, or The Finder of Lost Things, was finally coming at four in the afternoon. Who would've thought that a service like that would be in such high demand? Brundar had to offer twice the asking price to be put ahead of the other clients on the guy's schedule.

53

WONDER

*F*irst thing Wonder did when she woke up was to look out the window. The car from last night wasn't there, but that didn't mean that it wasn't hiding around the corner or somewhere further down or up the street.

She would soon find out.

Lying awake in bed for most of the night, she'd finally formed a plan. It wasn't foolproof, and it wasn't going to provide her with the measure of certainty she would've liked, but it was the best one she could come up with.

Wonder had made a list of questions, and she was going to fire them at Anandur one after the other. That way, he wouldn't have time to come up with lies between one question and the next. He'd be forced to either tell the truth or refuse to answer.

Unless he was an extraordinary liar, one who could make up stories on the spot, it would be difficult for him to fool her.

But first, she had to make sure no one was following her.

Fifteen minutes or so later, Wonder was dressed and ready for some evasive maneuvers. As soon as she pulled out of her parking spot, she checked her rearview mirror for the white Ford.

There was no sign of it.

So far so good.

Nevertheless, Wonder drove to the supermarket first, got inside, and then spent a good ten minutes peering through the window to see if the Ford showed up.

"Can I help you, miss?" one of the employees asked.

It must've seemed odd for a customer to stand by the front window and look outside, especially one that was stretching up to her tiptoes. If Wonder were a few inches shorter, she wouldn't have been able to see anything over the stacks of merchandise lining the front of the store.

"No, thank you. I'm waiting for a friend."

"If you need anything, let me know."

"Thank you."

She waited a couple more minutes before hitting the aisles for supplies. To feed her prisoners, she usually bought a twenty-pound bag of rice, a five-pound bag of black beans, another the same size of pinto beans, and a few seasonings to vary the taste. They kept complaining about the food, but given the quantities they consumed, it was all she could afford. And it wasn't as if she was eating anything better. Wonder's lunch was the same dish of rice and beans she served them daily.

Today, though, she splurged, buying a few extra treats for Anandur. If he thought she was into him, his guard would be down, and he would talk more freely.

And how was that for an excuse?

The sad truth was that she was into him for real. In a different universe, where she and Anandur had met under different circumstances, she would have loved to treat him to tasty things. She would have fed him the small morsels with her fingers like she'd done before.

For some reason, it had been oddly arousing, maybe because his lips had been so close. He had such kissable lips. Thick and fleshy.

Wonder closed her eyes and imagined herself wrapped in Anandur's strong arms, kissing him, him kissing her back.

Would he be a gentle kisser, or a covetous one, or a ravenous one?

All she had for reference were movies, and the few kisses she'd found exciting to watch. Most looked so fake it was obvious the actors weren't into them. But there had been a few she'd seen that had stirred something inside her. It wasn't about how handsome the male lead was, or how beautiful the female, and it wasn't even about the kiss itself. It was more about the chemistry between the actors.

Sometimes it looked so real.

There was no lack of chemistry between her and Anandur. In fact, there was so much of it that it was practically explosive. Unless she was imagining it and it was all one-sided.

Did he want to kiss her as much as she wanted to kiss him?

Stop thinking about stupid kisses!

Her life might be on the line, and instead of planning an interrogation, she was fantasizing about lips. Well, in her defense, there was a connection. Anandur would be using those to answer her questions.

Right. She was so full of dumb excuses today.

Adding a few snacks to her cart, including a six-pack of cola in addition to the beer, she headed for the cashier.

Before stepping outside though, Wonder peeked through the front window again, scanning the supermarket's parking lot for the white Ford. There was one, but it had a rack mounted on its roof. The one from last night had none.

"Do you need help outside, miss?" asked the same employee from before.

"No, thank you. I'm fine."

The guy eyed her big sack of rice. "Are you sure? This looks heavy."

"I'm sure." She pushed the cart out the door.

The guy followed. "It's really no trouble. It's my job to help customers with their groceries."

Why was he so insistent?

He must be new because she didn't remember seeing him there before. Maybe he needed to help her because his boss was watching?

Wonder knew all about wanting to impress an employer in order to keep a job. "Fine. That one over there is mine." She pointed at her car.

He took the cart from her. "I'm Scott." He pointed to the tag attached to his apron.

"Are you Scottish?"

He frowned. "No. Are you new around here?"

"Not really. I've been shopping at this supermarket for a while, but I didn't see you before." She eyed him suspiciously. Why was he asking her questions?

"I just got the job. It's part-time. I'm a student."

"That's nice." Wonder used her key to open the trunk. Hers was an old model that didn't come with a remote.

"Are you a student?" Scott asked as he hefted the sack of rice and dropped it inside.

"No, why are you asking?"

The guy tilted his head. "Isn't it obvious?"

"Not to me."

He shook his head. "Where have you come from, a

convent? Don't tell me you never had guys hit on you. Not with that face." He gave her an appreciative once-over. "And not with that body."

Wonder relaxed. Scott was coming on to her, that was all. It didn't happen often, but it had happened before. She should've recognized it for what it was.

Except, her head was somewhere else, imagining secret agents impersonating supermarket employees and trying to get information out of her.

She waved a hand. "It's too early in the morning for that. I work two jobs, and I don't have time for dating. Sorry."

Scott finished unloading her cart and closed the trunk. "Well, if you change your mind, you know where to find me. I work Tuesday and Thursday mornings, and the late shift on the weekend."

"Sure." She cast him a smile. "See you around."

54

BRUNDAR

"I'm calling Liam," Brundar told Magnus as they arrived back at the hotel. "I hope he has something for me."

He wondered whether he'd become more talkative because he was heading the operation with around thirty Guardians answering to him, or was it the influence of Magnus's easy-going attitude and optimism? The Guardian hadn't stopped believing they were going to find Anandur even when the situation seemed hopeless to Brundar.

He needed that to keep going. Sinking into despair was not an option.

Thankfully, Magnus seemed immune to the black hole effect Brundar's darkness had on other people.

"At eleven o'clock in the morning? I doubt it. The girl is probably still asleep."

"She has another job during the day. She can't stay in bed."

"Hard-working lass. I wonder what her story is." Magnus chuckled. "I wonder about Wonder. That's funny."

Brundar shook his head. No wonder Anandur and Magnus got along so well. The two were a match made in heaven.

He dialed Liam's number. "What's up, Liam?"

"Nothing interesting. I followed the girl to the supermarket. I'm watching her now talking to the boy who helped her load her groceries into her trunk."

"What did she buy?"

"A big-ass sack of rice and a couple of sacks of beans. The rest is in paper bags, and I don't have X-ray vision."

"Keep following her and let me know if you see anything suspicious."

"Like what?"

"You have the addresses of the places she cleans for her other job. If she goes anywhere else, let me know."

"Copy that."

"Why the hell does she need so much rice and beans?" Magnus asked. "And for whom?"

"Maybe she ran an errand for the shelter. It would make sense for them to buy in bulk."

ANANDUR

*A*s Anandur saw Wonder walk in, he took his first easy breath of the day.

"Where were you last night? I was worried."

"Boo-hoo," Shaveh teased.

Wonder ignored him and threw the shackles inside Anandur's cage. "Put them on."

"What? No good morning? No how have you been? Nothing?" Mordan pretended to pout. "You don't love us anymore?"

"Good morning." Wonder glared at him. "I hope you slept well. And now shut up."

Grud walked to the front of his cage. "Someone has woken up grumpy this morning. What's the matter, missed your lover boy?"

"Shut up, Grud, or you'll stay hungry today. You forget who feeds you." She pointed a finger at him, and then moved it to point at the other two. "And that goes for you as well. I don't want to hear another word from either one of you, or none of you eats today."

She opened Anandur's cage even though he wasn't done

attaching the chain that connected his leg restraints to the handcuffs. "Come on. I have a lot of questions for you."

He was surprised that the Doomers were keeping quiet. Apparently, they knew Wonder's threats were not in vain, and none of them wanted to go without food for a whole day.

Tough girl. He was so proud of her.

As he shuffled out of the cage and Wonder motioned for him to walk ahead of her, Anandur noticed that she stuffed the key to the cage in her pocket instead of returning it to its regular place under the stack of papers.

In his limited experience with her, Wonder struck him as a methodical person. It wasn't like her to deviate from a routine. That was why he'd been so worried when she hadn't shown up after her last shift in the club.

"What happened last night? Why didn't you come?"

"I was tired. I had to go home."

That sounded like a lame excuse. "Really?'

She pinned him with a hard stare. "The club is not my only job."

"I bet. You're a hard-working girl, Wonder."

She shrugged.

Anandur walked into the office they used for their talks and sat in his regular chair. "I see that you brought me more treats," he said as he noted the new assortment.

"This time I made sure to include a plastic fork." She leaned against the desk and crossed her arms under her impressive breasts, unintentionally giving them a boost.

Some women did that on purpose, but he was sure Wonder had no clue what that pose did to a male.

He made a point to stare at her face and not her chest. "I enjoyed eating from your hand."

Averting her eyes, she picked up a tray of cold cuts and cheeses, the same kind she'd brought yesterday, and then handed it to him together with a plastic fork wrapped in a napkin.

"Thank you." He unwrapped the fork, speared a chunk of cheese, and put it in his mouth.

"How many members do you have in your community?"

Anandur finished chewing. "Five hundred sixty-three, soon to be five hundred sixty-six."

"Who are the three newcomers?"

"One is a baby about to be born in a couple of months, the other one is a guy we suspect of being a Dormant, and the third one is you." He forked several slices of turkey and stuffed them in his mouth.

"Where is your community located?"

"We have three locations, but I'm not going to tell you where they are until you join us. We live in hiding."

"Because you're afraid of humans?"

"We need to keep our existence a secret from humans, but that is not why we hide as a group. The Brotherhood wants to annihilate us, and unfortunately there are many more of them than there are of us. We can't face off with them."

"Who is the head of your community?"

Anandur paused with his fork mid-air. "What's with the twenty questions?"

Wonder raised a brow. "Who said anything about the number twenty? I didn't count them."

"It's an expression. Why are you asking so many questions?"

"I'm curious."

Right. Well, he couldn't blame her. He was asking her to trust him based on very little information.

"Each one of the three locations is headed by a different person and for the most part is run independently. But when important decisions need to be made, all members who've reached their majority get to vote."

"What do your people do to earn a living? Do they all work together?"

"Yes and no. It's hard to explain in a few words. Each of our members does what she or he is interested in. But it's a choice. Our community owns several corporations, and the net profits are divided among the members. The basic share is not huge. It's enough to live on comfortably but not lavishly."

"So if I come with you, I will become a member and get paid whether I work or not?"

"No, you will become a member when you join with a member in a permanent relationship."

"Like marriage?"

"Something like that. It doesn't have to be official. But you have nothing to worry about. There are plenty of jobs for someone like you."

She narrowed her eyes at him. "What do you mean someone like me?"

"A hard-working girl that is not too picky."

Her shoulders sagged. "I guess I'll be the cleaning lady."

"Why would you say that?"

"I don't know how to do anything else."

"You're a bouncer, that's sort of a guard. You can become a Guardian, which is a cross between a warrior and a law enforcer."

She shook her head. "I'd rather clean houses. I might be freakishly strong, but that doesn't mean that I want to be a fighter. You may find it hard to believe, but I don't like violence."

"You can be whatever you want to be, Wonder. You can go to college and learn a profession of your choosing."

"I can't pay for that. Besides, I don't even have a high-school education."

Getting up slowly to avoid startling her, he shuffled to where she was leaning against the desk and lifted his hands to cup her cheeks.

Looking at him with wide eyes, she didn't recoil from his touch or even his stench. She didn't act scared in any way.

It was a very encouraging sign.

"Unlock my chains, Wonder, and say goodbye to all your worries. I'll take care of you. You'll get the schooling you need, and you will get to choose what you want to do with your future. I give you my word, and that's not something I do lightly."

56

GRUD

*A*s soon as Dur left with Wonder, Grud attacked the last concrete block standing between him and his freedom. Those two would be gone for hours, same as they had done yesterday, screwing each other's brains out no doubt.

Fucking Dur was getting all the fun. What did she see in that ugly redhead?

Eh, whom was he kidding?

The woman had the hots for Dur because he was tall and built like a pro-wrestler. Besides, the fucker knew how to be charming, cracking that smile of his like a whip. He probably never had to rape a female or beat her into submission. One smile was enough to make them spread their legs for him.

Some guys had all the luck.

But Dur's luck was about to run out. He was going to die today, and the female was going to belong to Grud.

The plan was simple, and even though he'd had to make some last minute adjustments, it was still a good one.

Grud wasn't coming back for his Brothers. They could

rot in there for all he cared. The idiots hadn't even noticed that this time Wonder had taken the key with her. He couldn't open their cages even if he wanted to. Not without wasting valuable time looking for it. She must've hidden it somewhere.

"Are you about done?" Shaveh asked.

"Almost. We get out of here today."

"Sweet," Mordan said. "So what's the plan?"

"Same as it always was. I squeeze through the hole to the other room, and if I don't end up in another cage, I find the exit, then come back for you, and we get the hell out of here."

"What about Dur and the woman?"

"We leave them. I'm not going to risk my freedom for pussy." Actually, he wasn't going to risk his freedom for the two of them.

"I'm willing to risk mine for payback," Shaveh said.

"Then you can stay behind for all I care."

Mordan grabbed the bars and stuck his nose into Grud's cage. "I'm with you, Grud. As much as I would've liked to fuck her, I'm not going to put myself in range of that Taser."

"She can get only one of us," Shaveh pointed out. "A Taser is not like a gun that can discharge many bullets. One shot and that's it. Then the other two can knock her out. If we cooperate, we can all have us some pussy. What do you say, Grud?"

"I'll think about it. Before I come back for you, I'll check what those two are doing. If Dur is screwing her, she can't Taser anyone. Right?"

"Unless she has the Taser on while he's fucking her, eh?" Shaveh seemed to think it was hot.

Sick bastard.

Grud attacked the block with renewed vigor, chipping

away at it even though his hands were bleeding all over the place. He was getting out of that cage today.

He only stopped when the hole looked large enough for him to squeeze through.

"Hey, Grud, if you get stuck in there, you stay stuck. We can't help you out," Mordan said.

"If my shoulders go through, I'll make it." Grud rose to his feet and walked over to the water tube.

First, he washed the blood off his hands, and then he took several long gulps of water to fill his empty belly. It was a pity that he had to run on an empty stomach, but it wasn't as if he could wait for Wonder to feed him lunch and then go.

Dur would be back.

There wasn't much the son of a bitch could do from a locked cage, but Grud's instincts were telling him to run while Dur was busy elsewhere.

"I'm going," he said to his jail mates.

"Good luck," Mordan said.

Shaveh cast him a questioning look. "You're coming back for us, right?"

"Of course."

Wiping his hands on his pants, Grud walked back to the back wall and the hole he'd made.

First, he picked up the rod he'd been working with and put it on the other side right next to the wall. It was the only tool and weapon he had, and he would need it to complete his plan.

Next, he pushed his arms through the opening, put his hands on the floor on the other side, and pulled himself forward. As he'd expected, his shoulders got stuck, but after a little wiggling and grunting, he managed to push through. The rest of his body followed with ease.

Thank Mortdh, he didn't end up in another cage.

With the glow from his eyes as the only illumination, he took a quick glance around. It was a long, narrow room with no furniture and no windows, but there was a door, not a reinforced one, but a simple one made from wood or particle board.

Grud smiled.

Luck was on his side today.

57

BRUNDAR

*B*rundar's phone rang. "What's up, Liam?"

"I followed the girl to one of the places she cleans, and I'm sitting in the car across the street from it."

"Anything interesting?"

"You tell me. She carried the things she'd bought in the supermarket inside."

"Is there anyone else with her?"

"I didn't check. But other than hers there are no other cars parked in front of the building."

That was strange. Why would the bouncer bring rice and beans into an empty building she was supposed to clean? It wasn't as if she needed a twenty-pound rice bag to make herself lunch.

Who was she cooking for?

"Stay in the car. Magnus and I are on our way."

"Perhaps you want to bring more Guardians with you? She brought enough supplies to cook for an army," Liam said. "If Doomers are using this building, they might have thralled the girl to bring them food."

That didn't seem likely. With all its faults and lack of

care for its soldiers, the Brotherhood was a well-managed organization. If they used the facility, they would have had cars parked outside and guards patrolling the perimeter.

"Did you see anyone at all in the vicinity of the building?"

"Not right next to it, but it's an industrial park, and there are cars in the other parking lots. There isn't much traffic, but there is some."

"No one who looks like he is patrolling?"

"Come on, Brundar, I'm not a greenhorn. I know what to look out for. It looks like there is no one here other than the girl. The only reason I'm calling you is that I thought it was strange that she brought the food supplies in."

"Maybe she is one of those survivalists who store food in case of an end of days annihilation event," Magnus said. "Like a nuclear bomb, or a massive solar flare, or a huge meteor hitting earth."

"That's even more unlikely than her being a Doomer pawn. I'm calling everyone in."

"What if it's a false alarm?"

"We move on."

"Right."

58

GRUD

*H*is luck was still holding. The door wasn't even locked.

Grud opened it carefully and peered outside. A single light fixture illuminated the long hallway in front of him, but coming from complete darkness, even that soft light managed to blind him momentarily until his eyes adjusted.

To his left were stairs going up, and to his right was the heavy door to the cage room. Ahead of him, the corridor was lined with several doors only on one side. They were all closed, but he could hear murmurs coming from the last one.

That was where Wonder had taken Dur. It sounded like they were talking, not fucking, which meant that the woman had her Taser gun on.

The corridor terminated with another reinforced door, which Grud assumed led to the outside. That door was most likely locked, and to get to it, he would have to pass by the room Dur and the woman were in.

His escape would be short-lived if he chose that route.

The choice was a no-brainer. Grud took the stairs, his bare feet making no sound as he climbed the concrete steps.

The staircase terminated in a landing and another door that was not only unlocked but left half open.

Peering from behind the door, Grud listened for a moment, reassuring himself that no one else was on the main floor of the building. When he stepped out into the lobby, he quickly scanned the layout. It seemed to bisect the main floor, with two corridors stretching away from it in opposite directions.

Ahead, double glass doors led to the outside.

It was tempting to push them open and run. But before doing that, he was going to take a look at what was out there.

Flattening his back against the wall, he leaned to peer out through the doors. His caution had been well justified. A car was turning into the building's parking lot.

Whoever it was, Grud wasn't going to hang around and find out.

Running down the corridor in the opposite direction from where the car was coming, he opened the door to the first office which looked out to the back of the building.

Thank Mortdh the room had a large window.

Quietly, he slid it open, and using his iron rod, he tore a hole in the screen. As he jumped out, Grud immediately crouched down and scanned the area.

The place was an industrial park of sorts, with big boxy warehouses occupying large lots, which was a problem. The wide open spaces didn't provide cover. He could be spotted easily.

That was the bad news.

The good news was that up ahead in the distance, he saw a hillside covered with what he was pretty sure were residences.

Up there he could get clothes and shoes and money to buy a decent weapon or two. Properly equipped, he could come back later and check whether the arrival of that car had anything to do with the woman.

It was possible that the driver had taken a wrong turn while looking for another address. If he left now, Grud might miss a once in a lifetime chance to own an immortal female, and possibly for no good reason.

Once Wonder discovered that he was gone, she would move the other two to a new location and quit her job. The T-shirt she wore most days had the name of the club she worked in. Wonder wasn't stupid. She would know that she needed to run because he was coming for her.

She would make sure that he could never find her.

It was a difficult decision.

Was the potential risk worth the potential reward?

59

WONDER

*I*t was hard to think with Anandur's big warm hands on her cheeks. His face was so close Wonder could have leaned just a little bit further and kissed him.

Instead, she looked into his beautiful eyes and said, "One last question."

"Ask me anything."

"Do you love your brother?"

"That's an odd question, but yes. Of course I love my brother. I would give my life for him."

"What if he hates me?"

"I don't see why he would, but it's his problem."

"What if he wants to hurt me?"

Anandur shook his head. "The only way Brundar would ever hurt you is if you were pointing a gun at my head, or anyone else he's tasked with defending. If you're worried about him wanting revenge, don't be. That's not the kind of man he is."

"Are you sure about that?"

"Positive. The only one he's going to hurt is me, for

worrying him needlessly, and I'll take the pounding because I deserve it. I could've gotten free yesterday morning. Except, that would've meant hurting you, and I couldn't do it. Brundar will understand." Anandur smirked. "After he beats the crap out of me."

Wonder doubted that. Despite his brother's deadly vibe, Anandur was bigger and looked stronger.

"What about my three prisoners? Would your people kill them?"

"We don't kill unarmed, defenseless opponents. They will get questioned and then put in stasis."

"What is stasis?"

"It's kind of like hibernation but deeper. The body retains only the most minimal of brain functions. Immortals can stay in that state indefinitely."

"And how is that state achieved?"

"With venom."

"That venom of yours has many purposes."

"Indeed." He waggled his brows. "But there is only one purpose I like to use it for."

He was such a flirt.

With a hand to his chest, she gave him a little push. "Sit back on the chair."

"Is it still a yes?" Anandur asked.

There was no way to eradicate all of her doubts. She could keep on asking questions from now until next week, and it wouldn't guarantee a right decision.

Now or then, in the end, she would need to trust her gut feeling.

Reaching inside her back pocket, Wonder pulled out the keys. "I'm going to release you and give you my phone to call your brother. But I want you to ask him not to hurt my prisoners or me when he gets here, and I want you to make him swear on it."

She should tell him that she'd met his brother.

Maybe later.

It was better if the guy didn't know she was the one responsible for all the trouble before he gòt there. That way there was a chance he wouldn't arrive foaming at the mouth with rage.

"It's a deal," Anandur said.

She handed him the keys. "You know what to do."

He seemed disappointed.

"You don't look happy. What's the matter?"

"I'm sorry for the stench. But there is nothing I can do about it."

He thought that was the reason she didn't unlock his restraints herself?

It wasn't that at all. It was the idea of getting so close to him that bothered her. She couldn't tell him that, but she couldn't let him think he repulsed her either.

"You don't stink. You have a body odor, but it's not unpleasant."

"That's very sweet of you to say." Anandur grimaced, evidently not believing her.

He unlocked the chain connecting his handcuffs to his leg restraints, and as he removed those as well, they clunked to the floor.

"Could you do the cuffs and save me some acrobatics?" He lifted his hands.

"Sure." She took the key and was about to insert it in the lock when she heard footsteps coming from above. "Someone is up there," she whispered.

"I heard it too." Anandur pushed to his feet and lifted his hands to her. "Quickly, unlock the cuffs."

She did, holding on to them so they wouldn't fall and make more noise.

"Stay here," he said quietly as he headed for the door.

"No way. I have a Taser. You have nothing," she whispered.

"I can handle whoever is out there. Do me a favor and don't argue with me. Stay here and hide behind the desk."

"Not going to happen." She gave him a shove. "Move. I'm coming with you."

His lips pressed tight, he nodded. "Can you at least stay behind me?"

"I can do that." She could, but it didn't mean that she would.

"Hallelujah. Can you walk without making a sound?"

Wonder pointed to her sneakers.

Anandur peered into the corridor before stepping outside.

Taser in hand, Wonder followed him.

60

ANANDUR

*W*hoever was up there, was making an effort not to make any noise. If he and Wonder were human, they wouldn't have heard a thing.

Was it a human thief?

Or had the Doomers somehow located their missing comrades?

The third option was that his brother had figured out Wonder's involvement and had her followed.

In either case, he needed to get upstairs and check who it was. If he found Doomers, he could pretend that he was one of them, but he couldn't allow them to get Wonder.

Her Taser would be no good against several attackers who were prepared for a fight, and he was just one unarmed man. Maybe he could sneak her outside and have her hide or make a dash for her car.

At least it would give her a running chance.

He turned around and whispered in her ear, "Is there another way out of here other than the stairs? What about that door?" He pointed at the reinforced door at the end of the corridor.

Wonder nodded. "The key is in the kitchen with the rest of my things."

"Where is the kitchen?"

"Upstairs. Second door to the left."

Great, that was no help, and they were running out of time. "Listen, I want you to go back and hide in the office. I'll try to sneak into the kitchen and get the key. If those are Doomers up there, I'll pretend I'm one of them and then find a way to open that door for you."

Wonder started shaking her head when the door at the top of the stairs creaked open. A moment later footsteps sounded on the stairs.

Fuck, they were too late.

Pushing Wonder behind him, Anandur turned around and assumed a fighting stance. But before he knew what had hit him, she pulled on his hand with such unbelievable force that he flew backward and landed on his ass.

He watched with horror as she got in front of him, her Taser clasped in her other hand, and pressed the trigger, shooting at no other than Brundar, who had just enough time to send a knife flying before hitting the stairs and rolling the rest of the way down.

His brother never missed.

Time slowed down to a crawl as Wonder went down, clutching at the knife embedded deep in her chest.

"No!" Anandur yelled as he caught her in his arms.

She wasn't going to die. She was an immortal. Even a knife to the heart couldn't kill her.

Or so he hoped as he yanked it out.

Wonder blacked out.

"What the hell?" Magnus yelled as he rushed to Brundar's side.

"She Tasered him. As long as she lives, he is going to be all right. If she dies, I'm going to kill him."

Magnus tore the barbs from Brundar's clothing. "I'm sorry, mate, but a knife to the heart is a deadly wound. She is dead already."

"She is an immortal." The bleeding had already stopped, and the terrible gurgling sounds were replaced with shallow breathing.

Thank the merciful Fates.

"What?" Magnus helped Brundar up. "Wonder is an immortal?"

"You know her?"

"Of course I know her. Brundar and I went back to the club and questioned everyone about you, including the lovely bouncer. How come I didn't feel anything?"

Rubbing his chest, Brundar groaned. "Neither did I. I can't believe she got me with a Taser. I'll never live it down."

Anandur smoothed his hand over Wonder's hair. "You and me both, brother. Isn't she magnificent?"

"I still can't understand how we missed her being an immortal." Magnus walked over. "We should've felt something." He crouched next to them. "I still don't feel anything. She smells and feels like a human."

Anandur could not have been happier to hear that. "There is no way to detect an immortal female. Not unless she is attracted to you. Apparently, she found both of you unattractive."

"I thought that was an urban legend."

"Nope. It's real." Anandur had smelled Wonder's arousal, and it was very different than that of a human's.

Magnus shook his head. "I don't know about the blond over there, but my feelings are deeply wounded."

Brundar got up on shaky legs, walked over to where they were sitting on the floor, and plopped down next to Magnus. "What I want to know is what's going on?"

Anandur waved a hand. "Look away. I want to check her wound."

As the two did as he asked, he lifted Wonder's T-shirt and wiped the blood with the hem. The wound closed, with only a narrow white line indicating where the knife had pierced her skin. Hopefully, her heart was doing just as well.

"She is healing remarkably fast."

"Who is she?" Magnus asked. "Where did she come from?"

"She doesn't remember. Wonder has suffered a complete memory loss. She doesn't even know her own name. She adopted the name Wonder because some kid thought she looked like the actress who played Wonder Woman."

"How did you end up here?" Brundar asked.

"Several months ago, during the height of the murders, Wonder caught a Doomer with his fangs in a female's throat. Assuming he was the killer, she Tasered him, knocked him out with a blow to the back of his head, and brought him here. This used to be some testing facility for big apes, and there is a room filled with cages that even an immortal male can't escape from. She locked him in one. After that she caught two more. When she saw me in that alley, she thought I was trying to murder the woman I was with and did the same to me."

"Where are the Doomers?" Magnus asked.

"Through that door. Wonder has the key. Don't worry, they are not going anywhere."

"Do I look worried to you?"

Brundar looked Anandur over. "How come you're out of the cage then?"

"I convinced Wonder that I wasn't one of them. She released me just as you guys showed up."

He wasn't going to tell them about the handcuffs, or that he could've gotten away on his own. Eventually, he would, but not right now.

"Only three Doomers in there?" Brundar tilted his head toward the reinforced door.

"Yes."

His brother pulled out his phone and dialed. "Onegus, cancel the alert. We got Anandur, and he is fine. There are three Doomers in here who need to be transported to the catacombs, and one injured immortal female who should be waking up any moment." He looked at Anandur. "I guess we are taking her too?"

"Naturally."

"I'm sending two teams to take care of the Doomers." Onegus sounded as excited as if he was talking about placing an order for office supplies.

Weird guy. But maybe that was why he was the chief Guardian. Nothing ever rattled him.

61

BRUNDAR

"*C*an you get the key to that room from her?" Magnus asked. "I should go check on the Doomers."

"My apologies," Anandur murmured as he reached inside Wonder's front pocket and pulled out the key.

"They are each locked in a separate cage." He pulled out another one. "This is the master key that opens all of them."

"Got it." Magnus took the keys and headed for the locked door.

Brundar was still woozy from the electric shock to his system, but he would be damned if he let it show. As it was, he felt shamed enough to have gotten hit by a bouncer with a Taser.

"She must've been well trained. Otherwise, I don't see how she could've hit me so fast and with such accuracy."

Anandur beamed with pride as if Wonder was his star student and not his abductor. "She is very strong too. She had me flying backward and landing on my ass with one pull. And I'm a heavy bastard."

"Is she interested in becoming a Guardian? She seems to have a natural aptitude for it."

Anandur shook his head. "Wonder doesn't know yet what she wants to do. She's been out of her coma for only nine months or so. I don't think she is ready for any major life decisions."

"Hey, guys?" Magnus stepped out of the cage room. "We have a problem. There are only two Doomers in there, and there is a big hole in the back wall where the third one was."

"Grud," Anandur hissed. "I bet he is the one missing."

"Don't you want to come in and question your jail mates?" Magnus asked.

Anandur looked down at the woman in his arms. "I don't want to leave her."

"I can keep an eye on her," Brundar offered.

"Right. As if she wants to see your scary puss when she first opens her eyes. I think the girl has been traumatized enough."

"You're joking, right? She got you locked in a cage. She got me going out of my mind with worry for you, and you think she has been traumatized?"

His brother was obviously delusional.

Anandur tightened his arms around the girl, lifted her to his chest, and pushed up. "She is just a kid who was trying to do the right thing and has gotten in over her head. Of course she's traumatized." He headed toward the cage room with the girl in his arms.

Brundar shook his head, got up, and followed Anandur. His brother wasn't thinking right, but then spending time locked in a cage could mess with a guy's head. He needed time to recuperate.

"What happened to Wonder?" one of the Doomers asked.

Anandur ignored the question. "Where is Grud?"

"As you can see, he escaped," the other Doomer said. "He was supposed to come back for us, but I guess you and your friends interrupted his plans. What did you do to the woman?"

Brundar wondered if the Doomer's concern for the girl was genuine.

"She is okay. Nothing irreversible. Do you know where he might have gone?"

The Doomer shrugged. "I don't know. Are you going to let us out, Dur?"

Dur? There was a story there, and for once Brundar couldn't wait to hear Anandur tell it, even if his brother was going to make a big production out of it and exaggerate lavishly to make it more interesting.

"Yes, Shaveh, I'm going to let you out. But I have bad news for you. I'm a Guardian and so are my friends here. We are taking you with us."

The Doomer named Shaveh sat on the floor and put his head in his hands.

"Are you going to kill us?" the other Doomer asked.

"No. We are not going to kill you, Mordan. We don't execute prisoners. But I don't know yet what will be done to you. I guess it depends on your level of cooperation."

"I will cooperate," Mordan said.

The other one seemed in too deep a despair to comprehend what was being said.

Anandur turned to Brundar. "Grud couldn't have gone far. He is on foot, and he was still here about an hour ago when Wonder got me out of the cage."

Brundar pulled out his phone and dialed Onegus. "Chief, change of plans. One of the Doomers escaped an hour ago at the max. He is on foot, unless he's already commandeered a vehicle."

"Get me a description. I'm sending all the Guardians back to your location."

"Will do."

The woman in Anandur's arms moved, tucking herself against his chest.

"Shh, everything is okay, sweetheart," Anandur said, in the most tender tone Brundar had ever heard him use. "Rest and get better."

"I need his description," Brundar said quietly.

"About six feet tall, one hundred sixty to one hundred seventy pounds, brown hair, brown eyes, and a short beard."

That general description could apply to too many males.

"What was he wearing?"

"No shoes, nylon training pants, black with a white stripe on the sides, and a faded yellow T-shirt."

Brundar group-texted the description to all the Guardians. "Anything else you can think of?"

"Just that his name is Grud and that he is a mean son of a bitch. If he offers any resistance, I suggest to take him out. This apple is too rotten even for stasis."

"Got it."

62

WONDER

*W*onder's chest hurt something awful. It felt as if she'd gotten stabbed in the heart.

Wait a minute, she had.

Should she check?

She tried to move, but something, or rather someone was holding her tight. It was okay, though, Wonder didn't need to open her eyes to know it was Anandur. She recognized his scent.

"Are you awake?"

"Where are we?" she murmured.

"In a car on the way to the airport."

She would've liked to sit up, but it hurt too much to move. It even hurt to talk. But she could listen. "Tell me what happened."

"You Tasered my brother, and he nailed you with a knife. Lucky for him, you're an immortal." He patted her back gently. "He's okay. Say hi, Brundar."

"I'm glad you're an immortal," Anandur's brother said from the front of the car. "I reacted on impulse and threw the knife before I knew it was you."

She needed to set the record straight even if it hurt like hell to talk. "I only saw your boots, and when the light reflected from your blade, I aimed and fired. I didn't know it was you either."

"Killer reflexes," Brundar said. "Are you sure you don't want to join the Guardian force?"

Anandur patted her back again. "Don't answer him. I know it hurts to talk when your heart is mending itself. Anyway, Grud escaped."

Wonder shifted in his arms so she could look at him. "How?"

"Very cleverly. He pried open the sewage grate, then somehow managed to remove one of the bars and used it to loosen the concrete blocks in the wall behind the cages. Apparently, he worked on it every time you took me out of the cage. He didn't trust me enough to do it while I was there. Smart son of a bitch, pardon my French. But that one is really vile, and now he is on the loose. Not for long, though. We have a force of Guardians looking for him."

Wonder had thought they'd been conversing in English this whole time, not French. Anandur was confusing her.

"What about Shaveh and Mordan?" Wonder whispered in an attempt to minimize the pain.

"They're coming with us."

Had Anandur said something about an airport? "Where are we going?"

"Not far. Only to Los Angeles."

"I can't. I need to go to work." Wonder tried to sit up, but Anandur only tightened his hold on her.

"No, you don't. With Grud on the loose, it's not safe for you to go back to work or to the shelter. Until he's caught, you'll stay under our protection. Naturally, I hope you'll stay for good, but it's your decision. No one is forcing you to join us."

"But…"

He put a finger to her lips to shush her. "Before you start arguing again, let me tell you something. That Doomer wasn't shy about expressing his intentions toward you. If not for the cages keeping me from tearing out his throat, he would've been dead already."

Given the vehemence in Anandur's voice, she could only imagine what Grud had been planning for her. In fact, she didn't need Anandur to spell it out for her because she'd seen the glimpses of hatred and lust in Grud's eyes but had chosen to ignore it.

He had the right to hate her. She would've been naive to think that feeding him and keeping him as clean as she could would diminish his hatred of her.

As much as she didn't like the idea of running like a coward, it was the prudent thing to do. She might have been able to take on Grud one on one, but there was the possibility that he would return with reinforcements. Besides, she only had a Taser gun that was good for one shot. He would probably be back with a real gun.

But what if Anandur and his people wouldn't let her go? What if they were planning something?

Once she was in their midst, escaping would be difficult.

Not that there was anything she could do about it. Already, she was surrounded by them, and she was still recuperating from a major injury. Running off was not an option. They would catch her.

Besides, it felt so good to be held that she didn't want it to end. Wonder couldn't remember ever being held. She needed that contact, she craved it, and it wasn't even about sexual attraction, although there was that too.

Who knew, maybe all that Anandur had told her was

true and she would stay, not because she had no choice but because she wanted to.

ANANDUR

$\mathcal{B}$y the time they arrived at the airport, Wonder had fallen asleep again. It was good for her, therapeutic.

Brundar opened the back passenger door and peered inside. "Do you need help getting her out?"

"No, I'm good. I'll manage."

As if he was going to let anyone else carry her. She would be frightened if she opened her eyes and saw a stranger's face inches away from hers. Fates only knew what the woman would do.

She might decide to head-butt the poor schmuck. For all her protests to the contrary, Wonder had excellent fighting instincts. The girl was born to be a Guardian.

Sliding carefully sideways, Anandur pulled out one leg, turned a little and got the other out. With both feet planted on the asphalt, he pushed up and away from the car.

Success.

Wonder continued sleeping peacefully in his arms. Thankfully, it was a small private airport with not many humans milling around. With him walking barefoot and

Wonder's T-shirt torn and covered in blood, they made one hell of a spectacle.

"Which plane did you get?" he asked Brundar.

"We used every flying machine we had. The two planes and three helicopters."

"Are you coming back with us?"

"Yes. Onegus can handle the Doomers without me. I want to get back to Calypso." He rubbed his chest. "I didn't expect the separation to be that difficult."

"Who is Calypso?" Wonder asked with her eyes still closed.

"Calypso, or Callie as everyone other than my brother calls her, is Brundar's better half. Were you pretending to sleep all of this time?"

She opened one eye. "Define all of this time."

Brundar chuckled. "You have your hands full, brother, literally."

"Fine by me. Couldn't have asked for a better charge."

"What's a charge?" Wonder asked. "Do you need to pay someone?"

Anandur chuckled. "I see that you are feeling better. I'll explain everything and answer your twenty questions once we are on the plane."

"Again with the twenty questions," she murmured. "What if I have more?"

Climbing the stairs up to the clan's private jet, Anandur tucked Wonder closer against his chest and then turned sideways to enter. She was a tall woman, and he didn't want to accidentally bang her legs.

Once inside, he sat with her in his arms.

"You should put Wonder in her own seat." Brundar entered behind them and took one of the seats across from them. "She needs to buckle up."

Anandur didn't want to let go.

"I'm better now." Wonder rubbed a hand over her chest. "It doesn't hurt as much anymore."

Reluctantly, Anandur lifted her and put her down in the seat next to him.

She looked around. "Wow, I've never been on a plane before. I thought they were bigger."

"It's a private jet." Anandur pressed on the side panel, and a table slid out. There was a mini fridge under it, and he opened it, hoping someone had remembered to restock it. "Snake Venom, I'll be damned. Remind me to kiss whoever put it in there."

He reached inside again, pulled out a can of ginger ale for Wonder, and popped the lid. "Here you go, sweetheart. I heard it's good for someone who's healing from an injury." Anandur cast his brother a baleful look.

Brundar crossed his arms over his chest and shrugged. The bastard. He wouldn't have been so calm if someone had turned Callie into a practice target.

Lifting the bottle to his mouth, Anandur took a long gulp, and then another. "Fates, I needed that. I also need a hot shower, a change of clothes, and several steaks with a mountain of mashed potatoes on the side."

"Sounds good to me," Wonder said. "Where are you taking me?"

Anandur and Brundar exchanged quick glances.

"Go ahead, tell her," Brundar said. "If she kept her own existence so well hidden not even Magnus and I suspected anything, she can keep our existence secret as well."

"Keep or village?" Anandur asked.

"Keep first, and from there to the village. Kian's instructions."

"Got it."

Sipping on her ginger ale, Wonder looked at Brundar and then at Anandur. "Who is Kian?"

Okay, that was question number what? One hundred and ten? It was time he started giving her some answers.

"Kian is the leader of the clan's American arm. His sister Sari heads the one in Scotland, and their mother heads a small sanctuary in Alaska that is hidden under a dome of ice."

Wonder frowned. "That seems extreme. Why hide under a dome of ice? And how is it even possible?"

Brundar was watching her with a stoic expression that only Anandur could decipher as amused. Well, by now Callie knew her mate well enough to decipher the slight variations as well.

"If you were the last goddess on earth, you would be cautious too."

That shut Wonder up. For about two seconds of wide-eyed staring at his face.

"Did you say a goddess?"

"Sounds unbelievable, I know. She is the Clan Mother. Everyone in the clan is her descendant, aside from a few newcomers."

"No, to me it sounds very believable." Wonder put the empty can of ginger ale on the table and lifted her hands in the air, then winced and clutched at her chest. "I thought I dreamt it."

"Did you dream about a goddess?" Brundar asked.

"Not one particular goddess. I just knew that there were three kinds of people, namely immortals, gods, and humans. I didn't know how I knew that, but it was like knowing that the earth orbits the sun and that the moon orbits the earth. It was a fact. But it seemed like no one ever heard of real living breathing gods or immortals. They were supposedly myths."

That was odd. If Wonder were a randomly activated Dormant like Eva, she would've assumed, just as Eva had, that she was a freak of nature or the product of some secret experiment. She wouldn't have dreamt about a world in which gods, immortals and humans coexisted. Except, it was possible that she had seen a movie or read a book that had influenced her subconscious, producing dreams of gods and goddesses.

"I knew I wasn't a myth," she continued. "Although at some point I started to doubt my immortality and thought I just had an abnormally fast rate of healing. That was until I encountered the first Doomer and discovered that there were more immortals out there. But the Doomers didn't know anything about gods either. They also thought they were a myth."

"They were lying," Brundar said.

Anandur scratched his beard. "Not necessarily. I talked a lot with Dalhu and he said the soldiers are not told much. All they know is that a clan of immortals exist who compete with them for the control of humanity. They don't want them to know the clan has a goddess while their supreme leader is only the immortal son of a god. Dalhu knew because he was smart and wasn't happy with the simplistic version he'd been fed."

"What about Robert?"

"Robert is more of a 'follow the commands and don't ask too many questions' kind of guy. He didn't know much until Carol told him."

Wonder lifted her hand to get their attention. "So let me get it straight. You guys are related to a real, living, breathing goddess?"

"Yes."

"And you know where she lives?"

"More or less. It's a secret not even her children are privy to. She and her people come and go using machine-piloted planes." He didn't want to get into a long explanation about the Odus. Wonder was having a hard enough time wrapping her head around all the new information coming her way.

"Is there any way I could meet her?"

Anandur shook his head. "It's up to her. The goddess does as she pleases. She might get curious about you and want to see you, but only if you become part of the clan."

Wonder narrowed her eyes at him. "You're not just saying that to make me want to stay?"

He scratched his beard again and smiled. "Maybe?"

The end... for now.

Dear reader,

Thank you for joining me on the continuing adventures of the **Children of the Gods**.

As an independent author, I rely on your support to spread the word. So if you enjoyed the story, please share your experience, and if it isn't too much trouble, I would greatly appreciate a brief review on Amazon for **Dark Survivor Awakened**.

Love & happy reading,

Isabell

COMING UP NEXT
DARK SURVIVOR ECHOES OF LOVE

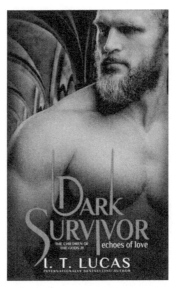

Dark Survivor Echoes of Love is available on Amazon

FOR EXCLUSIVE PEEKS

JOIN THE CHILDREN OF THE GODS VIP CLUB TO GAIN ACCESS
TO A **FREE** NARRATION OF GODDESS'S CHOICE, PREVIEW
CHAPTERS AND OTHER EXCLUSIVE CONTENT THROUGH THE
VIP PORTAL AT ITLUCAS.COM
CLICK **HERE** TO JOIN
(OR GO TO: http://eepurl.com/blMTpD)

THE CHILDREN OF THE GODS SERIES

THE CHILDREN OF THE GODS ORIGINS

1: GODDESS'S CHOICE

When gods and immortals still ruled the ancient world, one young goddess risked everything for love.

2: GODDESS'S HOPE

Hungry for power and infatuated with the beautiful Areana, Navuh plots his father's demise. After all, by getting rid of the insane god he would be doing the world a favor. Except, when gods and immortals conspire against each other, humanity pays the price.

But things are not what they seem, and prophecies should not to be trusted...

THE CHILDREN OF THE GODS

1: DARK STRANGER THE DREAM

Syssi's paranormal foresight lands her a job at Dr. Amanda Dokani's neuroscience lab, but it fails to predict the thrilling yet terrifying turn her life will take. Syssi has no clue that her boss is an immortal who'll drag her into a secret, millennia-old battle over humanity's future. Nor does she realize that the professor's imposing brother is the mysterious stranger who's been starring in her dreams.

Since the dawn of human civilization, two warring factions of immortals—the descendants of the gods of old—have been secretly shaping its destiny. Leading the clandestine battle from his luxurious Los Angeles high-rise, Kian is surrounded by his clan, yet alone. Descending from a single goddess, clan members are forbidden to each other. And as the only other immortals are their hated enemies, Kian and his kin have been long resigned to a lonely existence of fleeting trysts with human partners. That is, until his sister makes a game-changing discovery—a mortal seeress who she believes is a dormant carrier of their genes. Ever the realist, Kian is skeptical and refuses Amanda's plea to attempt Syssi's activation. But when his enemies learn of the Dormant's existence, he's forced to rush her to the safety of his keep. Inexorably drawn to Syssi, Kian wrestles with his conscience as he is tempted to explore her budding interest in the darker shades of sensuality.

2: Dark Stranger Revealed

While sheltered in the clan's stronghold, Syssi is unaware that Kian and Amanda are not human, and neither are the supposedly religious fanatics that are after her. She feels a powerful connection to Kian, and as he introduces her to a world of pleasure she never dared imagine, his dominant sexuality is a revelation. Considering that she's completely out of her element, Syssi feels comfortable and safe letting go with him. That is, until she begins to suspect that all is not as it seems. Piecing the puzzle together, she draws a scary, yet wrong conclusion...

3: Dark Stranger Immortal

When Kian confesses his true nature, Syssi is not as much shocked by the revelation as she is wounded by what she perceives as his callous plans for her.

If she doesn't turn, he'll be forced to erase her memories and let her go. His family's safety demands secrecy – no one in the mortal world is allowed to know that immortals exist.

Resigned to the cruel reality that even if she stays on to never again leave the keep, she'll get old while Kian won't, Syssi is determined to enjoy what little time she has with him, one day at a time.

Can Kian let go of the mortal woman he loves? Will Syssi turn? And if she does, will she survive the dangerous transition?

4: Dark Enemy Taken

Dalhu can't believe his luck when he stumbles upon the beautiful immortal professor. Presented with a once in a lifetime opportunity to grab an immortal female for himself, he kidnaps her and runs. If he ever gets caught, either by her people or his, his life is forfeit. But for a chance of a loving mate and a family of his own, Dalhu is prepared to do everything in his power to win Amanda's heart, and that includes leaving the Doom brotherhood and his old life behind.

Amanda soon discovers that there is more to the handsome Doomer than his dark past and a hulking, sexy body. But succumbing to her enemy's seduction, or worse, developing feelings for a ruthless killer is out of the question. No man is worth life on the run, not even the one and only immortal male she could claim as her own...

Her clan and her research must come first...

5: DARK ENEMY CAPTIVE

When the rescue team returns with Amanda and the chained Dalhu to the keep, Amanda is not as thrilled to be back as she thought she'd be. Between Kian's contempt for her and Dalhu's imprisonment, Amanda's budding relationship with Dalhu seems doomed. Things start to look up when Annani offers her help, and together with Syssi they resolve to find a way for Amanda to be with Dalhu. But will she still want him when she realizes that he is responsible for her nephew's murder? Could she? Will she take the easy way out and choose Andrew instead?

6: DARK ENEMY REDEEMED

Amanda suspects that something fishy is going on onboard the Anna. But when her investigation of the peculiar all-female Russian crew fails to uncover anything other than more speculation, she decides it's time to stop playing detective and face her real problem—a man she shouldn't want but can't live without.

6.5: MY DARK AMAZON

When Michael and Kri fight off a gang of humans, Michael gets stabbed. The injury to his immortal body recovers fast, but the one to his ego takes longer, putting a strain on his relationship with Kri.

7: DARK WARRIOR MINE

When Andrew is forced to retire from active duty, he believes that all he has to look forward to is a boring desk job. His glory days in special ops are over. But as it turns out, his thrill ride has just begun. Andrew discovers not only that immortals exist and have been manipulating global affairs since antiquity, but that he and his sister are rare possessors of the immortal genes.

Problem is, Andrew might be too old to attempt the activation process. His sister, who is fourteen years his junior, barely made it through the transition, so the odds of him coming out of it alive, let alone immortal, are slim.

But fate may force his hand.

Helping a friend find his long-lost daughter, Andrew finds a woman who's worth taking the risk for. Nathalie might be a Dormant, but the only way to find out for sure requires fangs and venom.

8: Dark Warrior's Promise

Andrew and Nathalie's love flourishes, but the secrets they keep from each other taint their relationship with doubts and suspicions. In the meantime, Sebastian and his men are getting bolder, and the storm that's brewing will shift the balance of power in the millennia-old conflict between Annani's clan and its enemies.

9: Dark Warrior's Destiny

The new ghost in Nathalie's head remembers who he was in life, providing Andrew and her with indisputable proof that he is real and not a figment of her imagination.

Convinced that she is a Dormant, Andrew decides to go forward with his transition immediately after the rescue mission at the Doomers' HQ.

Fearing for his life, Nathalie pleads with him to reconsider. She'd rather spend the rest of her mortal days with Andrew than risk what they have for the fickle promise of immortality.

While the clan gets ready for battle, Carol gets help from an unlikely ally. Sebastian's second-in-command can no longer ignore the torment she suffers at the hands of his commander and offers to help her, but only if she agrees to his terms.

10: Dark Warrior's Legacy

Andrew's acclimation to his post-transition body isn't easy. His senses are sharper, he's bigger, stronger, and hungrier. Nathalie fears that the changes in the man she loves are more than physical. Measuring up to this new version of him is going to be a challenge.

Carol and Robert are disillusioned with each other. They are not destined mates, and love is not on the horizon. When Robert's three months are up, he might be left with nothing to show for his sacrifice.

Lana contacts Anandur with disturbing news; the yacht and its human cargo are in Mexico. Kian must find a way to apprehend Alex and rescue the women on board without causing an international incident.

11: Dark Guardian Found

What would you do if you stopped aging?

Eva runs. The ex-DEA agent doesn't know what caused her strange mutation, only that if discovered, she'll be dissected like a lab rat. What Eva doesn't know, though, is that she's a descendant of the gods, and that she is not alone. The man who rocked her world in one life-changing encounter over thirty years ago is an immortal as well.

To keep his people's existence secret, Bhathian was forced to turn his back on the only woman who ever captured his heart, but he's never forgotten and never stopped looking for her.

12: Dark Guardian Craved

Cautious after a lifetime of disappointments, Eva is mistrustful of Bhathian's professed feelings of love. She accepts him as a lover and a confidant but not as a life partner.

Jackson suspects that Tessa is his true love mate, but unless she overcomes her fears, he might never find out.

Carol gets an offer she can't refuse—a chance to prove that there is more to her than meets the eye. Robert believes she's about to commit a deadly mistake, but when he tries to dissuade her, she tells him to leave.

13: Dark Guardian's Mate

Prepare for the heart-warming culmination of Eva and Bhathian's story!

14: Dark Angel's Obsession

The cold and stoic warrior is an enigma even to those closest to him. His secrets are about to unravel...

15: Dark Angel's Seduction

Brundar is fighting a losing battle. Calypso is slowly chipping away his icy armor from the outside, while his need for her is melting it from the inside.

He can't allow it to happen. Calypso is a human with none of the Dormant indicators. There is no way he can keep her for more than a few weeks.

16: Dark Angel's Surrender

Get ready for the heart pounding conclusion to Brundar and Calypso's story.

Callie still couldn't wrap her head around it, nor could she summon even a smidgen of sorrow or regret. After all, she had some memories with him that weren't horrible. She should've felt something. But there was nothing, not even shock. Not even horror at what had transpired over the last couple of hours.

Maybe it was a typical response for survivors--feeling euphoric for the simple reason that they were alive. Especially when that survival was nothing short of miraculous.

Brundar's cold hand closed around hers, reminding her that they weren't out of the woods yet. Her injuries were superficial, and the most she had to worry about was some scarring. But, despite his and Anandur's reassurances, Brundar might never walk again.

If he ended up crippled because of her, she would never forgive herself for getting him involved in her crap.

"Are you okay, sweetling? Are you in pain?" Brundar asked.

Her injuries were nothing compared to his, and yet he was concerned about her. God, she loved this man. The thing was, if she told him that, he would run off, or crawl away as was the case.

Hey, maybe this was the perfect opportunity to spring it on him.

17: Dark Operative: A Shadow of Death

As a brilliant strategist and the only human entrusted with the secret of immortals' existence, Turner is both an asset and a liability to the clan. His request to attempt transition into immortality as an alternative to cancer treatments cannot be denied without risking the clan's exposure. On the other hand, approving it means risking his premature death. In both scenarios, the clan will lose a valuable ally.

When the decision is left to the clan's physician, Turner makes plans to manipulate her by taking advantage of her interest in him.

Will Bridget fall for the cold, calculated operative? Or will Turner fall into his own trap?

18: Dark Operative: A Glimmer of Hope

As Turner and Bridget's relationship deepens, living together seems like the right move, but to make it work both need to make concessions.

Bridget is realistic and keeps her expectations low. Turner could never be the truelove mate she yearns for, but he is as good as she's going to get. Other than his emotional limitations, he's perfect in every way.

Turner's hard shell is starting to show cracks. He wants immortality, he wants to be part of the clan, and he wants Bridget, but he doesn't want to cause her pain.

His options are either abandon his quest for immortality and give Bridget his few remaining decades, or abandon Bridget by going for the transition and most likely dying. His rational mind dictates that he chooses the former, but his gut pulls him toward the latter. Which one is he going to trust?

19: Dark Operative: The Dawn of Love

Get ready for the exciting finale of Bridget and Turner's story!

20: Dark Survivor Awakened

This was a strange new world she had awakened to.

Her memory loss must have been catastrophic because almost nothing was familiar. The language was foreign to her, with only a few words bearing some similarity to the language she thought in. Still, a full moon cycle had passed since her awakening, and little by little she was gaining basic understanding of it--only a few words and phrases, but she was learning more each day.

A week or so ago, a little girl on the street had tugged on her mother's sleeve and pointed at her. "Look, Mama, Wonder Woman!"

The mother smiled apologetically, saying something in the language these people spoke, then scurried away with the child looking behind her shoulder and grinning.

When it happened again with another child on the same day, it was settled.

Wonder Woman must have been the name of someone important in this strange world she had awoken to, and since both times it had been said with a smile it must have been a good one.

Wonder had a nice ring to it.

She just wished she knew what it meant.

21: Dark Survivor Echoes of Love

Wonder's journey continues in *Dark Survivor Echoes of Love*.

22: Dark Survivor Reunited

The exciting finale of Wonder and Anandur's story.

23: Dark Widow's Secret

Vivian and her daughter share a powerful telepathic connection, so when Ella can't be reached by conventional or psychic means, her mother fears the worst.

Help arrives from an unexpected source when Vivian gets a call from the young doctor she met at a psychic convention. Turns out Julian belongs to a private organization specializing in retrieving missing girls.

As Julian's clan mobilizes its considerable resources to rescue the daughter, Magnus is charged with keeping the gorgeous young mother safe.

Worry for Ella and the secrets Vivian and Magnus keep from each other should be enough to prevent the sparks of attraction from kindling a blaze of desire. Except, these pesky sparks have a mind of their own.

24: Dark Widow's Curse

A simple rescue operation turns into mission impossible when the Russian mafia gets involved. Bad things are supposed to come in threes, but in Vivian's case, it seems like there is no limit to bad luck. Her family and everyone who gets close to her is affected by her curse.

Will Magnus and his people prove her wrong?

25: Dark Widow's Blessing

The thrilling finale of the Dark Widow trilogy!

26: Dark Dream's Temptation

Julian has known Ella is the one for him from the moment he saw her picture, but when he finally frees her from captivity, she seems indifferent to him. Could he have been mistaken?

Ella's rescue should've ended that chapter in her life, but it seems like the road back to normalcy has just begun and it's full of obstacles. Between the pitying looks she gets and her mother's attempts to get her into therapy, Ella feels like she's typecast as a victim, when nothing could be further from the truth. She's a tough survivor, and she's going to prove it.

Strangely, the only one who seems to understand is Logan, who keeps popping up in her dreams. But then, he's a figment of her imagination—or is he?

27: Dark Dream's Unraveling

While trying to figure out a way around Logan's silencing

compulsion, Ella concocts an ambitious plan. What if instead of trying to keep him out of her dreams, she could pretend to like him and lure him into a trap?

Catching Navuh's son would be a major boon for the clan, as well as for Ella. She will have her revenge, turning the tables on another scumbag out to get her.

28: Dark Dream's Trap

The trap is set, but who is the hunter and who is the prey? Find out in this heart-pounding conclusion to the *Dark Dream* trilogy.

29: Dark Prince's Enigma

As the son of the most dangerous male on the planet, Lokan lives by three rules:

Don't trust a soul.

Don't show emotions.

And don't get attached.

Will one extraordinary woman make him break all three?

30: Dark Prince's Dilemma

Will Kian decide that the benefits of trusting Lokan outweigh the risks?

Will Lokan betray his father and brothers for the greater good of his people?

Are Carol and Lokan true-love mates, or is one of them playing the other?

So many questions, the path ahead is anything but clear.

31: Dark Prince's Agenda

While Turner and Kian work out the details of Areana's rescue plan, Carol and Lokan's tumultuous relationship hits another snag. Is it a sign of things to come?

32 : Dark Queen's Quest

A former beauty queen, a retired undercover agent, and a successful model, Mey is not the typical damsel in distress. But when her sister drops off the radar and then someone starts following her around, she panics.

Following a vague clue that Kalugal might be in New York, Kian sends a team headed by Yamanu to search for him.

As Mey and Yamanu's paths cross, he offers her his help and protection, but will that be all?

33: Dark Queen's Knight

As the only member of his clan with a godlike power over human minds, Yamanu has been shielding his people for centuries, but that power comes at a steep price. When Mey enters his life, he's faced with the most difficult choice.

The safety of his clan or a future with his fated mate.

34: Dark Queen's Army

As Mey anxiously waits for her transition to begin and for Yamanu to test whether his godlike powers are gone, the clan sets out to solve two mysteries:

Where is Jin, and is she there voluntarily?

Where is Kalugal, and what is he up to?

35: Dark Spy Conscripted

Jin possesses a unique paranormal ability. Just by touching someone, she can insert a mental hook into their psyche and tie a string of her consciousness to it, creating a tether. That doesn't make her a spy, though, not unless her talent is discovered by those seeking to exploit it.

36: Dark Spy's Mission

Jin's first spying mission is supposed to be easy. Walk into the club, touch Kalugal to tether her consciousness to him, and walk out.

Except, they should have known better.

37: Dark Spy's Resolution

The best-laid plans often go awry...

38: Dark Overlord New Horizon

Jacki has two talents that set her apart from the rest of the human race.

She has unpredictable glimpses of other people's futures, and she is immune to mind manipulation.

Unfortunately, both talents are pretty useless for finding a job other than the one she had in the government's paranormal division.

It seemed like a sweet deal, until she found out that the director planned on producing super babies by compelling the recruits into pairing up. When an opportunity to escape the program presented itself, she took it, only to find out that humans are not at the top of the food chain.

Immortals are real, and at the very top of the hierarchy is Kalugal, the most powerful, arrogant, and sexiest male she has ever met.

With one look, he sets her blood on fire, but Jacki is not a fool. A man like him will never think of her as anything more than a tasty snack, while she will never settle for anything less than his heart.

39: DARK OVERLORD'S WIFE

Jacki is still clinging to her all-or-nothing policy, but Kalugal is chipping away at her resistance. Perhaps it's time to ease up on her convictions. A little less than all is still much better than nothing, and a couple of decades with a demigod is probably worth more than a lifetime with a mere mortal.

40: DARK OVERLORD'S CLAN

As Jacki and Kalugal prepare to celebrate their union, Kian takes every precaution to safeguard his people. Except, Kalugal and his men are not his only potential adversaries, and compulsion is not the only power he should fear.

41: DARK CHOICES THE QUANDARY

When Rufsur and Edna meet, the attraction is as unexpected as it is undeniable. Except, she's the clan's judge and councilwoman, and he's Kalugal's second-in-command. Will loyalty and duty to their people keep them apart?

42: DARK CHOICES PARADIGM SHIFT

Edna and Rufsur are miserable without each other, and their two-week separation seems like an eternity. Long-distance relationships are difficult, but for immortal couples they are impossible. Unless one of them is willing to leave everything behind for the other, things are just going to get worse. Except, the cost of compromise is far greater than giving up their comfortable lives and hard-earned positions. The future of their people is on the line.

43: Dark Choices The Accord

The winds of change blowing over the village demand hard choices. For better or worse, Kian's decisions will alter the trajectory of the clan's future, and he is not ready to take the plunge. But as Edna and Rufsur's plight gains widespread support, his resistance slowly begins to erode.

44: Dark Secrets Resurgence

On a sabbatical from his Stanford teaching position, Professor David Levinson finally has time to write the sci-fi novel he's been thinking about for years.

The phenomena of past life memories and near-death experiences are too controversial to include in his formal psychiatric research, while fiction is the perfect outlet for his esoteric ideas.

Hoping that a change of pace will provide the inspiration he needs, David accepts a friend's invitation to an old Scottish castle.

45: Dark Secrets Unveiled

When Professor David Levinson accepts a friend's invitation to an old Scottish castle, what he finds there is more fantastical than his most outlandish theories. The castle is home to a clan of immortals, their leader is a stunning demigoddess, and even more shockingly, it might be precisely where he belongs.

Except, the clan founder is hiding a secret that might cast a dark shadow on David's relationship with her daughter.

Nevertheless, when offered a chance at immortality, he agrees to undergo the dangerous induction process.

Will David survive his transition into immortality? And if he does, will his relationship with Sari survive the unveiling of her mother's secret?

46: Dark Secrets Absolved

Absolution.

David had given and received it.

The few short hours since he'd emerged from the coma had felt incredible. He'd finally been free of the guilt and pain, and for the first time since Jonah's death, he had felt truly happy and optimistic about the future.

He'd survived the transition into immortality, had been accepted into the clan, and was about to marry the best woman on the face of the planet, his true love mate, his salvation, his everything.

What could have possibly gone wrong?

Just about everything.

47: Dark haven Illusion

Welcome to Safe Haven, where not everything is what it seems.

On a quest to process personal pain, Anastasia joins the Safe Haven Spiritual Retreat.

Through meditation, self-reflection, and hard work, she hopes to make peace with the voices in her head.

This is where she belongs.

Except, membership comes with a hefty price, doubts are sacrilege, and leaving is not as easy as walking out the front gate.

Is living in utopia worth the sacrifice?

Anastasia believes so until the arrival of a new acolyte changes everything.

Apparently, the gods of old were not a myth, their immortal descendants share the planet with humans, and she might be a carrier of their genes.

48: Dark Haven Unmasked

As Anastasia leaves Safe Haven for a week-long romantic vacation with Leon, she hopes to explore her newly discovered passionate side, their budding relationship, and perhaps also solve the mystery of the voices in her head. What she discovers exceeds her wildest expectations.

In the meantime, Eleanor and Peter hope to solve another mystery. Who is Emmett Haderech, and what is he up to?

———

———

THE PERFECT MATCH SERIES

PERFECT MATCH 1: VAMPIRE'S CONSORT

When Gabriel's company is ready to start beta testing, he invites his old crush to inspect its medical safety protocol.

Curious about the revolutionary technology of the *Perfect Match Virtual Fantasy-Fulfillment studios*, Brenna agrees.

Neither expects to end up partnering for its first fully immersive test run.

PERFECT MATCH 2: KING'S CHOSEN

When Lisa's nutty friends get her a gift certificate to *Perfect Match Virtual Fantasy Studios*, she has no intentions of using it. But since the only way to get a refund is if no partner can be found for her, she makes sure to request a fantasy so girly and over the top that no sane guy will pick it up.

Except, someone does.

Warning: This fantasy contains a hot, domineering crown prince, sweet insta-love, steamy love scenes painted with light shades of gray, a wedding, and a HEA in both the virtual and real worlds.

Intended for mature audience.

PERFECT MATCH 3: CAPTAIN'S CONQUEST

Working as a Starbucks barista, Alicia fends off flirting all day long, but none of the guys are as charming and sexy as Gregg. His frequent visits are the highlight of her day, but since he's never asked her out, she assumes he's taken. Besides, between a day job and a budding music career, she has no time to start a new relationship.

That is until Gregg makes her an offer she can't refuse —a gift certificate to the virtual fantasy fulfillment service everyone is talking about. As a huge Star Trek fan, Alicia has a perfect match in mind—the captain of the Starship Enterprise.

FOR EXCLUSIVE PEEKS AT UPCOMING RELEASES & A FREE COMPANION BOOK

Join my *VIP Club* and gain access to the VIP portal at ITLUCAS.COM

CLICK HERE TO JOIN
(OR GO TO: http://eepurl.com/blMTpD)

INCLUDED IN YOUR FREE MEMBERSHIP:

- **FREE** CHILDREN OF THE GODS COMPANION BOOK 1
- **FREE** NARRATION OF GODDESS'S CHOICE—BOOK 1 IN THE CHILDREN OF THE GODS ORIGINS SERIES.
- PREVIEW CHAPTERS OF UPCOMING RELEASES.
- AND OTHER EXCLUSIVE CONTENT OFFERED ONLY TO MY **VIP**S.

Also by I. T. Lucas

THE CHILDREN OF THE GODS ORIGINS

1: GODDESS'S CHOICE

2: GODDESS'S HOPE

THE CHILDREN OF THE GODS

DARK STRANGER

1: DARK STRANGER THE DREAM

2: DARK STRANGER REVEALED

3: DARK STRANGER IMMORTAL

DARK ENEMY

4: DARK ENEMY TAKEN

5: DARK ENEMY CAPTIVE

6: DARK ENEMY REDEEMED

KRI & MICHAEL'S STORY

6.5: MY DARK AMAZON

DARK WARRIOR

7: DARK WARRIOR MINE

8: DARK WARRIOR'S PROMISE

9: DARK WARRIOR'S DESTINY

10: DARK WARRIOR'S LEGACY

DARK GUARDIAN

11: DARK GUARDIAN FOUND

12: DARK GUARDIAN CRAVED

13: DARK GUARDIAN'S MATE

DARK ANGEL

14: DARK ANGEL'S OBSESSION

15: DARK ANGEL'S SEDUCTION

16: DARK ANGEL'S SURRENDER

DARK OPERATIVE

17: DARK OPERATIVE: A SHADOW OF DEATH

18: DARK OPERATIVE: A GLIMMER OF HOPE

19: DARK OPERATIVE: THE DAWN OF LOVE

Dark Survivor
20: Dark Survivor Awakened
21: Dark Survivor Echoes of Love
22: Dark Survivor Reunited

Dark Widow
23: Dark Widow's Secret
24: Dark Widow's Curse
25: Dark Widow's Blessing

Dark Dream
26: Dark Dream's Temptation
27: Dark Dream's Unraveling
28: Dark Dream's Trap

Dark Prince
29: Dark Prince's Enigma
30: Dark Prince's Dilemma
31: Dark Prince's Agenda

Dark Queen
32: Dark Queen's Quest
33: Dark Queen's Knight
34: Dark Queen's Army

Dark Spy
35: Dark Spy Conscripted
36: Dark Spy's Mission
37: Dark Spy's Resolution

Dark Overlord
38: Dark Overlord New Horizon
39: Dark Overlord's Wife
40: Dark Overlord's Clan

Dark Choices
41: Dark Choices The Quandary
42: Dark Choices Paradigm Shift
43: Dark Choices The Accord

Dark Secrets
44: Dark Secrets Resurgence

45: Dark Secrets Unveiled
46: Dark Secrets Absolved
Dark Haven
47: Dark haven Illusion
48: Dark Haven Unmasked

PERFECT MATCH

Perfect Match 1: Vampire's Consort
Perfect Match 2: King's Chosen
Perfect Match 3: Captain's Conquest

The Children of the Gods Series Sets

Books 1-3: Dark Stranger trilogy—Includes a bonus short story: **The Fates take a Vacation**
Books 4-6: Dark Enemy Trilogy —Includes a bonus short story—**The Fates' Post-Wedding Celebration**
Books 7-10: Dark Warrior Tetralogy
Books 11-13: Dark Guardian Trilogy
Books 14-16: Dark Angel Trilogy
Books 17-19: Dark Operative Trilogy
Books 20-22: Dark Survivor Trilogy
Books 23-25: Dark Widow Trilogy
Books 26-28: Dark Dream Trilogy
Books 29-31: Dark Prince Trilogy
Books 32-34: Dark Queen Trilogy
Books 35-37: Dark Spy Trilogy
Books 38-40: Dark Overlord Trilogy
Books 41-43: Dark Choices Trilogy

BOOKS 44-46: DARK SECRETS TRILOGY

MEGA SETS

THE CHILDREN OF THE GODS: BOOKS 1-6—INCLUDES CHARACTER LISTS

THE CHILDREN OF THE GODS: BOOKS 6.5-10 —INCLUDES CHARACTER LISTS

TRY THE CHILDREN OF THE GODS SERIES ON AUDIBLE

2 FREE audiobooks with your new Audible subscription!

Printed in Great Britain
by Amazon